# THE BALLAD OF THOMAS PATRICK DOWNING

# THE BALLAD OF THOMAS PATRICK DOWNING

*A Memoir of one of
General Custer's Irish
Cavalrymen*

DES RYAN

TTT Press 2024

First Printing, 2024

Published by TTT Press

Verse of 'Oh, Sweet Adare' by Gerald Griffin (1803-1840)
Lyric of 'Garryowen' by Thomas Moore (1779-1852)

Cover photo - A headstone from the Keogh Crazy Horse sector of the Little Bighorn battlefield © Des Ryan (2024).

ISBN 978-1-0686728-0-4

For Dearbhla and Cormac

\*\*\*

For Thomas Patrick Downing (RIP)

\*\*\*

For the proud people of Limerick
Luimneach Abú

# Acknowledgements

I have studied the Seventh Cavalry, Custer and the Battle of the Little Bighorn for a number of years, and have visited the battlefield at the Little Bighorn in Montana but I am no Custer historian. I am indebted to the many Custer scholars who have dedicated their lives to studying and analysing this fascinating subject. Their work has facilitated my ability to piece together Thomas Patrick Downing's last few weeks. They have allowed me to put myself in his shoes on the battlefield. They have enabled me to make this a historically accurate account of his final hours. There are many of you. I have devoured your books and I thank you.

Thank you to the family of Thomas Patrick Downing - Lori Gagnon, Linda Yazzolino, Sandi and Taryn DeGraff. In particular, thank you to Linda Payne for sharing a family perspective, some family documents and her insights. I hope I have done him justice and I was glad to help fill in some blanks for you.

I would like to acknowledge award winning Limerick historian Sharon Slater for her support and for providing a foreword that lends her insight into Thomas Patrick Downing's place in Limerick and Irish history. Sharon is perhaps the most accomplished historian on all things Limerick. Thank you.

My thanks go to Bob Reece, President and co-founder of the Friends of the Little Bighorn who do tremendous work researching the battle and helping visitors to interpret the battlefield. He has been extremely generous with his support, insight and encouragement. Thank you also to Joanne Blair. She too has been very important in encouraging my passion for this work.

My gratitude goes to Gary 'BJ' Hayes, Damian Lane, Declan O'Reilly and Dave Cunningham for friendship, encouragement in this project and the odd bit of proof-reading along the way.

My beautiful sister Èadaoin.

My father was reared in Garryowen in Limerick. Perhaps because of the Garryowen connection to the Seventh Cavalry, he has always had a deep interest in Custer, the Seventh Cavalry and "Cowboys 'n' Injuns". He planted the seeds that, over time, have grown into my love of history, travel, music and the wild west. I hope this makes him proud. I am proud of him and always have been.

Mostly, thank you to Carol, Dearbhla and Cormac. 'There is a light and it never goes out'.

# Contents

# Introduction

The valley of the Little Bighorn, in the south eastern corner of Montana, is a spectacular setting. A ruggedly beautiful landscape of rolling grassland, pocked by hills that rise dramatically from the prairie and then fall away just as quickly. A hundred and fifty years ago, this was frontier country and barely explored by European settlers. Little has changed since then in terms of the landscape. It is still painfully remote, harsh, sparsely populated and it is still magnificent countryside.

This was Crow Indian country but the Sioux tribes were encroaching from their traditional lands farther to the east. The Sioux and their allies, the Cheyenne, were being pushed further and further west by the advancing European settlers. Manifest Destiny, a belief that the Europeans were destined to populate the American continent from coast to coast, was driving an insatiable appetite for land and resources. The Sioux were being backed off their land and into a corner. The discovery of gold in the Black Hills, located in the heart of Sioux territory, exacerbated the problem as floods of prospectors came in search of their fortunes. Driven from their land and being forced onto reservations, the Sioux culture and lifestyle faced an existential crisis.

It was here on 25th June 1876, less than two weeks before the United States celebrated the one hundredth anniversary of her Independence from Britain, that two cultures violently collided; one desperately trying to defend its way of life and hang onto land its people had lived on for countless generations, the other seeking to, lawfully or otherwise, expand its foothold on the American continent.

The battlefield itself is peaceful now and has been designated a national monument. Markers still stand, scattered across the vast field where US Cavalrymen fell and were butchered. More recently, a handful of markers were added where some of the Indian braves fell as they defended their way of life. Even with this evidence, it is hard to fathom that this beautiful and peaceful valley was the setting for such a titanic and bloody battle. It doesn't bear thinking about the experiences of those involved on either side.

George Armstrong Custer and his men rode into one of the largest Indian villages ever gathered on the plains. In doing so they rode into both oblivion and the history books. Those history books also include the names of other notable figures from the battle, Lakota Sioux Chief Sitting Bull and War Leaders Crazy Horse and Gall. A handful of General Custer's officers are also remembered; his brother Tom, Captain Myles Keogh, and Major Reno and Captain Benteen who both survived. But what of the two hundred and fifty or so regular troops in the ranks who also died that day in 1876? In most cases, the only remnant of their existence is a grave marker on the battlefield that says "U.S. Soldier 7th Cavalry. Fell Here. June 25 1876". Who were these men? How did they end up at the mercy of the Sioux and Cheyenne? Many were first generation immigrants from Ireland and Germany, many more were second generation. This can be deduced from the army enlistment records but beyond that little is known about any of their individual stories.

The Ballad of Thomas Patrick Downing is a true story. It traces the short life of one of those men, from his birth in Adare, County

Limerick, Ireland in March 1856, through to his death on the battle-field of the Little Bighorn in the mid afternoon of 25th June 1876.

The people, events, times, and places depicted in this story are all as they happened a hundred and fifty years ago. The details of Thomas' whereabouts and likely experiences have been meticulously pieced together, based on a range of sources including contemporary reports, officers' field diaries, eye witness testimony and a host of other historical records. None of the major facts in this story are fabricated. Of course, some elements have had to be fictionalised to fill gaps in the official records or to help create a memoir written in the first person. The core story, however, remains true to what actually happened to Private Thomas Patrick Downing, I Company, 7th Cavalry.

There are hundreds, maybe even thousands of books about General Custer and the events of the Little Bighorn. There is no book out there that traces the details of the life of one of his anonymous, Irish cavalrymen. Thomas Patrick Downing packed a lot into his twenty short years. Anonymous no more. What a life. What a death.

**"An honest man should always be remembered"**
*Inscription on the grave of Lakota War Chief Gall*

# Foreword

by Sharon Slater

Historian-in-Residence, Ormston House, Limerick

Des Ryan sets out to bring the story of Limerick man Thomas Patrick Downing back to the fore in this publication. Ryan takes the reader on the journey through Downing's eyes, from the place of his birth, the place he forever kept close to his heart, the picturesque village of Adare, County Limerick.

Today Adare is almost a place of pilgrimage for tourists from the United States trying to catch a glimpse of the lives their ancestors knew in pre-famine Ireland. Downing's journey from the Emerald Isle to the land 'where dreams are made' followed the same path as thousands of others.

After the Great Famine, Downing and his family formed part of the great exodus, although not for the reasons one would expect. This was to be a running thread in Downing's life. A thread Des Ryan weaved gracefully though the pages of his book.

Ryan's clever use of the first person narrative leaves the reader in no doubt over the physical and emotional toll this migrant son faced, not just upon reaching the new land but also during the journey to find a new place to call home. This home, in the southern state of Georgia, was a far cry from the lush green fields of

Limerick and Downing would quickly notice that those fields were not worked by the willing.

It is through this personal view, seen through Downing's eyes as a child, the reader can witness how quickly one can become swept away by powerful voices making impassioned speeches and how war infiltrates not only the lives of soldiers but the domestic lives of everyone who is in its path.

Ryan plays with Downing's youth and innocence at his first encounters with war. However, this does not deter the young boy, who as a teenager joins the ranks, serendipitously enlisting in a company with strong Irish ties. This connection highlighted by Ryan who plays with Downing's knowledge or lack thereof, of his native land.

This is not merely fictional portrayal of an Irish migrant's short life in the United States. Des Ryan uses and shares historical records to verify the timeline while taking the reader on a journey of the possibility, a journey that brings both joy and heartbreak in equal measure.

# I

## The Vengeance of his Ancestors

I heard from one of the other soldiers that the Sioux consider their hair to be a physical extension of their body's senses. They grow it long, down over their shoulders, to broaden their awareness of the world around them. It is as if their long hair is constantly sniffing the air, sensing what danger or opportunity might be nearby. They cut their hair only when mourning the loss of a loved one, dulling their senses while they recover from their bereavement. I wonder if he senses my resignation as he kneels over me here. I have all but given up. I am too weak now to fight him off. I am exhausted from weeks of riding in search of these Indians, from a lack of sleep last night, and from the exertion and adrenaline rush of our charge this morning.

He is straddling me. His right knee is on my left shoulder, pinning me to the grass. Weak from the exertion of the battle and in pain from my injured wrist, I don't even try to move him. He is too strong and I have nothing left. His left foot is standing on my right forearm. It is almost certainly broken at the wrist from the clatter he gave me with his war club. That had knocked me off balance and onto my back, leaving me here at his mercy on the long, coarse Montana grass. Even if he weren't holding me down, I don't think I could move my right hand. It is aching tremendously and I can feel a buzzing tingle coming from the bone on the outside of my wrist. It might even be protruding the skin. I can't see. There is no way I can defend myself from what I know is coming.

I never really feared what might happen to me in battle until we started to be overrun by these savages. I was so confident in General Custer and Captain Keogh that it didn't dawn on me that we might be in this situation. Adrenaline is powerful and I loved the energy it gave me as we charged this morning. I felt unstoppable and excited by what we would meet. It is only in the last twenty minutes or so that I felt any real fear. Now I feel as if the fear and adrenaline have drained from my body and left me feeling almost anaesthetised. I am surprisingly calm.

I look up at him. His long black hair is hanging down, dangling just inches from my face. His hairless face is obscured by the shadow of the hot, mid-afternoon June sun that is shining from behind his back. The sun briefly breaks through around the edge of his head, momentarily blinding me with a glaring halo. Then his head moves, blocking the sun again. After the flash of light, it takes a moment for my eyes to refocus and I can see his darkened face looking down on me again.

Just minutes ago, with my veins pulsing with adrenaline, I was struggling to take in the absolute chaos of the battlefield. It was overwhelming. I didn't know which way to look. There were Indians coming at us from everywhere. Thousands of them. All of them stirred up into an aggressive, vengeful frenzy. It was like they were springing up spontaneously from the grass, attacking us and then disappearing into the gullies that surround the highpoint we were defending overlooking the Little Bighorn river. The sound was deafening. Horses whinnying, Indians squealing in excitement, gunshots, men screaming and crying out in pain. This isn't what we were expecting, and in hindsight maybe it wasn't a clever idea to dismount from our horses to form a skirmish line. If we had stayed on our horses, perhaps we could have made a run for it. It's too late now. There are too many of them and we have been completely overwhelmed. I can still hear the screams and cries around me but the sound feels muted as my focus narrows. It feels as if I have withdrawn back into my mind and am observing my surroundings, looking out from deep behind my eyes. Now, it's just me and him. Both of us focused only on these last few, intimate moments.

This is the closest I've seen a hostile Indian warrior. I wonder if he is a Sioux chief or a Cheyenne leader of some kind. He looks distinguished. Bare chested except for some beads and a necklace made from a bird's claw, he has a wonderful physique. Lean. Muscular. Dark. It's hard to say but he is probably about the same age as I am, twenty years old or so. His long hair reaches down to his chest and is plaited below the ears on each side. Each plait is wrapped in leather and the fur of one of his previous kills, probably a rabbit. His ear lobes are adorned with carved animal bones. Even if I had the strength to fight him off, I know he would have been too strong for me. Years of living on the plains and living off the land was much better preparation for a day like today than I had growing up in Savannah. I have been in the army for nearly five years but the cavalry doesn't prepare you for hand-to-hand fighting like this. I haven't even been in a real battle before today.

Captain Keogh said he was sure their scouts knew we were in the vicinity, so they knew we were coming. Our scouts had only spotted their village late last night and we had hoped to make this a surprise attack by striking early in the morning as the sun was rising. They might have known we were on the way but the timing of our attack didn't give them much time to prepare. Many were still resting in their lodges as we started our charge down both sides of the Little Bighorn river, but this fellow had taken enough time to put on war paint before joining in the battle. The lefthand side of his face is painted a dark red. The righthand side is bare, coloured only by the sun's rays and an outdoor life. The Indians are formidable looking anyway but the war paint really makes them look wild and savage. I wonder does the red signify something. The blood of his ancestors perhaps. He has a single eagle feather woven into his plaited hair behind his right ear. I know the feather signifies honour and is supposed to give the warrior strength and freedom in battle. He has that alright. He is exactly what I had imagined a Sioux warrior would look like but I hadn't imagined I'd be helpless and at his will when I saw one this close up.

General Custer had ordered us to hold a high point in the field where Major Reno and Captain Benteen could see us and come join the battle with their men. With three companies under Captain Keogh, we were ordered to dismount and to form a skirmish line. There were three of us at one end of it. As usual, every fourth man held the horses behind, as the other three knelt in the line. 'Postie' had initially held our horses but when we started to be overrun, he had to let the reins go so he could join the line with us. God only knows where my horse, Sarsfield, is now. Bless him, he has served me well since I picked him out from the herd in Lebanon on my first few days in the cavalry. On my left, a few yards away, was my friend and fellow Irishman John Barry from Waterford and to my right, Canadian Darwin Symms. Just beyond Darwin was my closest friend, Ed Driscoll, also from Waterford. Captain Keogh wasn't far away either. He had been on his horse, Comanche, riding up and down behind us, barking orders until he took a bullet to the leg just a few minutes ago. Even though he had been shouting orders at us, we couldn't hear him properly in the deafening noise of the battle and now, with him down, we were quickly in complete disarray. They were coming at us from every angle and then a group of about fifty mounted Indians charged at us, yelping and screaming as the rode headlong at us. They came at us from down in a gully so we could only see them at the last moment. Completely overrun and with Captain Keogh down, there was pandemonium. I lost track of my position in the line as it disintegrated around me. Men ducked or jumped to get out of the path of the advancing Indian ponies as they galloped over us. I managed to get out of the way of one that hurdled over my shoulder as I fell out of its path. Its rider swung something at me, stooping to try and reach me but I was just out-side his reach. I don't know what has happened to the others, my friends, the men I have spent every waking hour with for months on end. They can't be much further than a few yards away from me but, in this catastrophic chaos, they may have run off looking for safety or worse still they could have already been killed.

The Indian charge had driven us off the high point we were defending and, disorientated, I found myself about twenty yards back. As some of the other men were engaging in desperate hand to hand fighting around me, I stumbled back to my feet and managed to find a small group of maybe six or seven men who had formed a protective circle around the wounded Captain Keogh. Hoping that there was some safety in numbers, I knelt in the line with them. I can't see them from where I am lying now. My only hope is that one of them is still close by, alive, and can come to my aid. I don't hold much hope though. It is bedlam around me and every man for himself.

Still pinning me to the ground, with his left hand he grabs a handful of the hair on the top of my head, and uses it to push my head back, down into the grass and slightly to the right. I try to pull against him, but my head is too tightly held in place. With his right hand he draws a knife from a sheath in his beltline. It's a serious looking weapon. Maybe eight inches long. He is tightly gripping its wooden handle backwards, with the steel blade pointing back up his forearm, sharp side out. He is comfortable with it in his hand. He's used it before.

A slight grin is briefly visible on his face but then he howls a high-pitched yell, as if claiming victory over me. This yell is more than a scream. He is channelling the years of pain his people have suffered at our hands. All the struggles and losses of generations of Sioux and Cheyenne Indians were compressed into this primal scream and while he was looking upwards at the skies, I know this scream is aimed at me. He is berating me as if I represent every white man who had ever set foot on their land, scolding me for every promise and treaty the US government has broken, every life a soldier has taken and for shaming his proud people by herding them onto reservations to live like caged animals, surviving on meagre government handouts. He hates me. He hates all of the white man.

Looking down at me again with venom in his eyes and flaring nostrils, he lowers the knife to the top of my forehead and starts to cut. I try to look him defiantly, dead in the eye, as he makes his first slice. Looking back into my eyes, slowly, starting at the left-hand side of my forehead, he begins to carve. It just feels like someone pulling my hair at first but I can feel the pressure as the blade pushes on my skin. Then, almost as if in slow motion, I can feel my skin split and explode on each side of blade as he cuts through my skin and into my scalp. Once through the skin a little, he pushes down hard with the effort showing with a grimace on his face. The sensation turns to a cold, numb freshness as the inside of my scalp starts to peel back and is exposed to the fresh air for the first time. I can feel the blade scratching across the top of my skull, bumping, and scraping over whatever parts of my flesh refuse to budge. With his left hand pulling my hair back, I can feel my flesh ripping free and the knife grating down over the bone. Slowly my scalp comes free of the top of my head. Then when he is more than halfway back my skull, with one final jolt and a flash of pain like I've never experienced, my scalp is cut through and comes free limply in his hand. Still kneeling over me, he raises it up to the sky as if to show his ancestors that he has avenged them. I can see my own bloody scalp hanging by the hair in his hand and my blood dripping through his fingers and down his forearm. A drop drips from his elbow and lands on my cheek. I feel no pain from the top of my scalp now, just a strange damp freshness and the sensation of a trickle of my blood dripping back down my bare skull, onto the grass.

I am lying prone, with my light blue shirt stained with sweat and now some blood from my scalp. I had abandoned the woollen tunic of my uniform before we started our charge because of the heat, and I had loosened the top button on my shirt to stay cool. I can feel my mother's crucifix laying on my bare chest. Today is Sunday and I had held it in my hand just this morning before we set off, praying to the Lord to keep me safe. I can't reach for it now but if I could I would do the same again now.

I am too far gone now to move. I am helpless. I know this is the end. There isn't even any point in playing dead. He lowers his arm and looks at me with pure hatred and contempt bursting from his dark eyes. With a sneering look on his face, he shows me my own blood-soaked scalp, as if I weren't aware of what he had done to me. Maybe he just wanted to exert one final show of power over me. I am nothing to him. My battle is over. Then, as he raises the knife again, I close my eyes and give in.  Still surrounded by turmoil, somehow the noise is filtered out and a calm silence comes over me. As I wait for the inevitable, I let my mind wander and picture my mother's loving smile and I can hear her soft Irish voice vividly whispering in my ear. She is reciting her favourite poem.

*Oh, sweet Adare! Oh, lovely vale!*
*Oh, soft retreat of sylvan splendour!*
*Nor summer sun nor morning gale*
*E'er hail'd a scene more softly tender.*

# II

⚜

# Oh, Sweet Adare

I'm not long after my twentieth birthday. I was born in the village of Adare in County Limerick, Ireland on 6th March 1856 and was baptised three days later at the Holy Trinity church on its main street. My mother used to say I was born with double luck. I was born with a caul covering my face. This layer of extra skin meant good luck would follow me on my travels through life. These good luck charms are often sold but my mother kept mine and swore it was lucky for us as a family. My second lucky win was that I was born during Lent. Easter was unusually early that year. My mother said that it was a sign I would have an exceptional life.

Even though I only lived there for a fleeting time, Adare feels like home and I have a very vivid and happy picture of this lovely village in my mind. I can't really tell which parts of my picture of Adare is from my own actual memory and which parts were implanted by my mother who talked about her hometown almost every day of her life. I was only three when we left and even after we moved to

America, my mother was always adamant that we were Irish, and that Adare was our home.

If I close my eyes, I can picture myself walking along the narrow winding road that leads out the twelve or so miles from the town of Limerick, passed the old St Nicholas Church ruins and graveyard on the left-hand side, where my mother's kin, the Harrigan family are buried. Then, with the road turning slightly to the left and down the hill, I come to the huge grey ruins of Desmond Castle. This has been in ruins for a very long time but it must have been some spectacle a few hundred years ago. Adare is a small, quiet village now with maybe a thousand people, but this castle was once an important defensive fortress on the banks of the majestic Maigue river. It must have been teeming with people and bustling with activity. Now it's deserted apart from the local children who use it as their playground.

Continuing, I cross over the bridge that leads across the river and up into the village. I can hear the rush of the river as it flows from right to left under my feet and under the six arches of the stone bridge below me. Salmon and eels from the river kept our family alive when the blight hit the potatoes causing the great famine. My grandfather had to be careful not to get caught by the water bailiffs. It was illegal to fish without a licence and our family was too poor to afford one of those. We weren't alone in poaching the odd fish to help us get by.

Rising the far bank of the river, I pass the "Black Abbey" on the right-hand side. It's a Protestant Church now but our family still call it Black Abbey because it was an Augustinian Catholic abbey for hundreds of years and their monks wore black robes. Adare was a deeply religious place over the centuries. The Desmond Castle made it a busy settlement and three different Catholic Orders had churches there. The Augustinian Black Friars, The Order of the Most Holy Trinity for the Redemption of Captives who still have the catholic church in the village and the Franciscans who had the "Poor Abbey" which is now also in ruins. The population is much lower now so there isn't a need for as many churches.

Continuing along the road, on the left-hand side, I come to the gates of the big house. Adare Manor, home of the Earl of Dunraven. True splendour. Whenever I was smartened up to go to Sunday mass, my mother would always touch my cheek, smile lovingly, and say *"Would you look at him. He's like the Earl Dunraven himself"*. His was the life she wanted for us all. There is no harm in dreaming, but we were vastly different from that.

**Adare Manor - Home of the Earl of Dunraven**

Wyndham Henry Quin, 2ⁿᵈ Earl of Dunraven, owned all the surrounding land and he leased it out to the local farmers and to labourers like my grandfather. He was the sixth generation of his family to own this massive estate. The Quins were old Irish Catholic gentry, but the Earl's ancestor Valentine Quin had to convert from Catholic to Protestant during the Penal Laws so that they could maintain custody of the estate. Together with his Countess wife Caroline, the 2nd Earl rebuilt the family manor house on the estate during the famine. In all it took them twenty years to complete with all the work being completed by labourers from the village. This was a real blessing during the years of the famine. While a lot of the landlords in Ireland were known to be cruel to their tenants, the Dunravens were fair minded and had the wealth to be able to create valuable work for their tenants when times were tough. The tenants on the land, while still extremely poor, liked them in return for this generosity and that made Adare a peaceful place when other parts of the country were rebelling.

Outside the walls of the manor house's vast estate is the village itself. On the left of the main street is a line of small cottages where some of the workers from the big house live. Across the road a few small businesses, a blacksmith, a stone mason, the baker, the grocer, and the local inn, named The Dunraven Arms in honour of the Earl. My grandfather's house, where we lived, is further on again, just outside the village on the road towards Rathkeale. It is an idyllic setting I was born into and it's no wonder my mother always felt she had left part of her heart behind when we left Adare.

My father, Thomas Bartholomew Downing, after whom I was named, was from the townland of Templenoe, just outside the town of Kenmare in County Kerry. I never went there and unlike my mother, my father didn't talk much about where he was from or about his family. He was a little bitter about how we came to leave Ireland and he became detached from his people in Kerry as a result.

My father was a police constable. He signed up to join the Irish Constabulary when he was my age. That was in 1844, just as the blight first started to hit the potatoes. For the son of a poor farmer, joining the constabulary was seen as a way of advancing themselves. While the pay was poor enough, being a police constable gave him some standing in the community. To be accepted into the force, you had to have a national school education, be aged between nineteen and twenty seven, be single or a widower and stand at least five foot ten inches. My father fulfilled all the criteria and had the endorsement of the local parish priest down in Kenmare. The priest had to attest to the authorities that not only was my father of good moral character but so too were his family. Once accepted, my father was happy to have work and was sent off to Dublin for his six months of training. Had he stayed down in Kerry, it would have been a different life for him no doubt.

**Adare Village**

The rules of the constabulary stated that a constable couldn't serve in his native county. As a result, when he signed up, my father had to leave Kerry and was first posted up the country in Queens County. He got on well there and quickly got the hang of the job but while he was there, he testified in a big court case against one of the leaders of the Fenian movement. Thomas Francis Meagher was being tried for treason against the Crown. My father was brought to Clonmel in County Tipperary where the trial was being held by Special Commission. The trial went on for three days during which my father testified that he had seen Meagher inciting a public crowd at Graignamanagh in County Kilkenny. My father's statement was only a small part of the testimony against Meagher, but unfortunately it was covered in all the newspapers and after Meagher was convicted, my father had to put up with jibes on the streets from the locals where he was serving. It was a tough time for him because his own family, including himself, would have quietly supported the Fenian cause. He felt he was just doing his job by testifying but I know he regretted it. Soon enough after the trial, my father requested a transfer and was moved to the barracks in Adare. It suited him to make a fresh start and Adare was a lot closer to his own family down in Kerry.

My father arrived in Adare in 1850, ready to make a fresh start in a new town. Ireland was emerging from the famine at the time so people were rebuilding their strength and their lives. Thanks to the Earl of Dunraven, Adare was a good place to be and my father was happy to have a quieter area to police. He was mostly there to keep the peace in the night time after people had too much to drink in the Dunraven Arms Inn on the main street or to issue fines for animals found loose on the road. The British Army would be called in if there was anything significant happening, so the police were mostly there to keep the peace and to make reports to headquarters at Dublin Castle. With time on his hands it wasn't long before Constable Downing met my mother, Ellen Harrigan.

My mother's family were from Adare. My grandfather, Patrick Harrigan, had a cottage on the Rathkeale road on the outskirts of the village. It wasn't too far from the police barracks where my father was now stationed. The Harrigan family had lived in Adare for generations and my grandfather rented the cottage from Robert Supple who in turn rented the land from the Earl Dunraven. His was a typical labourer's cottage. It was a small stone house with a thatched roof. It had three dark rooms, a bedroom at either end of the house and in between them was a kitchen. It had small windows but to maintain the heat, there were only a few and so it was a little dark inside. The stone floors were covered with straw in the winter to keep them dry and the kitchen had a big hearth with a fire that seemed to be constantly lit. That kept the family warm, and it was where my grandmother did all the cooking. Up under the thatched roof, over each bedroom, there was an elevated platform where the children slept. It was a simple, small cottage but it was all the family needed. My grandfather worked as a labourer on the Dunraven estate helping with the construction work on the new manor house and labouring around the grounds. There was plenty to do. The pay was poor but he got by. At home he had a small patch of land behind the cottage where he kept a few chickens and grew some vegetables. That along with a few poached fish from the river, got the family through the tough famine years.

My mother spotted my father soon after he arrived in Adare. She used to go out of her way to walk past the barracks in the hope that she'd see him and vice versa. She said he looked very handsome in his dark green constabulary uniform. Eventually she caught his eye and they started courting and, I suppose that is how I came to be. The constabulary rules meant that a young constable, like my father, had to have seven years of service before they were permitted to marry and once married, the couple would have to transfer to a county where neither had relatives. My mother wasn't keen to leave her family in Adare so when the time came that my father was eligible for marriage, they had to decide what to do. They held off for a little while but eventually they got married in the spring of 1855. In the hope that they wouldn't have to declare their marriage and so move away, they got married discreetly at St Michaels church in the town of Limerick, twelve miles from Adare. Nothing was said and my parents got on with their newly married lives. My father moved into my grandfather's house and the new couple took one of the two bedrooms. Of course, it didn't take long for nature to take its course and I was their first child, born in March the following year.

For the first three years of my life, everything was going well for the family. Our health was keeping up and we lived quietly in Adare. Surrounded by my grandparents, uncles, and aunts, I was absolutely doted on, and I loved the attention. My father enjoyed his police work and with plentiful work around thanks to the Earl, life was good for our family and the community in Adare. Then, out of nowhere, everything was thrown into turmoil and the trajectory of our lives changed dramatically.

# III

## The Phoenix Society

In early May 1859, my father was called into the constabulary barracks unexpectedly. Confident that it was just an operational matter and nothing to be concerned about, he put on his uniform and walked into the village, down the main street and entered the barracks as he usually did, via the carriage arch on the right-hand side of the main doorway. Most of the constables did this and they would go into the barracks by the side door away from the public reception. He said '*hello*' to the other constables there and then went straight upstairs to the head constable's office. He knocked on the door, entered and was surprised to be met by Head Constable Michael Sullivan from the neighbouring Newcastle district and the Limerick County Inspector of the Constabulary, John S Rich. He knew immediately that something was wrong. The County Inspector didn't get involved with trivial matters and Newcastle was the next district over. Why would Head Constable Sullivan be here? To confuse him more, his own head constable wasn't even present. This was very unusual. My father surveyed the room to see if there was any clues or indication as to what was up but saw nothing that might enlighten him.

My father had seen Inspector Rich around a few times, usually when he was appearing in court cases, but they had never had occasion to meet. Inspector Rich didn't mix with lowly constables, and it was very unusual for him to come out from the barracks in Limerick. He was in his sixties and coming close to the end of a lengthy career in the army and constabulary. He was typical of the officer class; wealthy, connected and disdainful of the Irish peasantry. Rich lived on a big estate in Castleconnell, on the far side of Limerick city.

My father's immediate thought was that it had become known that he had gotten married and not declared it officially. My father's record wasn't perfect but there was nothing else that he could think of that might have been an issue. He hadn't really been hiding the marriage and he lived with my mother and her family only a few hundred yards from the barracks. What didn't make sense though was who was meeting him today. If this were about his undeclared marriage, it wouldn't have been a matter for the County Inspector. He would have been reprimanded by his own head constable, fined, and then moved to another area at the earliest opportunity. It didn't make sense and my father was a little annoyed that he wasn't warned when he saw the other constables downstairs.

Both men were very formal as was always the case with the officer class. My father stood to attention, announced himself and saluted. His brain was racing trying to figure out what this might all be about. Inspector Rich didn't beat around the bush. He formally introduced first himself, then Head Constable Sullivan and he went on to announce in his very British upper-class accent, that my father was being *dismissed from his post, effective immediately, due to his connection with subversives within the Fenian movement*. My father was stunned. His jaw dropped open in amazement. This made no sense at all but with that, Inspector Rich and Head Constable Sullivan left the room and my father's career in the police force ended abruptly. There was no discussion, no opportunity for him to either understand the allegations or to defend himself. He was completely innocent of whatever this crazy charge was and had no idea what had just happened.

My father stood there for a moment completely stunned. Then he turned and walked out of the head constable's office. He was too upset to talk to his colleagues and was still annoyed with them for not warning him, so he slipped quietly back down the stairs and out onto the street. He walked home in a haze of confusion. He knew that there was no truth to whatever the allegation was. He wracked his brain as to what it might be or who might have made claims against him. By the time he reached home, he was none the wiser. He stopped outside the house for a moment to compose himself and then went in. With a tear in his eye, he told my mother what had just happened. He couldn't answer any of the questions that she naturally asked. He hadn't been given the opportunity to ask the same questions himself. She was confused about why my father didn't know any detail. How could he have been fired and not know why? She didn't really understand that when the County Inspector interacted with a mere constable, it was usually not a conversation, it was one way statement or order. Her questions made my father angry and in the end he had to go for a walk to clear his head.

That evening the Adare Head Constable visited the house and told my father that three of his cousins had been arrested for treason down in Skibbereen in County Cork. Patrick James Downing known as "PJ", Denis Downing and Simon Downing were first cousins of my father. Their own father had moved from Kenmare down to Skibbereen when he got married to a girl from there. Two years previous, together with another man named Jeremiah O'Donnovan Rossa, the three cousins had set up a secret society called The Phoenix National and Literary Society. They were Fenians and their aim was to enlist educated men and get them to join together to overthrow British rule in Ireland.

Down in Skibbereen, the Phoenix boys had been having regular meetings in a bar owned by another man named Mortimer Downing. Mortimer was not a relation of ours. Fenian societies were banned by the British and so it all had to be kept secret. Members were enlisted and had to be endorsed by an existing member to keep it secure. Unfortunately for the Phoenix boys, they were tricked into admitting an informer into their secret ranks; a man named Daniel O'Sullivan Goula. Like the Downing family, Goula was from Kenmare and knew all the Downings and he knew that they were all sympathetic to the Fenian cause. Unannounced, Goula had arrived down to Skibbereen and took lodgings in Morty Downing's bar. He befriended the group and managed to get himself admitted to the society. Goula attended some of the society meetings, gathered intelligence and then went to the British authorities with the information he had gathered. Five months earlier, in December, the police had swooped and the whole lot of them had been arrested and thrown in Cork Jail where they were still awaiting trial. In all Goula's information had twenty men arrested down in Skibbereen.

My father protested to the Head Constable that he knew nothing about this society. There was no doubt that Goula had also informed the authorities of the Phoenix Society's connection into the Adare constabulary via my father. There was no other explanation for what had happened. My father hadn't seen or heard of his three cousins since they were all children. Those cousins lived in Skibbereen which was about fifty miles from Kenmare and my father barely knew them. The Crown forces in Dublin Castle were taking no chances of having any connection to subversion within their ranks. My father was crying when the Head Constable told him there was nothing he could do. The orders for his dismissal came from Dublin Castle and had bypassed him completely. That is why he wasn't present that day for the meeting.

My father was crestfallen and very bitter about Goula and his own three cousins. While our family were all supporters of the Fenian cause, we had no part in the Fenian movement. He even reminded the Head Constable that he had, in fact, testified against the Fenian leader Thomas Francis Meagher in Clonmel a few years earlier but it was no use. It was all very unfair. All my father could do was quote the bible saying, "*God will help the king to judge the people fairly*" and try to move on. False accusations like these, that soil your character, are absolutely devastating to a man's integrity. While our family stood by him, I don't think my father was ever the same after this incident. He started drinking and would often get melancholy about it.

The loss of his livelihood was a big setback for my father. He was innocent of the claims against him but there was nothing he could do. My mother was devastated too. She knew there was no truth in it, but she also knew that there was no way to fight an order from Dublin Castle and that work around Adare would be difficult to find because of this episode. Anyone who gave my father work would immediately be suspected of being involved in Fenianism and would come under scrutiny. It wasn't worth it.

With my young stomach to feed and his chances of meaningful work badly dented by this stain on his name, my father had few options left. My mother didn't want to leave Adare or her family but eventually my father convinced her that we should all move to America to make a fresh start. He had other relations that had already gone to live in Savannah, Georgia. We could go there and make a fresh start. Within a few weeks it was all arranged, and we were off.

Later still, we heard that O'Donovan Rossa, the Downing brothers, and all that were in the Phoenix Society, were released from jail without even being put on trial. Goula's information had been exaggerated and while the Phoenix boys were guilty of being members of a secret Fenian society, they couldn't be convicted on his testimony. Goula's testimony against my father was also exaggerated, false in fact, but it was too late for him. So, it turned out that my father was the only one to be punished for the Phoenix Society, even though he had nothing to do with it at all. No wonder he was bitter and didn't talk about his family much while I was growing up. By the time the Phoenix boys were released from Cork jail, we were already on our way to America. I doubt my father would have been re-admitted to the police force if we had stayed anyway.

# IV

## The New World

The three of us set off on our search for a new life barely two months after my father lost his job in the constabulary. As the day of our departure came closer, a sadness came over my grandfather's house. My grandmother sat most of the last week in the corner of the kitchen with a black shawl over her head and shoulders. It was like she was mourning the death of her daughter. Most people who went to America never came home and so, in a way, my grandmother was mourning us. I know she loved having me around the house and she was probably mourning the fact that she wouldn't get to see me grow up either. The last two nights were like a wake for the living in the house. Relatives and friends, some of whom we rarely saw, came to visit to say goodbye. Some stayed in the house with us around the clock. There was a lot of reminiscing, drinking, laughing, and crying by all accounts. On the morning we left Adare, the priest came to the house to bless us on our travels and reminded my mother about the fact that I was born with a caul and that it would keep us safe.

My father didn't return to his family in Kenmare to say goodbye before we left. He was too bitter about his constabulary job loss.

My grandfather brought us by cart as far as the Limerick docks where we would start our travels. The three of us were accompanied on the journey into Limerick by my grandmother and what few possessions we had to take with us. It was unlikely my mother would see her parents again so there was silence most of the way into Limerick as everyone was quietly holding back their emotions. The only sound to be heard was the horse's hoofs on the ground and the clatter of the rickety old cart bouncing over the uneven and windy road below us. As we travelled in the road, we all took our last views of the Limerick countryside. Beautiful green rural land, plenty of livestock and honest, hard-working people.

After a short wait at Limerick docks, we boarded our first ship, bound for Liverpool in England. The scene at the gangway was one of utter sadness. We weren't the only family departing and the sad sight of other families breaking apart, loved ones leaving home and wailing in tears, made everyone even sadder still. The sullen quietness of the trip into Limerick ruptured and everyone was crying. Too young to understand but prompted by everyone else's tears, I cried too. The first generation of emigrant is never really at peace. Never fully settled in their new world, they are always torn, living in an emigration no man's land between two lives. They are destined to a life of heartache, remembering deserted loved ones, and dreaming of being home with them again. It is only the second generation, who are not as connected to the old country, that really reap the rewards of a new life elsewhere. I am sure that my parents were looking forward to the better life I would get to live in America. Once on board, we stood close to the top of the gangway and as we waited for the boat to depart, my mother watched as her parents, heads bowed in heartache, set off on the horse drawn cart, back along the twelve bumpy miles from Limerick to Adare. That was the last we would all see of one another.

The journey from Limerick over to Liverpool was a short trip of only twenty-four hours or so. It being summertime, the weather was good, and the seas were nice and calm. My mother cried most of the way as we crossed over the Irish sea. My poor father just sat silently with me in his arms, helplessly watching as tears dripped from her glassy eyes, and raced each other down either side of her nose. There wasn't anything he could say to console her; he just had to wait for the sorrow to lift. I was just a little over three years old, so I don't have many memories of our journey to America, but my mother's tears, I remember those for sure. She was utterly heartbroken.

Once we arrived in Liverpool, my father found the ticket office for the next leg of our journey and before long, we boarded the big ship William Stetson bound for New York City. The William Stetson was a large packet ship and it ferried both the mail and passengers back and forth to the new world. For the well off, this was a comfortable, if not luxurious, way to travel but for us down in steerage, deep in the bowels of the ship, it was a miserable experience. After we boarded, we descended a wooden ladder down into the hull. There we found a large room with hard wooden bunks, stacked one on another and five abreast down both sides of the ship. There was a small gap after every fifth bunk to give an illusion of some space, but it was cramped. The only light down there came from eight small portholes spread out along each side of the ship and the little bit that got in through the hole where the ladder was dropped from the deck down to where we were housed. We were packed in with hundreds of passengers from all corners of Europe. It was dark, it was noisy, it was unsanitary, and it was very poorly ventilated but, for the next few weeks, this was our home.

My parents found two bunks together near the foot of the ladder, and we settled in. I wasn't entitled to a bunk because of my age but we made do. Being near the ladder gave us some light and a little bit of much needed fresh air, but it also meant that we were in a high traffic area. Any time anyone was coming or going to the deck, they passed our spot. Privacy was extremely limited for us, but my father decided that fresh air was far more important than privacy. He was probably right. All steerage passengers were issued with a straw mattress, a steel cup, along with a plate, a knife, and a spoon. That, and whatever we were carrying with us, was all we had to make this trip as comfortable as possible.

Across the rest of steerage, our fellow passengers found their own space and made themselves as comfortable as possible. Stretched down the middle of the hull, there was space for luggage and absolutely every possible spot was taken up. Pots, pans, and all kinds of possessions were crammed in or hanging from the beams over people's bunks. Everyone had a few sentimental trinkets from home or a life's possessions headed for a fresh start. When the seas got rough, there was an awful racket from the jangling of the luggage, the creaking of the beams of the ship and the groans of the unwell passengers.

Initially the passengers all kept to themselves but slowly we got introduced to those around us and we formed into little communities, helping each other through the torturous and unpleasant journey. We were all equals. All any of us could afford was steerage and everyone had the same reason for traveling. We were in this together, so some friendships were made and there was a romance or two formed in these squalid conditions, I'm sure. Being young and wanting to explore, I was passed around between the families to keep me occupied. I think my parents were glad of a break from me trying to get out of their grips. We were allowed up onto the deck when the weather was clear, but a line of chalk just at the top of the steerage ladder, marked the end of the steerage area of the deck. We weren't to go beyond that mark for fear we would mix with the well to do passengers of first or second class. Our part of the deck was from that chalk line, down the side and around the back of the ship. We were thankful that our journey was taking place in the summer months so we could get fresh air up on the deck. If we were traveling during the winter, it would have been impossible. We would have been stuck below deck for weeks on end. Thankfully, we got plenty of clear days and people were able to spend hours up there, escaping the dark dungeon below the decks. Up on the deck people strolled back and forth, chatted, played cards, or snoozed in the sun while they had the chance. In poor weather or after dark, there was little that people had to help pass the time in the darkness below deck.

In steerage, one cooked meal was provided every day but in stormy seas the cook prioritised first and second-class passengers. Between that and the seasickness some people suffered from, some-times people went almost a week without eating. Mostly people managed though and the community spirit that developed meant that people shared what they had to help each other to get through.

During the passage there were two children born and four people died around us in steerage. These were below average numbers by all accounts. My mother often commented afterwards on the sad scene of a little English girl who died on board. Her family was on the bunks just down from us, and she had been sick with a fever for a few days. Initially she cried a lot but then my mother said she went silent. The surgeon on board came down to check on her but he said he couldn't help her. She died after a few days and her poor family had no privacy. Her mother was distraught but could find no outlet. She just had to manage through. The little girl died late in the evening. We heard her mother sobbing as she cradled her dead body through the remainder of the night. The following morning a funeral service was held for her, and the surrounding passengers tried their best to console her parents. One of my clear memories of the trip is standing on the deck, holding my mother's hand, as the little girl's body was laid out on a plank of wood propped up on the side rail of the deck. The poor girl was so small, and her mother was buckled over with the pain of her loss. We stood and watched as her little body was wrapped in a white sheet by one of the sailors, the sheet was then tied in a knot at each end and a weight was tied at her ankles. The ship's captain presided over proceedings as a Union Jack flag was placed over her. He said a prayer next to the body as all his crew stood with their heads bowed. A handful of us fellow passengers also stood quietly; mostly the ones who were nearby in the bunks below deck. After a moment of silence, one of the sailors raised the plank at the headend and the little parcel slid, feet first out from under the flag and down into the waves below. The little girl's mother quickly looked over the side, hoping for a last glimpse of her baby, but it was too late, the little girl was swallowed up by the seas. My mother was haunted by these scenes. She wouldn't let me out of her sight for the rest of the journey and talked about that experience for years afterwards.

After five weeks at sea, a wave of excitement spread as we came in sight of the new world. Newfoundland was the first land we'd seen for a while. Expectation grew over the following few days as we sailed down the coast of Nova Scotia and then after a few days along Long Island. The sailors would tell my father where we were and point out things on the shoreline. My father would then show my mother and me. He seemed to know a lot about America, and I could tell he was excited about what was in store for us. My mother was still a little subdued from the sadness of leaving home but she tried to be enthusiastic.

Slowly we sailed nearer and nearer to our destination, Castle Garden in New York City. This is where all emigrant ships dropped their cargo at the time. Tired and desperate for firm land, we finally landed on 20th July 1859. We still had another leg of our journey to go, down the coast to Savannah, Georgia but first we had to be processed as immigrants to America. We packed our few things, exchanged forwarding address details with the few friends we had made on the journey and disembarked. There were one or two tears, but it was nothing like saying goodbye at the start of the journey. It was a relief to be off the water for a while and we knew that the hard part of the journey was now behind us.

Castle Garden is a grand and welcoming sounding name, but it was originally known as Fort Clinton. It was an old stone fort situated at the very southern tip of the island of Manhattan in New York. The old fort had been turned into a reception centre for processing all of the newly arrived masses. To ensure no one entered without being processed, the fort was surrounded by a twelve-foot-high wooden fence. It was like a prison.

Having arrived, we unloaded but before we could enter America, we were first sent for a medical review on Staten Island. This meant we had to get on another boat. Having spent five weeks on a ship, another boat journey was the last thing we wanted but it was only an hour across to the hospital on Staten Island and at least we had the magnificent views of New York harbour to distract us. We spent most of the day at the hospital waiting in line to be seen. Eventually we were called forward and we each were given tests for tuberculosis and other diseases. We were also washed and deloused which was much needed after our long journey over on the boat. Thankfully, we were all passed fit to enter the United States. Many others, clearly unwell, weren't so lucky and were sent for quarantine or worse still some were sent back to where they had come from. With our medical certificate secured, we were shipped back across to Fort Clinton for processing. It was late when we got back, and processing had already finished for the day, so we found a corner of the big hall, set up camp and tried to get some sleep. Even though the processing had finished for the day, there were lots of people milling around. Like us, they had just arrived and were jostling for a position that would see them at the top of the line when the processing started again in the morning.

I often wondered what we all dreamed that night, our first night in America. The following day we would be processed and would enter the new world. The land of opportunity where anything was possible. The anticipation of what was waiting for us must have stirred up excitement in our minds. My mother probably dreamt about her parents and Adare.

The following morning, we took our place in the lines. The hall was enormous but quickly became packed with more and more newly arrived immigrants. It was a hectic scene as every kind of humanity tried to get ahead in the line. At one end of the hall, there were raised desks where the officials presided over the fate of these lines of newcomers. It took hours, but eventually my father made it to the top of the line, answered the immigration officer's questions and shortly after, we were finally cleared to enter The United States of America.

Once we showed our papers to the guards, we were allowed through the high wooden fence. With trepidation, we emerged into Battery Park and the hustle and bustle of New York City. It was quite overwhelming for my parents. My father had been told to look for someone from the Irish Emigrant Aid Society and not to listen to people offering transport or shelter. Newly arrived immigrants were easy picking for enterprising nativists and criminals. My father was warned that many a fresh arrival was naively swindled out of their life savings within hours of landing in America, often by someone who pretended to be from their homeland. We were also cautioned to stay close to the water and to stay well clear of the area known as Five Points which was just a short walk north of Castle Garden. Five Points was a notorious tenement slum where, my father was informed, more crime is committed every day than in all of Ireland and England combined.

It was very crowded, and we were approached by lots of people saying they would help us. Some would ask where we were from and then claim to be from Limerick too but thanks to the warning, my father waved them all away. After a little while, my father managed to find a man from the Irish Emigrant Aid Society, and after a short conversation with him, we were directed to walk west, around the southern coast of the island, to a pier on the Hudson River. Clear on our directions, we walked for about forty minutes, dragging our belongings, and ignoring many offers of help for fear that we would be robbed. When we reached the pier in question, my father went into the ticket office and bought us tickets on the New York and Savannah Steam Ship Company's 'Mitchell Line'. The next sailing wasn't until the next day, so we spent the afternoon and night in the waiting room of the steam ship company. My father didn't want to spend money and risk being robbed in a hotel. Anyway, having spent weeks sleeping in discomfort on the William Stetson, we could have slept anywhere.

The next day, we were off on the seas again, boarding the steamship 'Star of the South' which ran the Mitchell Line down the coast to Savannah. With a small crew and about forty passengers onboard, this final leg of our journey only took us three days and with less crowds, it was far more pleasant than the big ship we had been confined to previously. It was also interesting to hear the new American accents and to see our new surroundings as we sailed south.

Never far from sight of land, we sailed south along the coast of the new world. As he had done on the other ship, my father would talk to the sailors and get updates on where we were. We sailed passed New Jersey, Delaware, Virginia, North Carolina. Once my father pointed out the lights of the city of Charleston, South Carolina on the horizon, we knew we were getting close to our destination. Finally, we rounded Hilton Head and turned up the muddy Savannah River. As we got closer to our destination our interest in the surroundings became more focused. We passed Tybee Island, then we sailed along the southern side of Fort Pulaski. Fort Pulaski was an impressive stone fort that guarded the mouth of the Savannah River. Going further upstream, on our left was the State of Georgia where our destination, Savannah, was. On the right-hand side was the state of South Carolina. The river was no more than seventy yards wide in places, but it was muddy so we couldn't tell how deep it was. Along the way there were a lot of marshes and swamps on both sides of the river and lots of small tributaries flowing down and joining the river. Within an hour or so of being on the river, we had docked in Savannah harbour, seventeen miles upstream from the coast. It was hot and muggy, and we were absolutely exhausted but finally our travels were over. We had reached our new home, Savannah in the State of Georgia.

Once the steamship had tied up, we gathered our possessions and disembarked onto the cobbled street that ran along the waterfront, River Street. It was like stepping out into New York all over again. Different accents, different languages, different coloured faces, different smells. It was buzzing with energy. The city was scarcely a hundred years old, but Savannah was the second busiest port in the southern states of America and River Street was its epicentre. Passengers like us unloading their luggage onto the street, others waiting for their turn to board one of the fifteen or so boats tied up on the wharves, cargo being ferried on carts to and from warehouses along the waterfront, and music coming from rowdy bars where sailors were being entertained by working women. It was alive with activity, and everything was new to us. These were sights and sounds like we had never experienced. It was vastly different from our life in the quiet village of Adare. I sometimes wonder about how my parents adapted to such a different setting. I was too young to know different but the contrast between Adare and Savannah was extreme.

We were met at the wharf by a relative of my father who had arranged a house for us to rent. It was just a short walk from the dock on River Street to our new home on St Julian Street. First, we had to climb up steps and onto the bluff. River Street is down on the waterfront, Savannah itself sits up on a bluff about twenty feet higher. It is a steep climb up the steps that led up to Bay Street but we managed it ok. Up there, there was just as much activity as down below on River Street. Businessmen marching in and out of City Hall, auction prices being shouted at the cotton exchange, carriages being driven up and down. As we walked through the busy streets, we got our first glimpses of beautiful Savannah. It felt so advanced compared to Adare. White wooden houses, tree lined streets, everything laid out in a neat grid and lots of park squares where people were shading from the hot Georgia summer sun. It was wonderful. Even though we were exhausted, our new surroundings gave us an energising lift that powered us on the final, short walk from the waterfront to our home at 31 St Julien St.

# V

# Antebellum Savannah

Having come from my grandfather's cold three-room cottage in Adare, 31 St Julian St was like a king's palace to us. A two-story wooden house with three bedrooms and a small porch out front, it was more than my mother had ever dreamed of. We had fireplaces upstairs and downstairs to keep us warm in the winter, large windows to let a breeze through in the hot sticky summer months and window shutters for hurricane season. Out the back was a small garden where my mother could grow flowers and out front was a quiet tree lined street. Situated just three blocks in from Bay St and the harbour front, and on the northeast corner of Price St, our new home was really central to all the exciting new things we had seen on our way from the docks. This little section of St Julian St was only two blocks long and was bookended by Washington Square at one end and Warren Square at the other, both of which were beautiful, tree shaded parks. It was like a little oasis in the middle of this bustling city.

Next door on one side were Con and Bridie Donovan and their

two daughters, Honora and Katie. They were from Ireland too. Con worked as a labourer, and Bridie worked in the local laundry. The couple became good friends with my parents. On the other side was an old lady, Celia Burke, who was from England originally. Her Irish born husband had died in a yellow fever epidemic a few years before we arrived in America. She kept to herself a lot and had a house slave named Lucy to help her, but my father would also keep an eye out for her and do any house repair work she needed done. Lucy had a son my age, but he kept to himself. Sometimes I would see him watching me playing with my friends. Once or twice, we invited him to join in, but he never did. Five doors up from us was the Sullivan's house. The Sullivans also had a son my age. His name was Tim. Tim and I became best friends and got up to all kinds of mischief together. We were close from the first time we met on my second day in Savannah, right up until I left town over ten years later.

Savannah was a wonderful place to live. Even though my mother loved Adare so much, she agreed that this was a marvellous place and after a while she didn't feel as lonely for her family. Life was definitely better. Savannah was a wealthy enough city, it was kept well and crime was fairly limited. Wages were higher in America and so people seemed to have just a little bit more money to keep the pressure off. On top of that, it was good just to feel warm most of the year around compared to Ireland which was only sunny for a few months a year. We just had to get used to the humidity and the mosquitoes which drove us demented during the sweltering summer months.

My father got a job working as a bookkeeper for the newly formed Southern Express Company. The company was owned by a man named Henry Bradley Plant who was from the northern state of Connecticut. He first came down to Georgia a few years prior to our arrival, as the southern superintendent for the New York based

Adams Express Company. He had done an excellent job on behalf of Adams, establishing them on all the railroad and steamboat lines and opening forwarding offices across all the major cities of the south. As a civil war was looming between north and south, the Adams Express Company feared losing all their southern interests, so a deal was cut with Mr Plant. Plant would establish his own business, The Southern Express Company, and he would take over all the southern operations and assets of the Adams Express Company. It was an incredibly lucky break for Plant who went on to make a fortune from this new venture. The Savannah office of this new company was its crown jewel. It was alive with activity as Savannah sat at a crossroads between the shipping routes of the Atlantic coast and the newly laid railway lines that ran across the growing economy of the south states. Plant used to say that he had a licence to print money.

This was the kind of job my father would never have had the chance to get back in Ireland after he was forced to leave the constabulary. No one would have taken the risk on him there. Southern Express was a wonderful way for my father to get started in Savannah life and he was happy there even though he was still bitter about having to leave Ireland.

Over the following weeks and months, we settled into our new home. Savannah was a busy, emerging city but it was a city of strange contrasts and contradictions. Savannah was a wealthy city. Some people, like Henry Bradley Plant, had made their fortune in industries like the cotton industry or the shipping industry. Those industries were exploding in the southern states and if you were in the right place, there was a lot of money to be made. That wealth was there on display for all to see around Savannah. The wealthy were lavishly dressed, riding in plush horse drawn carriages and generally showing their wealth at every opportunity. But Savannah also had the other extreme. There were hundreds of poor Irish and

German labourer immigrants trying to find a foothold in this new world there. The work they did at home or in the cities of the northern states, labouring mostly, here was done by African slaves for no wages. Why would anybody pay a labourer when you could get a slave to do the work for free? These poor immigrants found it difficult to make ends meet and their poverty was also very visible on the streets of Savannah. The poorer residents tended to live on the western side of the city. We were nestled in the more affluent part on the eastern side of Bull Street which divided the city down the middle. While we lived in the richer side of the city and were surrounded by slave owning elites, we were not wealthy. My father had a decent enough job, but compared to those around us, we struggled to get by.

Another contrast that we had to learn to adapt to was that of freedom and slavery. We were free to come and go as we pleased but all around us were people who had owners; masters who decided what they ate, what they did, and who they interacted with. The population of Savannah at the time was about twenty thousand people and that included about eight thousand slaves. One in three families owned one. Most of the families that lived on the eastern side of town, around us, had at least one. These negro slaves in Savannah, while starved of their freedom, were mostly treated well, unlike their counterparts out on the plantations that surrounded the city. City slaves would come and go, running errands for their masters. They were well dressed because nobody wanted society to think they couldn't afford to dress their negro well. So long as they behaved and wore their tag, city slaves had relative comfort. City slave owners had to find the right balance between allowing their slaves freedom to do their work around town and giving them too much freedom. Occasionally the authorities would pay someone a visit and say they were giving too much slack to their slave and, for the good of all and to prevent a rebellion, they should tighten the

leash a little. Meanwhile, out on plantations, their slave counterparts were just treated as beasts of burden. They were there to do
the hard labour of picking cotton or running the farm. They were
treated poorly, and it didn't matter what rags they were dressed in,
no one was looking out there anyway.

The last ship carrying African captives to Savannah arrived just
seven months before we did. Even though it was illegal by that time,
the ship "Wanderer" had landed just down river from town and
smuggled over four hundred captives ashore. Each slave had been
bought from a slaver in East Africa for fifty dollars and could be
sold in the auctions of Savannah or Atlanta for many times that.
There was a lot of money at stake and the cheap labour was needed
to keep fuelling the growth of southern industry. Then, just four
months before we had arrived there, the biggest ever slave auction
in US history took place in Savannah. Four hundred and twenty-
nine slaves from the Butler plantation not to far out of town, were
sold off by their master who had run into financial difficulty. The
horse racing course was used to house the slaves the week of the
auction which also took place at the site. Butler got just over three
hundred thousand dollars, or seven hundred dollars a head, for his
chain gang. Slavery was very much part of living in the south, and
you couldn't walk on the street without being confronted by it.
Most southerners were more than supportive of slavery. It was part
of their culture they would say.

My father used to say that the Irish were treated like slaves
by the British for hundreds of years and that it wasn't right that
these people were treated so poorly. He had to keep his thoughts
to himself though because most southern people had strong views
to the contrary and there was trouble brewing across America because of it.

One of my first experiences of this side of Savannah came one afternoon when I was out walking with my mother. We were crossing

over Johnson Square not too far from our house. Johnson Square is the main square in the centre of Savannah. It is just in front of City Hall and is usually the centre of any activity that is going on in town. Whether it is a celebration or a protest, Johnson Square is where the crowds gather. That particular day there was a lot of activity over by the courthouse, so we walked over to see what was happening. As you would expect of an important building like this, the courthouse is a big, impressive building. Painted white and with high roman columns out front with sweeping steps up to its front door.  It is a fabulous looking building. Outside the courthouse and all along one side wall was a permanent wooden platform. About five feet off the ground, there were steps leading up to it from the lefthand side and a guard rail surrounded the front and the right-hand side. The platform was snug up against the wall of the building so didn't need a rail at the back. Underneath the platform were two cages with strong wire mesh and padlocked gates. This platform was used every other day for slave auctions.

As we approached, there was a negro girl standing on the plat-form. Scarcely dressed at all, she had chains around the ankles of her bare feet. She looked dishevelled and worried about what was happening to her. Meanwhile, a well-dressed white man with a suit, waistcoat, and top hat, was on the platform beside her. He was presenting her to the crowd. Gathered around, there were five or six men inspecting her and a few other spectators like ourselves. The men would shout up to the man on the stage who would, in turn, tell the poor girl to show various parts of her body so they could all see better. With her dignity completely stripped, she would comply, even when the inspection was of an intimate area. She was ordered to show her breasts, for what reason no one said. The well-dressed man then pulled her dress down to the waist, leaving her standing there topless for all the world to see. By the end of the show, she was standing there naked and crying. At one point she was asked to turn around and show her rear to one of the onlooking men. As she did so, the auctioneer told her to lean over. When she did that, he took his cane, placed it between her cheeks and pushing, he prised her buttocks apart to allow her cleanliness to be inspected. To these prospective buyers, she was just meat. To most of those watching, this was a normal occurrence around Savannah.

A man yelled up at the poor girl, *"Hey, what's your name girl?"*.

*"Betsey, Sur"*, she answered.

*"Show me your leg. What is that scar?"*, he asked.

*"Disy here hole on my leg is where a snake dun bite me Sur. I dun took a knife an cut the jus out. It lef me with dis here mark"*, she responded to him.

*"What happened to your forehead?"*, he then asked.

*"Dat der scar on my head frum my missus. She done hit me with a club cause I run away"*, she responded.

*"Sur, if you buy me, an be good to me, I won't run away none, an I promise to work up atil I die."*, she added sensing a touch of kindness in the man's voice.

*"Yes. Yes you will"*, said the man as he agreed to buy her for six hundred and ten dollars.

With that, the poor girl was pulled from the stage, dragged down the wooden steps and was thrown into the holding pen under the platform where a dozen other negroes were waiting for their turn to be displayed, inspected and sold on the platform.

With the paperwork complete for the sale of poor Betsey, next up on stage was a fine strong looking fellow. Naked from the waist up, barefoot and with britches that were ragged at the knee, he was introduced by the auctioneer as George. For a man of his size, George was holding himself in a rather meek manner.

*"Listen up everyone. Y'all looking out for good bone and strong muscle. The crop will be heavy this year and you all need strong hands to pick it. This is George. Ladies and gentlemen, you won't find a better specimen of a field hand anywhere this side of the Mississippi.",* he said.

*"What age are you, George?",* he asked the negro.

*"Twenty-two sur",* replied George.

*"Show them your teeth boy",* he was ordered. George grinned widely so his teeth were visible.

*"You see, all his own teeth and not a scar on his body. This is a prime negro. Twenty-two years old. You'll get at least fifteen years of field work out of him.",* announced the man.

As George stood there in chains on the platform, there was lively bidding for his ownership. He was finally sold for eight hundred and fifty dollars, a good bargain according to the auctioneer. That was when the pain of slavery became plainly visible to those crowded around. As soon as the purchase price was agreed, George spoke up.

*"Mas'r, Mas'r. 'scuse me Mas'r",* he said.

*"I loves Mary, Mas'r; I loves her true, an she love me. Mas'r please buy Mary sur; good lord knows she a good woman and a real good house servant; keep us togetha sur; we wants to get married sur and we have chilrun for you sur; fine healthy strong chilrun; please sur",* he begged.

Sensing that his new owner wasn't interested in another purchase that day, he added *"Mas'r; please mas'r; Mary a prime slave sur; she strong; please sur; we bout to me married sur".*

Still there was no sign from the new owner that he was empathetic to George's plight. Wails started to come from under the stage as Mary began to realise her beloved was being sold away. The tension rose as George was dragged down from the platform. With the auctioneer's assistant pulling on his chains and Mary's cries getting louder, George got visibly angry. Trying to look back and have his words heard, George gave it one last try and yelled, *"Please mas'r. Please"*. With that the auctioneer hit him a wallop on the side of the head with the same cane he had used to prise apart poor Betsey's buttocks. As George was dragged off to his new owner's awaiting transport, there were roars and cries as the young couple were separated and most likely never saw each other again.

After watching for half an hour or so, we moved along with my mother muttering under her breath *"Those poor people"* as we left the sad scene. The crying and begging left a mark on my young mind. Auctions like this were an almost daily occurrence as J. Bryan and Son, Elisha Wylly and C.A.L Lamar, all agents in the sale of people, took turns selling their wares on that platform in the main square or in their auction rooms scattered across the city.

It took some time for me to understand some of the differences but there were four distinct kinds of slaves kept in the city. The first were family servants. Mostly female, they were well treated and lived with the family. Every piece of food consumed by the family was purchased and cooked by these servants. They did all the house chores and took care of the children. The second kind was the hired servant. A slave cost about seven hundred dollars to buy. That is a lot of money, so some people rented a slave. For about ten dollars a month, you could use the slave as you wished. They could be used for labouring work or housework. So long as you paid the monthly fee, you had your slave. Then there were the nominal slaves. These were slaves who had somehow managed to gather some money together and with some good fortune, they were able to pay their master a monthly fee to live like free men. They lived in poor dwellings out in the swamps away from the white people and didn't have much money left after paying their master, but they were free and used their time to find ways to earn the next month's fee. The last kind of slave was a waterman. All around Savannah were marshes, streams, and swamps. Watermen knew the terrain and were used to help navigate about the place. They slept on their owners' boat and spent all their time out on the water. Of course, there was a fifth kind of slave, the plantation slave. Purely there for labouring, you only saw plantation slaves in the city if they were being brought into town to be bought and sold.

All slaves wore a badge specifying what their status was. They could be accosted at any time by the police or by bounty hunters looking for runaways. They would have to prove their status by showing the badge they carried. There were also a small number of negroes in Savannah who had been granted their freedom by their masters. Even though they were 'free', they had to wear a badge that proved so and they had to adhere to a nightly curfew. All freed slaves had to be sponsored by a white person, usually the master that gave them their freedom, and they had to do one month of compulsory community service every year, like work in the fire brigade. My father said they weren't free at all.

Every now and then there would be a disturbance around town when someone's slave would run off. Savannah was a destination for runaway slaves from all over the south. Slaves felt that if they could get to Savannah, they could blend in with the freer city blacks before stowing away on a boat to New York or Boston, where there was freedom to be had. Many managed to get away. Most were hunted down and captured though. No master could afford to lose his seven-hundred-dollar investment, so they would get slave hunters to track them down. In the marshes down river and on some of the many small islands along the Georgia coast, there were plenty of slaves who had managed to get free. Occasionally, they would be caught and brought back to town. Sometimes they would get whooped but mostly the punishment was to put them in the slave jail at the edge of town or worse, sell their family out from under them. To me that must have hurt more than any whooping.

Not too long after we had arrived in Savannah my brother Francis was born. My mother had been getting close to the birth for a few days. She couldn't get around the place so was resting in bed a lot. Our neighbour Bridie Donovan helped and cooked our meals for a few days and tended to my mother. The child came during the middle of the night. I was awakened by the sound of my mother's screams. Being young, I could hear my mother was in pain but couldn't understand why. I didn't know how the baby would come out of my mother's stomach. I went to my parent's room to see what was happening. My father turned me around at the bedroom door and sent me next door to quickly wake-up Bridie and get her to come and help. I was five years old, and my father told me to stay outside the door and to allow nature to take its course. It was hard not to look in the door especially when the screams got louder. After what felt like hours, my little brother came out and I could hear him crying in the room. At that point, I couldn't hold back any longer and dashed in to meet him. He was covered in a towel and was in Bridie's arms when I met him first. He had a little tuft of fair hair on the top of his head. It was a little matted and red with blood. He was so small. I turned to my mother in the bed in excitement. She was exhausted and there was a lot of blood on the blankets around her, but she smiled at me and told me it was a boy, and that I was a big boy now that I had a little brother. I was absolutely thrilled. I couldn't wait to tell my friend Tim. He already had a little brother called Dennis. Francis was the first of our family born in America. Things were going well for us. We didn't know it at first, but Francis was a little bit handicapped and was a little bit slow. When it became noticeable after a few years, it was sad for my parents.

With my father settled into a respectable job, my parents wanted me to get a good education. So, when I turned five years old, I was enrolled in Chatham Academy. This was a private school and my father paid ten dollars a quarter for me to attend. That was a lot of money. Most other children I knew didn't attend school at all and I couldn't understand why my friend Tim couldn't come with me. I didn't understand the sacrifice my parents were making for me. I didn't have much choice, so I went along. Chatham Academy was a big three-story stone building on Bull Street, not too far from our house. Inside were classrooms all fitted out with wooden benches and desks for the students, a blackboard hung on the wall up front and there was a desk for the teacher. The school had a focus on classical subjects like Latin, history, and mathematics. I didn't like it much. I would rather have been with Tim playing in one of Savannah's squares or exploring down around the harbour front. Chatham Academy also had a military part of the curriculum where we learned to march and drill like soldiers. I liked this part much more than sitting in the classroom. In the end, I only went to school for two terms as the school closed when the civil war started, and I didn't go back afterwards.

A little over a year after we arrived in America, on November 6th, the 1860 Presidential Election was held. With the trouble brewing between the northern and southern states, this election was a flashpoint that could ignite a civil war. Ahead of the election, Minnesota, Kansas, and Oregon joined the Union. This gave the northern states a numerical advantage in terms of population. Previously, with each slave only counting as two thirds of a person, the southern states had the higher population. That year there was also a change in the electoral college system. This time there would be three hundred and six electoral votes, with one hundred and eighty-six from northern non-slaveholding states, and just one hundred and twenty from slaveholding states. There was a lot of people in the south unhappy about these changes. To them it felt like it was being stacked in favour of the anti-slavery states. The result, that an anti-slavery northern candidate would win, was being set up and then, they felt, the southern way of life would be gone forever.

Abraham Lincoln, a lawyer from the northern state of Illinois and a vocal slavery abolitionist was selected as the Republican candidate. The democratic party was divided. At their national convention, the northern democrats put forward abolitionist Stephen Douglas, while the southern democrats put forward John Breckinridge. Breckinridge was the serving Vice President under President James Buchanan. With the split in the democratic party, there were ultimately four names on the ballot sheet. Lincoln and Douglas were abolitionist and from the northern states, Breckinridge was pro-slavery and felt the states should decide for themselves. The fourth candidate was John Bell from the Constitutional Unionist Party. Bell had no position at all on the main talking point of the election, slavery.

With the country's future delicately balanced on the outcome, Abraham Lincoln was elected. Lincoln hadn't even received a single vote in Savannah and the same happened in other polling districts across the south. Two thirds of the votes cast in Savannah were for pro-slavery Breckinridge and the balance were split between Douglas and Bell. The country and Savannah braced itself for what might happen next. It was almost a certainty that Lincoln would emancipate the slaves.

News of the election of Abraham Lincoln prompted a public demonstration in Johnson Square. A huge crowd turned out to protest. There were speeches and placards calling for Georgia to leave the Union. During our usual Sunday mass at St John the Baptist Church, the following Sunday, Father O'Neill took to the altar and in his sermon, he condemned the election and urged the congregation to support a confederacy. Most people in the church nodded approvingly as he spoke. My father sat with his head in his hands.

Within weeks, South Carolina seceded from the Union. A few days later, on December 26th, a rally was held in Savannah to honour South Carolina's brave step. Almost every house in the city was lit up with lanterns. Bonfires were lit and, as usual, a crowd descended on Johnson Square in front of city hall where they called for Georgia to follow suit and leave the Union.

Crowds gathered in Johnson Square, Savannah, celebrating
Georgia's secession from the Union.

The effects of South Carolina's action were felt almost immediately across the south. Trade between north and south ground to a halt. Dock workers started to lose their jobs in Savannah and people started to horde supplies in anticipation of a civil war. Several slaves decided the time was right for them to make a break for freedom, hoping that people would be preoccupied with the inevitable conflict. In response the Savannah city council ordered for more policemen to be recruited to help keep the peace.

Suspicion and anger also came against any northern person who happened to be living in the city. A hateful mob set upon a shoe dealer. He happened to have been born in Massachusetts but had lived in Savannah most of his life. Unfortunately for him, he had made the mistake of expressing anti-slavery views. The mob tarred and feathered him and left him for dead. Thankfully, my father had never openly expressed his views, outside of to a very close friends, but he was still impacted by the anti-northern sentiment that blew up after the election. Some people were suspicious of the ownership of the Southern Express Company. Henry Plant was from the north and people questioned the legitimacy of his new company. Was it all a ruse so that the Adams Express Company could retain their southern assets? For a while business slowed as a result and my father's job was jeopardised temporarily but it passed once people saw that Southern Express were shipping confederate supplies.

# VI

❦

# Civil War

Even as we were settling into our new life in Savannah, it was obvious that there was trouble brewing. As recently as February 1859, the Union was expanding with Oregon joining as the 33$^{rd}$ State but there was a real divide between the northern states and southern ones. The southern states relied on slaves to be able to harvest cotton at a low price. Slavery which had started as far back as 1619, had been phased out in the north. Pennsylvania was first to ban it in 1780 and by the time we arrived in America, a total of seventeen states had abolished it. The fifteen other states, the southern ones including Georgia, held firm.

When we arrived in Savannah, the tension between north and south had reached fever pitch and it was clear that something had to happen to solve the standoff. My father was an ardent slavery abolitionist. He didn't see how any Irishman could stand by and watch the negroes be treated like they were. How could you 'own a man' for the price of seven hundred dollars? To him it was just cruelty and we Irish had had enough of that at the hands of the British.

However, the Irish in the southern states were divided on the subject. Many of the poor Irish emigrants found it difficult to compete with the free labour provided by the slaves. Some Irish resented them and wanted slavery abolished so they would have better access to work. Others had found work on plantations policing slaves and were known for their cruelty in punishing them for any reason they could find. To them slavery gave them the opportunity to treat others as they felt they had been treated back in Ireland. With most of the population of Savannah being pro-slavery though, my father kept his head down and his opinions to himself.

As young boys, myself and Tim weren't really aware of what was happening around us but there were things happening that we watched with the innocent eyes of children. Sometimes my parents would tell me what was happening or warn me to say away from certain things. Tim and I shared everything we learned as we tried to piece together what the mounting anxiety all around us was about.

## 1861

January 3$^{rd}$ 1861 was a rainy Thursday. It was two months after the election and I wasn't at school because of the new year's holiday. There was so much excitement around the town that I don't think we would have been in school even if it wasn't a holiday. Tim and I were attracted by the sound of military drums and walked up to Johnson Square. There was a big crowd gathered there. Then a procession of military men marched, three abreast, down Bull St, around us in the Square, then along Bay St on their way to River Street. The men were from the Oglethorpe Light Infantry of the Georgia militia. Dressed in their uniform, knee length dark blue frock coats buttoned from collar to the waist, leather utility belts with the letters 'OLI' on the buckle, grey trousers, and cap, they were an impressive sight. They were each carrying a rolled-up blanket strapped on their backs, had rifles over their shoulders and their bayonets were strapped to their belts. Along with them were six artillery pieces being pulled on carriages by big black horses. There must have been a hundred and fifty men in all. They were marching under a white flag with a lone red star on it. I learned later that it was the flag of Georgia. Tim and I followed them along Bay Street and, as young boys would, we pretended to march as if we were part of the moving garrison.

As they got closer to River Street, the crowd got so thick that the soldiers could hardly keep their marching formation. There was great excitement around them. When we reached the waterfront, the men boarded a steamship called 'Ida'. As they boarded, some climbed on the roof of the cabin. Others went into the cabin and found their place as black smoke billowed from the single chimney of their steamship. After a little while, there were loud cheers from the crowd as the ship set off down the river. Me and Tim watched the boat sail away down the river towards the ocean from up on the bluff at the end of River Street.

It was a fun morning for us. We had no idea that they were sailing off down the river to "attack" Fort Pulaski. Fort Pulaski was a disused fort at the mouth of the Savannah River seventeen miles downstream. It had been built in the 1840s to provide a strategic defensive spot on the Savannah River but it was never really used. The army kept a handful of soldiers there to keep the fort operational but at the sight of the Georgia Militia arriving that day, they simply downed their weapons and surrendered the fort. Within a short while, the Georgia flag was flying proudly over the fort's ramparts. This was the first piece of aggression that Georgia undertook in the impending Civil War. The Georgian politicians felt that if they hadn't taken the fort, the northern army would increase their presence there and take control of this strategic location. Better to strike first, they thought.

The days following that military parade and the taking of Fort

Pulaski were full of anticipation as first Mississippi seceded from the Union on January 9th. The following day, Florida followed suit and then the next day, Alabama. With the southern states falling like dominos, everyone wondered what Georgia would do. A week later, on January 19th, a convention was held in the town of Milledgeville. Milledgeville was the state capital and was midway between the three big cities of Atlanta, Augusta, and Savannah. Late that evening news broke in Savannah that a vote to remove Georgia from the Union had been easily passed. Georgia, the fourth state to join the Union back in 1788, became the fifth state to secede in response to the election of Abraham Lincoln.

That night there was a street party in Savannah. There were fireworks in Johnson Square and speeches made on the steps of City Hall. Everyone, it seemed, was pleased with this decision. My father was disconsolate. *"They are going to bring war on us. We have just started to make a new life here in America. Now what? And all because of slavery?"*, he said to my mother when he heard the news. That night we stayed home. My father didn't think we had anything to celebrate, and he wasn't even curious to see the revelry. I spent the evening looking out my window. Every now and then there would be a flash of fireworks and as the evening got later, revellers would stumble along the street outside our house, drunk and cheering our independence from the 'nigger loving Union'.

Over the next few weeks, a call went out for men to join the militia to help defend the newly independent State of Georgia. Forsyth Park on the outskirts of town was taken over for the new recruits to be trained and drilled. I was warned to stay clear of it by my parents. Tim was still allowed go or at least hadn't been told not to, but we decided to stay away from that part of town anyway. Needless to say, my father didn't volunteer his services.

By the end of the month, Georgia had been followed by Louisiana and Texas in leaving the Union. Then on February 4th, representatives from each of the seceded states met down in Alabama. A week later, on February 11th, they agreed to form the Confederate States of America. A man named Jefferson Davis was elected as our new president and a new constitution was agreed. That constitution included a commitment to continue the practice of slavery in all the confederate states and territories. When news reached Savannah, there was another celebration party with a military parade and more fireworks in Johnson Square.

During those first few months of 1861, there was a real tension in the air. There was a lot of coming and going around River Street. There were shipments of guns arriving, northern vessels being commandeered, units of the militia marching through the Savannah streets. It seemed like there was something happening every day and I was happy to skip school to explore the events of the day with Tim. We were spending all our time down on River Street or around Johnson Square. Those two seemed to be the best locations for whatever activity might be happening on any particular day.

Things became even more tense after Abraham Lincoln was inaugurated as the 16th US president in Washington, D.C. There were shouts of "*Not my president*" and "*I'll defend Georgia with my life*" to be heard regularly on the streets around Savannah in the build up to it. On the day of the inauguration, military officials called on all able-bodied men to come and enlist at Forsyth Park. My father refused to go but about fifteen hundred men presented themselves, perhaps attracted by the prospect of a fifty-dollar signing on bonus that was on offer.

One Thursday afternoon in late March 1861, we were playing in Warren Square at the end of our street. There was a lot of people hanging around and it felt like there was something going on. As curious children do, we followed along to see what the excitement was about. We followed as far as Chippewa Square, a few blocks from our street. When we got there, we could see hundreds of people lingering around the square and a large crowd outside the Atheneum Theatre on the corner. The Atheneum was an impressive three-story stone building. Out front of the main doors, an ornate veranda gave summer shelter, and it had a sign announcing what was playing in the theatre that week. Along the side of the building there were a few steps that led up to the side door. We decided to use them to sneak inside to see what was happening. Inside, the hall was lined with plush red audience seats and above them two balconies held space for more viewers. We found a stairway that led up to a gantry high over the stage. We hid up there where we could see down into the hall.

The audience seats were all packed and there was a buzz of anticipation in the room as if something important was going to happen. Behind the stage was draped a huge flag. The flag had a blue square in the top left corner with seven stars in it. The rest of the flag was three stripes, two red and with a white one in the middle. I'd never seen this flag before. It turned out to be the new flag of the Confederate States. Sitting on the stage, under the flag, were a line of men all dressed well in suits and all looking very official. We were too young to recognise any of them but one of them stood out. He was a strange looking fellow. He must have been about fifty years old. Dressed in a dark suit with a smart waistcoat and the stiff collar of his white shirt was held in place by a bow tie. He was a very sickly-looking man. Very frail and with wispy fine fair hair down over his ears and a fringe that cut across his forehead.

As we watched, another man strode up from the back of the hall and mounted the stage. In a loud voice, so as he could be heard, he introduced himself as the Mayor of Savannah, Charles Jones. He made a few remarks before inviting the frail man to step forward to address the crowd. His name was Alexander Hamilton Stephens and the mayor introduced him as the new Vice President of the

Confederate Republic. He stepped forward to tremendous applause from the eager and attentive crowd.

Mr Stephens was obviously a very well-educated man and despite his frail appearance, his voice was loud enough to carry in the room. No sooner had he begun than a muttering could be heard coming from the back of the hall. Then someone shouted up from the back that there were more people outside the theatre than inside and perhaps Mr Stephens would be better off standing at the theatre door to make his speech. The mayor rose and asked for silence. After a few minutes during which Mr Stephens had returned to his seat, it was announced that Mr Stephens health would not permit him to speak in the open air and that he would proceed from the stage. There was an immediate clamour from the back as people wedged themselves inside so as the hear the imminent speech. Again, there was a call for silence from the stage and after a few minutes Mr Stephens returned to his feet.

With myself and Tim eagerly watching down between the wooden posts of the gantry guardrail, Mr Stephens began to speak. He started, *"When perfect quiet is restored, I shall proceed. I cannot speak so long as there is any noise or confusion. I shall take my time; I feel quite prepared to spend the night with you if necessary"*. There was loud applause to this last line. Once the applause subsided, he continued, *"We are passing through one of the greatest revolutions in the annals of the world. Seven states have within the last three months thrown off an old government and formed a new. This revolution has been signally marked, up to this time, by the fact of its having been accomplished without the loss of a single drop of blood"*. Again, there was tremendous applause from the crowd.

Mr Stephens was a fine orator; he had no speaking notes, but he kept the ear of all who were within listening distance of him. He spoke passionately about the confederate states and the new constitution that they had agreed to down in Alabama. He said there were some things that he himself didn't fully agree with but that, it was a better path for the nation than the constitution written by the founding fathers nearly a hundred years ago. He went through several points where the new Confederate constitution was better than the previous one. A lot of this was lost on our young ears but the crowd were very vocally supportive any time there was a break in Mr Stephens' words.

Then, to the packed room, he delivered a message that was very loudly approved of. "*The new constitution has put at rest, forever, all the agitating questions relating to our peculiar institution, African slavery as it exists amongst us, the proper status of the negro in our form of civilisation. This was the immediate cause of the late rupture and present revolution. Jefferson in his forecast, had anticipated this, as the 'rock on which the old Union would split'. He was right. What was conjecture with him, is now a realised fact. But whether he fully comprehended the great truth upon which that rock stood and stands, may be doubted. The prevailing ideas entertained by him and most of the leading statesmen at the time of the formation of the old constitution, were that the enslavement of the African was in violation of the laws of nature; that it was wrong in principle, socially, morally, and politically. It was an evil they knew not well how to deal with, but the general opinion of the men of that day was that, somehow or other in the order of Providence, the institution would be evanescent and pass away. This idea, though not incorporated in*

Confederate Vice President Alexander H Stephens who delivered the 'Cornerstone Speech' in support of slavery in Savannah on March 21st 1861 *the constitution, was the prevailing idea at that time. The constitution, it is true, secured every essential guarantee to the institution while it should last, and hence no argument can be justly urged against the constitutional guarantees thus secured, because of the common sentiment of the day. Those ideas, however, were fundamentally wrong. They rested upon the assumption of the equality of the races. This was an error. It was a sandy foundation, and the government built upon it fell when the storm came, and the wind blew. Our new government is founded upon exactly the opposite idea; its foundations are laid, its cornerstone rests upon the truth, that the negro is not equal to the white man; that slavery, subordination to the superior race, is his natural and normal condition".* To that there were loud cheers. Some of those seated in the hall, arose, and waved their hats in jubilation. Again, there was a clamour from the back as Mr Stephens words were relayed to the crowed amassed outside and another loud cheer could be heard from outside.

Mr Stephens spoke for a while more and then thanked the crowed for listening. He finished by saying *"If we are true to ourselves, true to our cause, true to our destiny, true to our high mission, in presenting to the world the highest type of civilisation ever exhibited by man, there will be found in our lexicon no such word as fail".* He then returned to his seat, amid a burst of enthusiasm and support from all present. Myself and Tim didn't understand most of what he had said, but we knew from listening that the people of Savannah agreed with him.

It was getting late so, after Mr Stephens spoke, we went back down the stairs from the gantry and slipped out the door, and back into the street. As we made our way through the jubilant crowd to go home, we could hear everyone dissecting their recollection of the words they had heard. That night my father came home; he was drunk, and I heard him telling my mother about it. He was in the crowd and told my mother that there was *"a lot of trouble brewing over the fate of those poor negroes".* He must have been the only one in the hall that night not shouting his approval and he must have gone drinking afterwards to calm himself down.

One afternoon a few weeks later in April, Con Donovan from next door, came bounding in the door of our house.

*"It has started"*, he told my father.
*"The war. It has started"*, he clarified when he saw a confused look on my father's face.
*"Idiots. The lot of them are idiots"*, my father yelled.
*"How many men will have do die because of this? Its not worth it. Slavery is wrong"*, my father added. He was wasting his breath; Con was one of the few people who agreed with my father.

The Confederate Army had attacked Fort Sumter in Charleston harbour in the neighbouring state of South Carolina. Unlike Fort Pulaski, which was taken without a fight, Fort Sumter had been shelled for two days by confederate forces before the Federal troops withdrew and gave up their stronghold. My father was furious.

In the following days, four more southern states withdrew from the Union. Virginia, Tennessee, Arkansas and then North Carolina. The Union was falling apart, a civil war had begun, and my school days were over. Chatham Academy was closed to allow people to sign up for the war and so that it could be used as a field hospital for the many soldiers who would be wounded over the next four years.

In the first week of May, two US army officers were discovered to be staying at the Pulaski House Hotel on Johnson square. Someone had seen their names on the hotel register and word spread quickly. The two were holed up in their room as a large crowd gathered outside. People were shouting about them being spies and calling for them to be lynched. To quell the panic and to prevent the baying crowd storming into the hotel, the mayor was called. When he arrived, he went into the hotel and requested to meet the two visitors. He went up and knocked on their door. The men opened the door and agreed to meet with him. It turned out they were recent graduates from West Point military academy, and they had been traveling back north from a trip to Florida when they both became very unwell. Both had contracted consumption and needed a place to rest because they were so weak. They were inevitably dying and were therefore no threat to Savannah. Relieved that it wasn't part of a Union plot, Mayor Jones told the men they could continue their travels unhindered once they had the strength. He then went down and informed the crowd. They were still wanting the men to be hung but eventually they agreed with the mayor's position that the men should be allowed to continue their travels if and when they were strong enough. Both men died within a week. They were buried in Savannah and never made it home.

On 21st May 1861, one of the grandest sights of the war took place in Savannah. The Oglethorpe Light Infantry's "A" Company was heading off to the battle front in Virginia. They assembled at their parade ground and marched to the railroad depot. A brass band played "Bold Soldier Boy" and other military tunes as they marched along. The streets were lined with civilians waving hankies and cheering as local boy Colonel Francis Bartow led his men proudly by. Bartow was a local attorney, politician, and a member of a prominent family. He was the epitome of what a brave southern man was expected to be and there he was, setting an example for all local boys to follow.

Having arrived at the railway, the troops boarded a train at 2PM. Before boarding himself, Bartow was presented with a confederate flag which he promised not to dishonour saying *"I pledge to you this day on their behalf, that should they fail to bring back to you this flag, it will be because there is not one arm left among them to bear it aloft".* To loud cheers, he took the flag, boarded the train, and saluted as the train pulled away from the platform. Two months to the day later, Bartow and many of the men we watched march proudly out of Savannah that day, were killed during a confederate victory at Manassas during the First Battle of Bull Run. Bartow was shot in the chest. His final words to his men were "*Boys, they have killed me, but never give up the field*".

A week after his death, on 26th July, Bartow's body arrived back in Savannah. His body was presented to the Savannah public as he lay in state at the city exchange building. Hundreds watched as his black hearse, drawn by four grey horses, clip-clopped through the city carrying his coffin. Bells rang out and cannon salutes were fired, as his body was brought to Christ Church for his funeral. The city was brought to a standstill as sixteen different military companies marched alongside him in the cortege. My father and mother were discussing it afterwards and they agreed that it was a sad spectacle, but both questioned why Bartow's body was the only one to be brought home. The other brave Savannah boys who died with him, were buried on the battlefield in Virginia without fanfare or even grave markers.

From around May, the Union navy had started to block off access to the Savannah River and the effects on the local economy was starting to bite. Then, in September, Tim and I were down on River Street watching what was happening as a steamship named "Bermuda" arrived in the docks with a cargo of supplies for the Confederate Army. Somehow, it had managed to evade the Union navy's blockade to deliver these much-needed supplies. Boxes were taken off the ship containing rifles, ammunition, and other provisions. They also unloaded about a dozen cannons. Then, with my limited Chatham Academy reading skills, I was able to read "Tait Clothing Company. Limerick" on the side of big canvas bags being unloaded. I was so excited to see 'Limerick' written on them that I dashed home to tell my parents. My father was a little bemused by my enthusiasm and told me that the Tait factory in Limerick City made clothes, so the bags probably contained Confederate Army uniforms. I don't think he was too happy about it. The "Bermuda" was shortly followed by another blockade runner named "Fingal" which also landed in Savannah with confederate supplies. The arrival of both ships was a cause for celebration in Savannah as the blockade had begun squeezing the life out of Savannah's trade. The crews of both ships were celebrated and acknowledged as heroes. As usual, they were feted by a big celebration on Johnson Square. The "Bermuda" and "Fingal" were amongst the last ships to make it to Savannah during the war. In November, the Union Army sent a flotilla of ships to block off access from the Atlantic up the Savannah River completely. They also sunk several vessels to make navigating the mouth of the river difficult for any ship that managed to evade the blockade.

On the night of November 24th, the Union army landed troops on Tybee Island right out on the coast and just a mile from where the Georgia Militia held Fort Pulaski. The confederate troops could see the Union soldiers landing and raising their colours on the beach. There were no confederate troops on Tybee Island to defend it. With the Union Army now just miles from Savannah, a lot of people decided to move inland away from any possible Union attack. We had nowhere to go and, anyway, my father said it would all be over soon, and things would be better once Georgia was back in the Union.

### 1862

Some people wondered if Savannah might be the site of a major battle. There were about ten thousand confederate troops in city throughout the war. Even though the Union Army was now just up the coast from Savannah, the anticipated attack never came. A stalemate took hold. The Union were happy just to blockade the port, to stop supplies reaching the city and the confederates. Life in Savannah just continued relatively normally over the next little while but the threat just up the coast always loomed large. With the Chatham Academy closed, I spent my days with Tim checking out what changes each day brought. There was always something happening to entertain our young minds, troops moving, defences being built, ships being re-enforced with steel so they could try and run the gauntlet of the blockade. My father's work was busy as The Southern Express Company was always shipping things on behalf of the Confederate Army. He was happy to have work to do, even if he didn't agree with the confederate cause.

About 8 o'clock in the morning of 10th April, we were awoken by the sound of distant heavy gunfire. My father said it must be a Union attack on Fort Pulaski. He was right. For the next twenty-four hours we stayed indoors as the Union artillery rained down on Pulaski from six big guns across on Tybee Island. All day we could hear the guns and wondered what was happening and would there be a simultaneous attack on the city. We all sheltered in the house and waited for word to come. That night I struggled to sleep because of the distant booming. Then, almost exactly twenty-four hours after it started, the guns fell silent. Slowly people emerged out onto the streets to see if anyone knew what was happening. In the late afternoon word reached Savannah that Fort Pulaski had fallen to the Union. The news was greeted with consternation on the streets. What now? What was there to prevent the Yankees from sailing up the river and taking Savannah? A panic spread through the city. Some were packing up to move inland, others were calling for every man to be ready to defend the city, house by house if necessary. My father just said that we should wait and see what would happen next.

The panic was misplaced; the Union Army never came. With the blockade in place and Fort Pulaski now in Union hands, Savannah's main strategic value was nullified. The Union General, Ulysses S

Grant, preferred to focus on other parts of the country for his strategic gains, safe in the knowledge that Savannah and the Savannah River couldn't do any damage to his cause.

The rest of 1862 passed by with Savannah stuck in the Union naval blockade. In the town, people went about their usual business. Everyone followed the updates as to what was happening in the battles that raged across our fractured country. Every now and then, word would reach town that one of the local boys who had gone off to fight for the confederates had been killed in action. Occasionally, a gravely wounded and disfigured local boy would come home to Savannah, half the man he was when he left.

In September, Abraham Lincoln let it be known that he was going to announce the emancipation of the African slaves on 1st January 1863. Savannah was on tenterhooks for the remainder of the year as Savannahians and their slaves waited to hear his words and wondered what might happen if he did emancipate the slaves. Many slave owners warned their slave that they would sooner shoot them than see them run free.

On New Years Eve, the Donovans from next door joined us as we counted down to this momentous event. Con was probably the only person my father was open with about his anti-slavery views. Con agreed with him, so it was safe for them to discuss it amongst themselves. The city was like a powder keg that night. No one knew what would happen at midnight. With a candle burning by the window of our drawing room, we ate and counted down the minutes. My father told us to *"Always remember Freedom's Eve. From tomorrow, things will be different"*, he said.

## 1863

True to his word, Abraham Lincoln issued the Emancipation Proclamation on 1st January 1863. In it he stated that *"all persons held as slaves"* within the rebellious states *"are, and henceforth shall be free."*

In the safety of our house, my father was jubilant. He had always said slavery and the treatment of the slaves was wrong. He was happy that it was now official US policy, in the northern states at least. He sat me down in the kitchen and read the proclamation to me. He ended it by saying to me, *"Son, there is injustice in the world, and you will at times be a victim of that injustice but remember, that doesn't mean you should be part of the injustice. Always try and do the right thing."*

Thursday 1ˢᵗ January was greeted with protests and unrest in Savannah. Down at Johnson Square a crowd gathered to condemn Lincoln for his treachery. There were noticeably fewer negroes on the street that day. Their masters kept them under watch for fear of an uprising. Around mid-morning, Celia Burke, the old lady next door, came knocking on our door. When my father answered it, she was angry.

*"Lucy has run off. I've been good to that girl, and she run off the first chance she got"*, she said.

*"I'm sorry to hear that but you know Lincoln has freed the black folks, right?"*, my father replied.

*"He has no authority here; we have left the Union. What am I supposed to do now?"*, Mrs Burke said.

*"I'm sorry Mrs Burke but there is no point lookin for her now. She could be anywhere and I'm sure lots of black folks have run off today"*, my father replied.

With that Mrs Burke grumbled under her breath and walked off. Not knowing my father was an abolitionist, she was hoping that my father would help look for Lucy. There was no chance that he was going to help track down someone and return them to servitude. Some Africans did run off that day. All they had to do was find a company of the Union Army and they would be freed. I would wager that most of those that ran off this day, went down towards the coast and tried to get to Fort Pulaski or Tybee Island. Those that didn't run would have to live under the laws of the confederacy for a while longer.

In January and February, the Union Navy made repeated attempts to capture Fort McAllister on the Ogeechee River to the south of Savannah. Despite these attempts, the fort held firm in confederate hands. With much sad news around, this stout defence gave the citizens of Savannah something to cheer about. Even though a long-anticipated attack on Savannah from Tybee Island hadn't materialised, these fresh attacks raised concerns that the Union had turned its eyes on us and again there was a little panic in the streets of town.

Through the summer of 1863, the people of Savannah eagerly followed news of the battles that raged across the country. The second battle of Fredericksburg, Vicksburg in Mississippi, Gettysburg in Pennsylvania. Increasingly, it looked like the Union Army had the upper hand in the war. In August, a call went out around Savannah to strengthen the city's defences and to prepare for a Union attack. As usual my father ignored the pleas for support, instead keeping himself busy at work. The city's defences were built up primarily along the river and to the east on the presumption that, when it came, the Union attack would be from the coast.

Confederate President Jefferson Davis

My father did turn out in late October to hear what visiting

Confederate President Jefferson Davis had to say. Davis, a man in his fifties from Mississippi, had been elected to lead the Confederacy in part because of his military experience. He had spent six years serving as a lieutenant in the army in his youth and as a colonel during the Mexican American War. A talk, gaunt man, Davis inspected the city and its defences before addressing a large crowd outside the Pulaski House Hotel where he was staying. I watched from on top of my father's shoulders as he addressed the gathered crowd. He looked weary and tired. He spoke of the tremendous effort of the troops in fighting a righteous battle and said that the confederates were winning the war. He got a good reception from those who were gathered around. On the way home my father said he felt that Davis had already given up the war.

## 1864

In early new year of 1864, our family grew again. By now I was seven years old, but the procedure was much the same as when Francis was born. Bridie Donovan was called during the night to act as midwife. As I was a little older than last time, I knew to expect the screaming, so it was easier for me, and I sat with Francis to try and reassure him. My second brother arrived in time for breakfast the following morning. My parents named him Denis. He looked the very same as Francis when he was born with a little bit of fair hair at the top of his head. With all the difficulty that was happening in the world, Denis was some welcome good news for us, and we were all delighted with our new little brother.

A few months later, at the end of August, we were all home. It was evening time, and my father was reading, I was playing with Francis and my mother was tending to Denis upstairs. The house was quiet, and we had the windows open to try and quell the late summer humidity with a cross breeze. Suddenly, my mother called out to my father to come quickly. He dashed up to her and, of course, I followed to see what was going on. When we got to the bedroom we found baby Denis in his cot shaking violently. My mother started to get upset and asked my father what was happening. My father said he didn't know and sent me to run and fetch Dr Yonge as quick as I could. I dashed down the stairs, out the door and up the street to Dr Yonge's house. Within about fifteen minutes I was back with the doctor rushing as quick as he could. Denis was still convulsing in the cot but more slowly than before I had left, and he seemed a lot weaker. Because of the heat he didn't have a vest on, and I could see his little heart fighting for life in his chest. His chest would raise up, his tummy momentarily bloat and then his little chest would collapse back down again. As we were watching, his breathing slowed right down. The doctor looked at him for a few minutes without saying anything. My mother was sobbing, watching on helplessly. The doctor checked Denis' temperature and listened to his chest with a stethoscope. We all stood around the cot, anxiously watching. My mother cried out *"Do something. Do something"* but there wasn't anything the doctor could do. After a few minutes, Denis stopped convulsing and his breathing seemed to stop too. He just lay there. Helpless. The doctor again checked him with the stethoscope. Then, putting the stethoscope down from his ears and onto his shoulders, he said, *"I'm sorry"*. He didn't need to say any more. We knew what he meant. Denis had died right there in front of us. My mother let out a wail and grabbed poor Denis up in her arms. My father quietly ushered me out of the room and closed the door. After a few minutes, the doctor emerged, looked down at me, patted me on the top of the head without saying anything and let himself out. I didn't know what upset me more, the fact that my little brother had died or the fact that my mother was so upset. She cried all evening and through the night.

The following day my father went to the undertakers and we put

Denis in a little coffin. He looked peaceful lying there in his little white dress and shawl. His face was very pale, and I bent down to catch the last possible glimpse of it as the cover was placed over his coffin and then nailed shut. It was incredibly sad. At ten in the morning, we held a funeral at St John the Baptist church. A few friends and neighbours came along. Denis was the first of the family to die in America, so my father had to buy a burial plot for him at the cemetery. It cost twenty dollars and he had to pay another three to have the gravediggers open it up for poor Denis. It was mournfully sad to watch his little coffin being lowered down into the freshly dug ground. Father O'Neill said some prayers over the open grave as we watched on. My parents were grief stricken by it. Once the prayers were finished, the gravediggers started to throw dirt on top of Denis' coffin, so we turned and left him there.

It was sad around the house for the next little while. My mother fell into a melancholy that lasted for a few months. To try and lift herself out of it, she focused on making sure Francis was ok. He was still terribly young, and my mother was worried that whatever had happened to Denis, might happen to him. Francis was also starting to show signs of a problem with his development so my parents were concerned for him anyway. We visited Denis' grave every Sunday morning after mass and every Sunday when we got home my mother would go to bed for the afternoon with her tears. It took a long time for us to recover from losing Denis.

Throughout 1864, the long blockade of the city and the years of war took their toll on the people of Savannah. People were stressed about what might happen but even more so about the shortage of supplies that has started to happen. In April, there was a riot outside a bakery as local women mixed with some of the remaining house servants, in trying to get the few loaves of bread that the bakery had enough ingredients to make. Thankfully, we weren't in that position thanks to my father's work. We weren't rich by any means, far from it, but we had more than most people who relied on labouring jobs or who had no work at all. The cost of the few supplies that were available in the city was high but we got by.

From July, it was evident that the Union would be victorious in the war. The confederate leadership, perhaps trying to gain some redemption, began a prisoner exchange with their northern counterparts. We watched as pitiful, skeletal and ragged Union soldiers, many wounded or missing limbs, were marched, through the streets of Savannah from the train station, to boats waiting down on River Street. They had been shipped from the two main prisoner of war camps in Georgia, Andersonville and Millen. Through the war we had heard rumours of the tough treatment of Union prisoners, particularly at Andersonville. As we watched these near dead troops stagger passed us, we knew they had been through hell. Even those Savannahians who viewed them as the enemy could barely watch these poor wrenches and the condition they were in. A few months later, reciprocal troops from the confederate army began arriving in the city. They too were defeated, forlorn looking, malnourished, and dirty but the locals gave them a cheer and thanked them for their bravery.

By September, the Union Army under General Sherman had captured Atlanta just two hundred and fifty miles away. As they continued their march towards the sea, they plundered and ruined everything in their path. Knowing the importance of the railway to Savannah, the Union troops pull up the train tracks. With that, my father lost his livelihood. He received a telegram from Atlanta to say that, with the railroad closed and the river blockaded, there was now little being shipped and therefore the Southern Express Company was temporarily ceasing operations. My father wasn't surprised, and he reassured us that the war was nearly over, and everything would be fine. *"General Sherman will shortly be here to liberate us from this madness"*, he said. He spoke as if we were amongst the African slaves that needed to be liberated.

As December came, Sherman was closing in on Savannah and there were still thousands of Confederate troops now trapped in the city. They knew that they were going to be no match for the approaching Union Army but for a time, there was concern that a major battle would take place over Savannah. While people waited to hear what the confederates would do, there was a lot of construction work at the far side of the city from our house on St Julian Street. We didn't go down there but the word was that they were building a pontoon bridge across the river into South Carolina. That would be a good seventy yards long so it would be a big undertaking.

Union Army General William Tecumseh Sherman

On the night of 20th December, the city erupted in explosions that lit up the night sky. My father went out to see what was happening. When he returned about an hour later, he told us that the confederates were escaping across the river into South Carolina. The pontoon bridge that was being built was for them. Anything they couldn't carry was burned and the few confederate boats in the harbour were blown-up so that the advancing Union army couldn't use them. By the following morning, the confederate army had completely deserted the city. For the last five years the city had had thousands of confederate troops in the city, this morning there wasn't even one to be seen. The city was now left defenceless to an attack from the advancing Union troops. I took a walk around the city streets with my father. He was so happy. He knew that Sherman wouldn't attack a defenceless city. It was over for us now.

Early the next morning, General Sherman's army arrived on the outskirts of the city. Sherman himself wasn't with them so General John Geary was in command. Through the day, the city's politicians frantically debated what they should do. In the end there was no option but to surrender the city to avoid it being destroyed. So, that evening Aldermen John O'Byrne, Robert Lachlison and Christopher Casey were sent out to meet the advancing troops and to offer up Savannah to the Union. As they travelled out in a small black horse drawn buggies, there was a real sense of gloom and resignation around town. The weather was atrocious and that matched to mood of the confederate supporters all across the city. As dawn broke, the Aldermen returned along with General Geary and his troops. They arrived in, along the western end of Broad Street, at the far side of the city from where we lived, and they then marched up along Bay Street to Johnson Square. My father woke me up and we went down to see them arriving. While my father was jubilant, he still suppressed his desire to cheer them into town. We watched the Union soldiers marching in formation. They were as ragged as the confederates who had occupied the city just days before, but they were victorious, and it showed in how they held themselves. Before long, the Union flag was unfurled over the cotton exchange and the customs house. The following day General Sherman himself arrived triumphantly into Savannah.

Looking around, Savannah had changed a lot over the years of the war. The railroad was damaged, the river was blocked up so was unpassable, most people had dropped to barely existing financially and many of the buildings had fallen into complete disrepair. It was pitiful to see our once beautiful city like this, but thankfully, at last our civil war was over.

# VII

## Postbellum Savannah

When we awoke on Thursday 22nd December 1864, the world was certainly a different place. The days between then and Christmas were quite chaotic around the town. There were sixty thousand Union soldiers who needed to be fed and accommodated. They took over all of Forsyth Park and any open grass space they could find, and they commandeered whatever food stores were left in the town. Also coming into town in those first few days were the thousands of negroes who had been liberated by General Sherman's army as they marched east. As they were freed, many didn't know what to do, so they tagged on along behind the advancing army to get away from their old masters. They felt safe in Sherman's shadow.

Amidst the contrasting fortunes of the newly freed slaves and the recently defeated supporters of the confederacy, there was no change really for us. We were happy the war was over but now had to restart our lives again. Money was tight but my father was confident that he would get his job back, just as soon as the railroad was opened again. In the meantime, we kept ourselves busy and looked forward to Christmas.

General Sherman took up residence on Madison Square, close to where his men were camped in Forsyth Park. He ordered that any food supplies left behind by the Confederate Army should be given to the population of Savannah and he ordered that fresh supplies be shipped in to offset the inevitable hunger that would take hold while Savannah got back on her feet. It took three weeks but eventually a ship arrived in the harbour laden with food and other supplies. It was much welcomed. Over the next month, we occasionally saw the General around the town. He was a smart looking forty-five-year-old and seemed to have a line of people wanting to shake his hand every time we saw him. My father would always comment that people were suddenly union supporters when he was around.

### 1865

We celebrated New Year of 1865 with more gusto than we had in previous years. With the war behind us my father was confident that 1865 was going to be a good year. He announced at midnight that my mother was pregnant again. That was a good start to the year alright.

A couple of weeks into the new year, there was a commotion around the town as a group of negro children, hundreds of them, marched through the streets. The children were aged from about five years and up and were marching with a real conviction and intent. These early days after liberation were a nervous time around the city. The white population were on edge as they anticipated how the newly liberated negroes would react to their newfound freedom. Some feared retaliation attacks. As these children marched through Savannah, they became quite a curiosity for everyone. People looked on to see what they were up to as it certainly didn't look like the start of a revolution or retaliation. It was more like a festival of children. Starting at the First African Baptist Church on the western end of the city, they paraded through Franklin Square, then along the other end of St Julian Street, and up to the slave mart on Old Bryan Street.

Joseph Bryan owned the slave mart building. He had previously run a slave mart on Bay Street but had bought what had been the Wright Slave Yard just before the war. These premises had a wooden building in which the auctions took place and a holding pen out the back where the negroes were chained up while they awaited their turn on the auction block.

With just a handful of adults amongst them, these negro children commandeered the building and declared that this was now their new school. One of the adults, the teacher, took up position at the front of the room where a slave auctioneer's lectern was and immediately repurposed it into a teacher's desk. The children assumed positions sitting on wooden benches that were previously used by waiting prospective slave buyers. There, surrounded by remnants of the trade that had taken place in the hall up until just a few weeks earlier, these children started their formal education. There was an energy about these children, they ignored the chains on the floor and they sang their slave songs with pride. When I spoke to my father about it later that evening, he said it was a statement of intent for how the world should be. In my entire life, I had just a couple of terms of education at Chatham Academy. Most of my friends had no schooling at all but now it seemed like education was going to be for everyone who wanted it.

Through those first weeks there were lots of examples of negroes standing their ground with defiance and taking what was previously forbidden. Not all of them passed off as smoothly as the children claiming the old slave mart. Savannah was filled with negroes from across the south who had followed Sherman, they now had to decide what to do. Many went in search of family members who had been sold off to new owners, often hundreds of miles away. Others, not confident in the south's stability, were looking for a path to the northern states where there might be more security for their new-found independence.

Every inch of open space had been commandeered by the army or the freed slaves. The army even let their horses free on the city's graveyards, so they had some grass to eat. Outside our own door, on both Warren and Washington Squares, the army troops had divided out the squares amongst each other and built camps for themselves. Some even erected wooden huts to try and get some warmth from the cold January nights. These new neighbours annoyed my parents. It was very rowdy at night which made it hard for us to sleep but we knew it would pass and that they would move on once their new orders were received.

On January 16th, General Sherman issued Special Field Order No.15. This was his way of dealing with the issue of what to do with all the newly freed men and women. He ordered that all the islands along the Savannah River and a huge parcel of land in both South Carolina and Georgia be divided up and given to the negroes. Each would be allocated a patch so that they could begin farming and building their own futures. It had an immediate impact as there was a dash out of the city as people went to claim their plot of land. A week later, General Sherman himself packed up and left the city by steamboat leaving General Foster in command of the city. Within days of that, orders came for the army to move north into South Carolina, which was still in confederate hands. Slowly but surely, in miserable weather, the troops packed up and, in their companies, marched out of town.

A few days after Sherman left the city, at about eleven at night and while we were all asleep, we were awoken by a huge boom. It was so loud it nearly bounced me out of my bed. I ran to my parent's room where we all hid under my parents' bed. The boom was shortly followed by another and then another. The explosions seemed to be coming from the western, far side of town. After a little while, my father was confident enough to go and see what was happening. There were continued explosions as we waited for him to return. When he did, he reassured us that the war hadn't restarted which had crossed our minds. The remains of the confederate weapons arsenal had caught fire and then exploded. Through the rest of the night there was an occasional explosion as another box of ammunition exploded sending shrapnel everywhere. The explosions caused a massive fire to break out that was still smouldering the next day.

Early the following morning, Tim and I went to explore what the damage was. We were both excited to go, as we could hear the excitement during the night and were both frustrated that we weren't allowed to go to see it unfold. There was a heavy smell of smoke in the air and as we got closer to it, we started to see what had previously been nice white wooden houses, now all stained black from the smoke of the fires. Then we got to some houses that had been completely destroyed by the fire. Over a hundred buildings had been destroyed that night and because they were wooden, they were all reduced to piles of ash and burned-out rubble. Most of the western side of the town was gone. As we walked along Zubly Street, which was at the centre of the explosions, we looked at one particular house. Tim pointed to a charred body in the rubble. Both of our eyes widened, and my heart skipped a beat when I realised it was a burnt corpse. We both stood there and stared, unable to look away. Its skin was blackened so you couldn't tell if it was a white person or a negro. There was some exposed bone on the leg. I looked at the face and saw a twisted expression, its mouth open as if still screaming from death. Its eyes wide open but the eyeballs were gone. A piece of half burned wood lay across its chest. It was awful. We wondered who it was but even a family member wouldn't have recognised them. Seven people were killed that night in the explosions and in the fires that followed during the night.

In April 1865, what was left of the confederate army was beaten and General Robert E Lee finally surrendered. The war was officially over. Then within a week, news broke that a man named John Wilkes Booth had assassinated President Lincoln in Washinton D.C. My parents took us to St John the Baptist Church for a prayer vigil for the soul of the dead president. My father was full of praise for that man. He said he gave his life so that all Americans could be free. His vice president, Andrew Johnson, was now president. We prayed for his wellbeing too while we were at the church. The following day a huge crowd turned out in Johnson Square to mark the death of the late President. Both whites and negroes were there to pay tribute to him. Gunboats in the harbour fired a one-hundred-gun salute and there were black ribbons hung from the front of many of the buildings around the square. It felt a bit strange. Just a few months prior, Johnson Square was the scene of slave auctions and Lincoln was the enemy. People spat his name, called him a *"nigger lover"* and condemned the cause for which he was fighting. People are fickle.

My father returned to work once the railroad was reopened and the port was unblocked. Finally, we were able to start getting on with our lives. It felt like the war started just as we had arrived in America, and we wondered what might be in store for us. Then in May, my sister Mary Ellen was born. She was beautiful. We were all thrilled to have a little girl in the house. After what had happened to poor Denis, and with Francis showing increased signs of difficulties, we were all extra gentle and concerned about Mary Ellen's wellbeing. We were starting to fill our house. I was twelve, Francis was eight and now our first sister, Mary Ellen.

The rest of 1865 passed by without incident. The city slowly settled back into normal life. With the railroad and harbour reopened, cotton and timber exports resumed. There was still uncertainty and mistrust between whites and negroes but by the autumn it appeared as if Savannah had started to recover from the brutal damage of the war.

## 1866

The new year got off to a rocky start. My father had never really been the same after he was let go from the Irish Constabulary. He occasionally had bad bouts of melancholy and he would withdraw into himself. It was hard for my mother because, sometimes for weeks at a time, it was like he wasn't really there. In his place was a sullen shadow of himself, a man who was easily agitated and who's temper was on a short fuse. The setbacks of Francis being born handicapped and then the war costing him his job, had both rocked him further and his bouts of melancholy became more frequent. To ease the pain he was very obviously feeling, he would drink straight whisky. Sometimes that would dull his pain, other times he would go too far, and he would get aggressively drunk.

On 22$^{nd}$ January he had one of those episodes where, after two weeks of being melancholy, he started to drink and, on this particular day, he got very drunk. In the afternoon he came home from one of the saloons down on River Street. He started to shout at my mother that it was her fault that Francis had a problem, and that Denis was dead. He got louder and louder. I was down the street in Washington Square and heard him. As I walked closer to the house, I could see him at the front door of the house. I couldn't make out what he was arguing with my mother about, but I saw him raise his hand to her, slap her on the side of the head and send her flying back onto the floor. I ran towards them, but he shouted once again and then stormed off. I ran up the steps to the house and asked my mother if she was ok. She said not to worry it was just one of my father's episodes. A police officer had been passing though and saw what happened. He went after my father and arrested him for domestic assault. My father didn't go easily and was very abusive to the young officer who was arresting him. This added to the problems my father had when he was brought to court five days later.

He was kept in the jail until his court case. When he appeared in the court, he was really dishevelled and sorrowful looking. The charge was read out, *"Improper conduct, beating his wife and abusing officer in discharge of his duty at 2 o'clock PM Jan 22nd, 1866"*. My mother was called as a witness and had to say what had happened. It was extremely hard for them both. In his defence my father just said he was deeply sorry. He didn't even try and make an excuse. He was found guilty of the offense and fined five dollars.

His melancholy had lifted while he was in custody and when my parents met outside the courthouse, they embraced, and my father again apologised for his actions. We all put it behind us and tried to get on with things, but Francis was always a reminder that things were going to be hard for them.

After the civil war, there was still a lot of animosity between the races. One evening in May 1866, we were home when we heard a calamity outside the door of our house. We went out to see what was happening and found a group of five or six white men dragging a negro man down the street towards Washington Square. My father asked one of the crowd what was going on and got a response that enraged him. *"We're going to tie him up. Damn nigger wouldn't give up right of way on the street to Lawrence. Then he called Lawrence 'a rebel son of a bitch'"*, was the reply.

My father and I ran out, but the crowd was in too much of a frenzy. There was nothing we could do to help. We followed the group to Washington Square where the poor negro had a rope put around his neck. He was crying out for help and apologising in vain to the rabid crowd but it was no use. He was just the unlucky one they would take their frustrations out on. He had been in the wrong place at the wrong time and found himself amongst the wrong people.

The other end of the rope was thrown over a branch of an oak tree in the square. Then three of the men slowly pulled the rope until it was tight and starting to lift the negro from the ground. He had to stand on his tip toes. You could see he was trying to stay calm and focused on his desperate struggle to catch a breath as the noose tightened. One of the men, presumably Lawrence Craney who had been insulted by him, looked the negro in the eye and said *"What do you think now nigger boy? Still think I don't have right of way?".* With that, the three men pulled back the rope and the poor negro was pulled three feet in the air by the neck. With his hands and legs untied the negro struggled desperately to survive. His hands naturally reached up and held the noose under his chin, trying to keep it from crushing his throat. His legs swung back and forth as he tried to gain some upward momentum from his body to ease the strain on his neck. It was useless. Gravity always wins. For a few moments, the poor guy struggled, fighting desperately for his life while the others watched on with glee. Then, sensing that it would take too long, the men lowered him back to the ground again. With a man taking each of his hands, they stretched him out, pulling hard on each arm. They pulled so hard that it appeared as if his arms would come out at the shoulder sockets. His arms were face down, with the elbows facing up. Then one of the men took an iron club and smashed it down on the man's outstretched left elbow. A whelp of pain was left out as the man's arm obviously shattered. He begged for mercy to no avail. Then, still pulling the broken arm on one side, the same was done on the other side. Both arms were broken and just lay limply down by his sides. The negro fell to his knees in pain and began to fall further but he was held up by the noose that still hung him loosely from the tree. With that, the men pulled back the rope again. As the poor misfortune was lifted by the neck this time, he couldn't struggle. His two broken arms dangled by each side. There was a little life in his legs, but it was no use. With the noose tight behind his left ear, his neck was stretched and pulled. The strain on his neck muscles and the whimper of his voice were the only sign of any fight as he dangled there. He was frothing at the mouth as he continued to keep his neck muscles from relaxing. After a minute or two the neck muscles gave away and he gave up. With no strain for survival, his neck gave way to the weight of his own body, and he began to choke. He was still breathing for about five more minutes as his aggressors watched on. Occasionally, his body would twitch just a little showing that he was still alive. Then, when they were sure that he was dead, one of the men spat on the ground under the man's dangling feet and they all walked off chuckling. Once they were out of sight, my father and I cut the rope and lowered the man down. He was obviously dead. There wasn't any point calling for police. If we reported the men, who knows what kind of trouble we would be bringing on ourselves. We said a prayer and left the man laying there on the grass at the foot of the oak tree. His body was gone by sunset the following day.

Events like this were common in the years after Lincoln's liberation of the slaves. Nearly four million slaves had been set free. There was no way that all the whites, many of whom had fought a war to keep slavery, were going to give up their land and live side by side with them.

## 1868

Things got particularly tense when in April 1868, the freed slaves first had the opportunity to vote. This election was one of the steps required before Georgia and the other confederate states would be allowed to rejoin the Union. The terms for readmission were that all rebel states had to hold free elections, enact state constitutional change to uphold the 13th amendment to the constitution, which had abolished slavery, pay off war debts and swear allegiance to the Union. There was a lot of concern amongst the confederate supporters around Savannah about this vote. They didn't want the negroes to have a vote and worse still, they didn't want to have a freed slave elected to represent them in congress. Groups emerged that started to intimidate both races in an attempt to control the vote. It was around this time that we first began to hear about a mysterious organisation calling itself the Ku Klux Klan. Notices started appearing saying that any white who voted republican would pay a consequence and there were also threats against ex-slaves who put themselves forward for election. Despite this intimidation, over twenty of the ex-slaves were elected in Georgia that April and in July, Georgia was re-admitted to the Union.

Our family was delighted with this outcome. My father said we were back where we belonged, in the Union and we all hoped that it would be the start of a peaceful future. However, within months there was a a legal challenge made by ex-confederates. They claimed that the Georgia constitution didn't allow black representatives. This challenge was upheld by the supreme court meaning that the twenty-eight newly and fairly elected black members of the Georgia legislature had to be evicted. Congress immediately expelled Georgia from the Union again. It took another two years before things got straightened out. On July 15th, 1870, Georgia was finally and permanently re-admitted to the Union. We were the last of the confederate states to officially rejoin.

Our family grew again in 1868. Another little brother named John came along. I knew the routine at this point and took care of Francis and Mary Ellen while my mother was in labour, and Bridie Donovan cared for her as was the custom at this stage. John was a big child. It took a long time for him to come out and my mother's health was in danger during the birth. My father and Bridie both looked very worried as the night wore on and became morning and the baby still hadn't been delivered. Thankfully, after a mammoth labour, John was born, and both he and my mother survived the birth.

## 1869

At the age of thirteen, I got my first job. As I hadn't been going to school, my parents said it was time that I started to contribute to the household. I went down to the shipping wharves and asked around if anyone had any labouring work that I could do. Eventually, I got a positive response, and I became an employee of 'J Henderson & Co.'. John Henderson was a successful businessman around Savannah. He had an import and export business and he also had shipping interests. His office was on the corner of Commerce St and Pratt St, not too far from St Julien St. He took me on as a labourer. My job was to help load and unload goods at his warehouse. The kind of things that he had me labouring over included Italian or Manilla hemp which was shipped and sold in big bales that took three of us to unload or Russian cordage which was sold by the yard but was quite heavy and so took two of us to handle. It was tough work, but I was happy to be earning some money and it made me feel like an adult.

A little later, I got a second job. This one was for 'Beard and Wardell' who were the publishers of the Savannah Advertiser newspaper. It was still labouring but it wasn't as hard going as the work with Hendersons. After I got the second job, I was earning nearly twenty dollars a month which was a lot of money and every month I handed it all straight to my mother who used it to support our growing family. By this time, my father had started to be unwell and wasn't able to work as much as before. He had trouble with his left leg. He developed ulcers in his thigh which would weep continuously. He had to keep them bandaged up and there were times when the pus would seep out through the bandage and become visible on his trouser leg. It got progressively worse and unfortunately the doctor wasn't able to offer him any comfort other than to keep the wounds clean and change the bandages regularly. It was difficult for him but at least now I had a job and could contribute to supporting the family.

## 1870

At the start of 1870, my mother had another pregnancy but had a stillborn child. Had he lived he would have been another boy but instead we gave him up to the Lord and buried him with his brother Denis. That was another sad day for us. If it weren't for the fact that John was still young and needing my mother's attention, I'd say she would have fallen into another depression like she had when Denis died.

By this time, I was fifteen years old, a grown man and was starting to think about what to do with my life. I had been labouring for a couple of years. The pay was good and it helped to keep the family going while my father wasn't able to work but I was keen to go and find adventure. I guess because I grew up with soldiers all around me during the war, I had a hankering to join the army. It had the allure of adventure, I'd get to see some of the country and with the war now over, it was safer than it had previously been to be a soldier. I talked to my father about it. We were always close and he always gave me good advice. He didn't want to see me leave Savannah and was worried a little about how the family would survive without the money I was bringing in labouring, but he was happy that I wanted to do something and that I wanted to go off and fend for myself. He agreed to let me go and join the army and I agreed to send home some of my wages to support the family.

## 1871

In January 1871, after we'd celebrated the new year, I took off to find some adventure in the army. It was sad to say goodbye to my friend Tim. Since I had arrived in America, he and I were always the absolute best of friends. We had a lot of fun growing up together and I knew that I wouldn't see much of him while I was in the army. I had hoped that he might decide to come with me but he said he'd rather stay in Savannah with his family. We pledged to stay in touch by letter and said our goodbyes.

I said my farewells to my parents, and to Francis, Mary Ellen, and baby John. I visited my two dead brothers in the graveyard before I left too. My mother was pregnant again when I was going so, I promised I'd come back first chance I got to take leave. Just as I was about to turn and leave, my mother reached out her hand and handed me a small wooden crucifix on a leather necklace. She said that her father had given it to her as she was leaving Adare and that it would keep me safe on my travels. I teared up a little and said thanks. It meant a lot to me to have something belonging to my grandfather and something that connected me to the town I was born in. She also reminded me about the good luck I was due because of my caul. With that, I turned and walked up along St Julien St, towards the railway station.

Not long after I left, my mother gave birth to my sister Katherine. I never got to meet Katherine or my two other sisters, Anastasia and Alice, who were born after I left home.

# VIII

❧

# Kentucky and the Klan

After the civil war, there weren't many people from the southern states enlisting in the US army. Most still considered them to be the enemy. Not me. I was looking for adventure. I was told that the best way to join up was to travel north, out of the confederate states, to find an army fort, and to present yourself there. Kentucky was north of the Mason Dixon line and was the nearest non-confederate state. I decided to go there to sign up. With my father's blessing and the few dollars he gave me, I headed off. After I had said my goodbyes, I walked through Savannah's streets and beautiful squares on my way to the railway station. As I walked in the early morning through the battered city, I wondered how it compared to the northern cities that didn't have the same war experience. I hoped that I'd get posted to or at least get to visit some of them to find out. I really didn't have any idea where the army might take me, but I was excited to go and find out. I was only fifteen years old so was a little worried that they wouldn't let me enlist, but I had been told that if I was refused at one fort, that I could get accepted at another so I was confident that I would get in one way or the other.

From Savannah, I took the train to Atlanta. It was my first time taking a train journey. As I waited on the platform, with the rhythmic chugging of the steam engines reverbing around the station, I looked at the train on the platform, admiring the size and power it had and I watched as the fireman shovelled coal into the engine's fire. He was filthy from head to toe in coal dust and sweat. That looked like a hard job. I climbed aboard and took a seat on one of the wooden benches by the window and watched the final preparations happening on the platform outside. After a short wait, a whistle blew and the train started to move. Slowly at first but then gradually, with the engine puffing smoke out from the chimney, we picked up speed. My first stop was the new state capital of Georgia, Atlanta. Atlanta had only just recently become the state capital which was previously in Milledgeville.

Other than the trip out from Ireland, I had never been more than twenty miles out of Savannah and the closest I'd come to going to another state was a boat ride on the river with Tim when I was younger. As the train sped across the Georgia countryside, I admired the view and soaked up all the new sights. We passed through cotton plantations with their fields still being harvested by Africans. Just a few years earlier they were slaves and laboured under duress in these fields, now some were back doing the same work but, thanks to the war, they were being paid for their efforts.

It was about two hundred and fifty miles from Savannah to Atlanta. The journey took all day and most of the night. There were lots of stops along the way and each one was new to me. We arrived in Atlanta as dawn was breaking. I was already further away from Savannah than I had ever been, and this was my first taste of a city other than my own. I took a room at the Silver Dollar Saloon on Montgomery Street. It was rowdy downstairs with a piano playing most of the evening as revellers sang and danced the night away. It had been a long day and I slept easily through the noise. I spent a couple of nights in Atlanta just soaking up my newfound freedom and the surroundings of a new city.

After a few days, I was off again. This time I took the 'Nashville, Chattanooga and St Louis Railway' headed to Chattanooga, Tennessee. It took twenty-four hours to travel that distance. As I looked out the window of the train, I saw the names of towns like Calhoun, Dalton, Rocky Face, and Tunnel Hill pass by. It was a long journey with stops in over thirty different towns in all but thankfully there were some stops where I was able to get off the train, stretch my legs and get some food.

I arrived in Chattanooga in the middle of the day. After the long train journey, I decided to stay there for a few days. I took a room at the Phoenix Saloon on West 9th Street. After I got myself settled, I went downstairs to the saloon. I sat up at the bar and ordered a whisky from the bartender. I was a month shy of my sixteenth birthday and this was the first time I had had a whisky. I made small talk with the bartender. His name was John Allen. He had been born in England and came over to America as a child. He'd been as far west as San Francisco and had some interesting stories to tell about his travels, gold prospecting, and even some skirmishes with Indians. I could have listened to him all night but after a few hours he told me I'd had enough whisky for a young man and that I should go sleep it off. He was probably right, I was feeling a little drunk.

In a haze, I walked out onto West 9th Street with the intension of taking some air and walking a little to clear my head. Once out in the air, I started walking along the dimly lit cobblestone street. I got no more than a few feet when I met Miss Grace.

*"Hello young man"*, she started.
*"Hello"*, I responded with a smile.

*"Are you having fun tonight?"*, she asked. *"I can make it a lot of fun for you"*, she added.

It was then that it dawned on me who and what Miss Grace was. Standing there, swaying just a little, I could hear the muffled music and revelry coming from the saloon I had just exited. I looked at her. Her figure was shrouded in the folds of a woollen shawl. Her dark hair, with long looping curls tentatively tied up behind her head and hanging limply around her shoulders. She was about thirty years old. It was hard to tell for sure. She had a confidence about her that can only come from having done this work for a while.

*"I am sure you can."*, I said.
*"I have a room upstairs in the saloon, but I need to get some fresh air"*, I added.
*"Come with me"*, she said.

She took me by the hand, ignored my need for some fresh air and led me back into the saloon. I could tell that she had been in there before. She led me straight around the back of the bar, nodding at my friend John Allen behind the counter. He nodded back to her and then smiled at me. I was no longer in control of the situation, so I followed along meekly. As we climbed the stairs Miss Grace asked what room I was in and before I knew it, I was sitting on the end of my bed, helpless and looking at this woman as she made herself comfortable in my room.

I sat there and watched as she untied and took off her boots and then threw her shawl to the side. She turned towards me and took offer her blouse exposing a light blue corset that was bursting at the seams. Then, as she walked back towards me, she reached around her back and opened her petticoat and let it slide down her slender body. Without breaking her stride, she stepped out over the crumpled petticoat and stood before me in just her underwear. I didn't know where to look. I knew where I wanted to look but I was a little shy. For the next twenty minutes Miss Grace taught me the beauties of a woman's body and by the time she left the room, I was no longer a boy.

Next morning I didn't wake up, preferring instead to roll over and bury my aching head in the pillow. In the afternoon I came round. My head was still pounding but I sat up in the bed and pieced together the events of the previous night. I'd never been drunk before, and I'd never been with a woman before. I lifted my blanket to confirm that I was naked and hadn't dreamed it all. Then I sat back in the bed and contemplated if I was now, officially, a man.

After another night in the Phoenix, it was time for me to move on from Chattanooga. I packed my bag and walked down to the station. From Chattanooga my next destination was Lebanon, Kentucky where I was told there was a barracks where the army were temporarily headquartered. To get there I had to travel first to Nashville and then take the Monterey line for about ten stops.

On the Chattanooga to Nashville train, I got talking to another man who was about my age, maybe a little older. He was from England and his name was George Day. It turned out that he was also going to join up with the army, so we agreed to travel together the rest of the way. We had a brief stop in Nashville and then, on the Monterey line, we passed through Belle Buckle, Winsted, Wade and Kimbro before arriving at Lebanon. That last leg of the journey was only four hours, so it passed quick enough, and George and I were starting to get excited about signing our enlistment papers.

Lieutenant Andrew Nave who enlisted
Thomas Patrick Downing at Lebanon,
Kentucky

We arrived in Lebanon, Kentucky on 12<sup>th</sup> February. Lebanon was a major train junction point, so it was a big town though still a lot smaller than Savannah, Atlanta, or Chattanooga. George and I got off the train at the depot at the south-western end of the town and walked up along Main Street to see if we could find where the army barracks was. Eventually, we were directed to Hoods Avenue on the northern outskirts of town where the US Government Barracks were. It took us about fifteen minutes to walk there. We nervously approached but we needn't have been. It was obvious why we were there and, within a few minutes, we were standing in the recruitment office in front of Lieutenant Andrew Nave. Nave was a remarkably tall man, over six feet I estimated. He was from Knoxville, Tennessee and had just been assigned to join the Seventh Cavalry who were shortly to arrive in Kentucky. Still a young man in his twenties, Nave had a large bushy moustache and a long narrow beard hanging down from his chin. We both stood with our chests out as if to stand to attention. I was only fifteen years old, and George was only seventeen. We knew we were going to have to bluff our age, or we'd be sent home.

Nave looked us up and down from his deep-set blue eyes.

*"So, you want to enlist boys?"*, he started.
*"What age are you?"*, he asked.

"*Twenty-one*", we both immediately blurted out.

I am almost certain he knew we were both younger than we were saying but he chose not to be concerned. So long as we were fit and willing to commit, we were always going to get in.

"*Ok. You first*", he said pointing in my direction.
"*Name?*", he said.
"*Thomas Patrick Downing*", I replied.
"*5 years Downing?*", he asked, to clarify the length of my commitment to the ranks.
"*Yes Sir*", I said without even thinking about it.
"*Place of birth?*", he asked.
"*Limerick, Ireland Sir*", I said proudly.
"*Limerick, eh? You will have to join the Seventh Cavalry with me*", he said.
"*Yes Sir. Why is that Sir?*", I queried.
"*Do you know Garryowen in Limerick?*", he asked, a little impatiently.
"*No Sir*", I said.
"*Do you know Garryowen the song?*", he asked next.
"*No Sir,*" again I replied.
"*You will learn, Downing. The regimental tune of the Seventh Cavalry is a song called Garryowen. It is named after a place in Limerick.*", he informed me.
"*Excellent Sir. I didn't know*", I said sheepishly.
"*Aged 21 you say?*", he asked sceptically.
"*Yes Sir*", I said more forcefully than previously.

He then went on to record my blue eyes, sandy hair, and florid complexion on my enlistment record. He measured me to be five feet eight and a half inches.

"*Sign here Downing*", he said, pointing at the completed enlistment form. *"I will put you in I Company under Captain Keogh. He's an Irish-man. He'll like you."*, Nave finished.

And that was it. I was in the US army. For the next five years, I was committed to army life and whatever that might have in store for me. I was delighted with myself. Lieutenant Nave then repeated the same routine he had run through with me but this time with George. Almost all the answers were the same for George other than place of birth. George was born in Suffolk in England. He too committed to five years of service, and I was glad that he was told he would also be joining Captain Keogh's I Company.

When George was finished answering the questions and had signed the paperwork, we were shown by a corporal to the quarter-master's building where we would be issued our uniform and pack. The quartermaster had a tough job, supplies were scarce and so he had to cobble together what he could to match what the uniform was supposed to look like. There were parts of the uniform in the store that were left over from the civil war, but we managed to get ourselves kitted out. We were issued a pair of long johns that covered us from our mid-calf up to our neck. They buttoned up from the crotch to the neck. Over the backside there was an opening that would allow us to use the toilet without having to undress. On the cold nights, this was a very welcome feature. We were issued two pairs of woollen socks, a grey wool shirt with long sleeves and sky-blue trousers and braces to hold them up. The trousers were double lined on the inside around the crotch because of wear from the saddle. In the cavalry we were also issued black leather riding boots to just below the knee. We were issued a dark blue necker-chief which was useful to keep dust from your face when riding but also had other uses. A dark blue jacket, white leather gloves and a heavy double-breasted overcoat completed the uniform. Finally, we were issued a wide brimmed felt hat with the seventh cavalry insignia brooch pinned to it. The insignia was two crossed swords and had been selected by General Custer himself. I was proud as punch when I put the uniform on. I couldn't wait to ride home to my mother and to let her see her son the soldier. Replacements were hard to get so we had to really look after the uniform and often we had to supplement what was issued with civilian clothes that looked similar. So long as it was a close match to the official uniform, we wouldn't get punished.

Once we were all kitted out, we were shown to the privates' quarters where we made ourselves at home on two bunks at the end of the room. Nave said Captain Keogh and I Company of Seventh Cavalry would arrive in a few weeks' time. In the meantime, we would do some basic training with him.

That evening, around the camp's fire, we got talking to some of the other troops. They all seemed to agree that joining the Seventh Cavalry was a lucky break for us. The regiment was led by Lieutenant Colonel George Armstrong Custer. The name rang a bell when it was mentioned first and then I was reminded of the stories I had heard about him during the civil war. Custer was known to be a bit of a maverick and for his bravery in battle. He had fought during the First Battle of Bull Run, the Battle of South Mountain, the Battle of Antietam, and at Gettysburg. I was quietly pleased that I would get to serve with a man of his reputation and looked forward to his arrival in Kentucky. While he was officially a Lieutenant Colonel, during the civil war he had been a General, so everyone called him General Custer.

That night we also learned the Seventh Cavalry's regimental song, Garryowen. We'd be singing it a lot over the next few years. No one seemed to know why General Custer selected that song, but I was delighted that there was a connection for the whole regiment to my hometown. Every time it was sung, the other troops would

make a special effort to stress the line that mentions Limerick and
look at me with a wink.

> *Let Bacchus's sons be not dismayed,*
> *but join with me each jovial blade,*
> *come booze and sing and lend your aid,*
> *to help me with the chorus.*

> *Instead of spa we'll drink down ale*
> *and pay the reckoning on the nail,*
> *for debt no man shall go to jail*
> *from Garryowen in glory.*

> *We are the boys who take delight*
> *in smashing Limerick lamps at night,*
> *and through the street like sportsters fight,*
> *tearing all before us.*

> *We'll break windows, we'll break doors,*
> *the watch knock down by threes and fours,*
> *then let the doctors work their cures,*
> *and tinker up our bruises.*

> *We'll beat the bailiffs out of fun,*
> *we'll make the mayor and sheriffs run,*
> *we are the boys no man dare dun,*
> *if he regards a whole skin.*

> *Our hearts so stout have got us fame,*
> *for soon 'tis known from whence we came,*
> *where're we go they dread the name,*
> *of Garryowen in glory.*

The following day we were sent to the stables to be allocated our horses. Growing up in Savannah, I didn't have much need to a ride horse, so I was a little nervous. At the stables we were asked which company we had been assigned to. When we said "I Company", we were told to select a light brown horse from the corral. In the cavalry, the horses were colour coded to the troop and I company all rode light brown horses. George and I gingerly approached the corral and to pick out our horses. There was plenty to choose from, all of them nice geldings. For cavalry troops, all horses had to be geldings. Officers were allowed a mare if they chose. Stallions were too independent and hard to break, mares a little too soft. Geldings were preferred for long rides and ambushes as they were somewhere in the middle.

I selected a beauty and knew immediately he was the one for me because of his temperament. He sensed my nerves and made it easy for me. He had a gorgeous light brown coat as directed but with a slight amber tint to it and a white stripe on his nose. His mane was mahogany brown, as was his tail. As I approached him, he took a step toward me, and I could see into his dark, whisky coloured eyes. It was like he was selecting me and consenting to spending the next five years with me. With a little assistance, I saddled him up and took him for a walk around the corral first and then out of the barracks and I chanced a gallop out in the open. As someone who wasn't a confident horseman, it felt fluid and comfortable, so I was happy with my choice.

I decided to christen my new horse, Sarsfield, after Patrick Sarsfield who had defended Limerick bravely during the Williamite Wars. Sarsfield was famous for his horsemanship, and he led a daring mission on horseback to blow up an arms cache belonging to Prince William's army in 1690. It was a fitting name and Sarsfield served me well over the next few years.

For the next few weeks, myself and George, got to know how a soldier was supposed to act. There were a lot of regulations to learn, and we had to learn to ride our horse like cavalry troops. Discipline in the army is important and everything is regimented by bugle calls. Every day was more or less the same, 5AM was reveille with its roll call and inspection, then we would drill for an hour. This involved us ride in parade formation both mounted and walking our horses, we'd practice our horsemanship and learn battle tactics. After drill was breakfast where we would get a chance to relax. After breakfast we would have our camp work to do. We would alternate between various cleaning or camp maintenance jobs. We'd drill a second time just before lunch which was called by bugle at noon. After lunch we'd tend our horses, clean equipment, and get prepared for another drill session at about 4PM. Supper was called at six. Then we'd have a little down time. At 8.30 the bugle for tattoo would be sounded. That meant that we had to secure the camp or fort and prepare for bed. We drilled a lot but that was where we learned the most, so I was happy to do it and I soon became an expert at handling Sarsfield. Once I knew what to do, drilling became more of an annoyance. The bugle would sound 'taps' at nine and that was lights out and no further talking. It was a monotonous routine but there was good camaraderie amongst the men, and I soon settled into the rhythm. The hardest part for a new recruit was remembering which bugle call was for what task. There were over twenty different calls; church, fire call, mail call, mess call, pay day, school, stable, to arms, each one was different, and some were not used often so you couldn't just know by the time of the day what it was likely to mean. In the first few months I had to keep asking what the call was or I would just follow one of the other troops.

Discipline was rigidly enforced in the army. Any infraction had consequences so when the bugle sounded, we were always quick to respond. At inspection we would have to have everything spotless and perfect for fear of punishment. Minor punishment might be something simple like extra weeding of the parade ground or extra water duty. As the crime got more significant or repeated, the punishment also got more extreme. Sometimes the punishment was to humiliate you, like forcing you to carry a sign that had your crime written on it. Other times it was very severe. Desertion was sometimes punished with a man being stripped naked and being branded on his hip with the letter 'D'. Thankfully, I never really had any real problems with discipline and kept my record pretty clean.

A month after we enlisted, the official orders came out from Fort Leavenworth that the Seventh Cavalry would be officially transferred from Fort Hays in Kansas to Kentucky where we were waiting for them. When the order was made, a notice was posted on a board in Lebanon barracks, so we were able to read it. It was from the commander, and it was full of praise for our new regiment. We were thrilled. It sounded like we were joining an elite bunch.

*Headquarters Department of the Missouri*

*Fort Leavenworth, Kansas,*

*March 8, 1871*

*General Orders NO.4.*

*Orders transferring the 7th Cavalry from this Department having been received from Headquarters of the Army, the Commanding General deems it his duty to express to the officers and soldiers of the regiment his high appreciation of their soldierly qualities and of the conspicuous services performed by them in this department.*

*The regiment carries with it a noble record of faithful services and gallant deeds. During the four years which it has been in this Department it has experienced all of the hardships, dangers and vicissitudes attendant upon military operations on our wild frontier. It has made many long and toilsome marches exposed to the severest storms of winter and has gone for days in that inclement season without shelter and almost without food for man or animal. It has been engaged in many bloody combats with the Indians in which its valour has been thoroughly tried and proved. It has met all dangers and privations with firmness and intrepidity and has been distinguished throughout for steady discipline and efficient performance of duty.*

*The present soldierly condition and high state of discipline of the regiment give assurance that in the new field to which it is ordered it will be distinguished for the same high qualities which have so justly earned for it its brilliant reputation in this command.*

*With sincere regret the Commanding General sees this regiment leave this Department. It is needless to say, that it will carry with it his hearty good wishes and his confident hopes that its future will be as successful as its past history.*

*It will be long remembered in the Department as a model of soldierly discipline and efficiency.*

*By command of Brigadier General Pope:*

*(Signed) W.G. Mitchell*

George and I were delighted. The sooner the regiment arrived in Kentucky, the sooner we would be able to get started with our real army life. Within weeks, nine of the twelve companies of the Seventh Cavalry had arrived. The other three companies followed on two months later. The regiment was split up and spread across various towns across Kentucky and South Carolina. Regimental headquarters were established in Louisville and General Custer took up residence there. Our I Company had been assigned to the town of Bagdad. They arrived there by train on March 26th. As soon as we got word that they had arrived, we immediately left Lebanon barracks and rode out the forty miles to join them. Lieutenant Neve came with us. Our excitement grew as we got closer to Bagdad. We wondered what the commander would be like and how we'd measure up to the rest of the troops under his command.

We were a little nervous at first, but we were welcomed warmly by Captain Myles Keogh, commander of I Company. He said he was delighted to have us in the company and that reinforcements were much needed. Keogh was a tall man with obvious military credentials, and he carried himself with the authority of an officer. I looked at his dark eyes and could see a calmness that I instantly liked. He spoke with an Irish accent and, for an officer, was quite casual. He asked where we were from and instantly there was a glint in his dark eyes when I said I was Irish.

*"Where in Ireland are you from Private Downing?"*, he asked.
*"Limerick, Sir"*, I replied.
*"Excellent. Beautiful city with a proud fighting tradition. I am from Leighlinbridge in County Carlow"*, he said.
*"Don't know it Sir. Sorry."*, I said meekly.
*"Do you know Garryowen"*, he asked.
*"Yes Sir"*, I replied, not letting on that I had only recently learned it.
*"Very good. We will have you singing it a lot. Welcome aboard. I am glad to have you as one of my boys"*, he finished before telling us to find a spot for our tent and to make ourselves at home.

Captain Myles Keogh - Commander of I
Company

Over the next little while I got to know Captain Keogh. He was quite informal and seemed to have a soft spot for the Irish boys under his command. Keogh was in his early thirties but had already built up an incredible military record. He had left Ireland in his late teens to go and fight with the Papal army in Italy defending Pope Pius IX. He served in the St Patrick's Battalion which was mostly made up of Irish volunteers and he rose through their ranks quickly. During his service in Italy, he was awarded the Pro Petri Sede Medal for gallantry and was issued an elaborate broach which he would occasionally wear on his army uniform. After the papal war, the civil war was just starting in America, and the Archbishop of New York went to Rome to recruit experienced officers. Keogh answered the call and was soon in America and enlisted in the Union army. He was known for his bravery in civil war battles like Gettysburg and he ended the war with the rank of Brevet Lieutenant Colonel. After the war, he decided to stay on in the army and was transferred to the Seventh Cavalry when it was first established in 1866. None of the men had a bad word to say about Captain Keogh and I was happy to have a commander who was so experienced and had such a formidable reputation. He always referred to his men as his 'boys' and it certainly felt like he considered us as adopted sons at times. I liked him. It helped a little that he was an Irishman like me.

George and I found a spot to pitch our tent and threw down our kit. As the new guys, we were an immediate curiosity from the other men. When you spend as much time together as soldiers do, any new character that comes along breaks up the monotony and new friendships are formed quickly. I was immediately drawn to a couple of Irish accents and was introduced to Patrick Lynch from Carrigaholt in County Clare, just across the Shannon estuary from Limerick. He was only a few months in the army having joined the previous October. He was a labourer before he enlisted and like myself, he was looking for some adventure in the army. I was also quickly introduced to James McNally, another Irishman. James was from Kildare. He was three months into his army career. Two other Irish lads were also quick to say hello that first day. Patrick Kelly from Mayo and John Mitchell from Galway had enlisted together the previous year. I was delighted to meet these Irish fellows and they made me feel at home and explained what was what.

The entire company was very welcoming. It was a mix of Irish, German and US born soldiers. Most were in their mid-twenties. They came from all kinds of backgrounds. There was a confectioner, an upholsterer, a cigar maker, a boatman, and a machinist amongst them. There were also fellows whose previous jobs made them popular amongst their colleagues. William Miller was a saddler and was always good to help with any leatherwork we needed. James Troy had been a shoemaker; John Parker had been a gunsmith, and the oldest Private Henry Bailey was previously a blacksmith. They all put their skills to good use around the camp. I had little to offer in return as a barely sixteen-year-old with no real work experience other than labouring a bit back in Savannah.

Bagdad in Shelby County, Kentucky was in the north central part of the state. During the civil war there had been some skirmishing here because it was on the Louisville and Frankfort railroad and so was a key location for both sides to control. Bagdad is bluegrass country, named for the kind of grass they had but it was farming country and tobacco country. It was also the area where the Ku Klux Klan had been most active since it emerged after the end of the civil war.

The Ku Klux Klan had first started in the town of Pulaski in Tennessee back in 1865. Pulaski was named for Casimir Pulaski, a Polish General who fought in the American Revolution. I found it kind of strange that the town was called after the same man that the fort in my hometown of Savannah was named after. Over the few years since the civil war ended, the influence of the Klan in the former confederate states had grown substantially. While Kentucky was never a confederate state, it had been suffering from strong Klan activity, with intimidation, beatings and murders all becoming regular occurrences. That is why the Seventh Cavalry had been sent there in 1871.

In the weeks just before we enlisted, a former slave by the name of William H. Gibson was working as a clerk on the Lexington to Louisville train line. The train he was working on stopped at Benson, not far from Frankfurt, and members of the Ku Klux Klan boarded. They found Benson and beat him badly before pulling him from the train and leaving him for dead. In another example, a group of about fifty Klansmen on horseback took a man named George Duncan, another former slave, from a jail cell in Brookville, and hung him from a tree about a mile out of town. The local marshals struggled to keep these kinds of crimes from happening and so needed army presence to back them up.

In the month we arrived in Kentucky, this unrest led to a letter being sent to the US Congress by the coloured citizens of nearby town of Frankfort. The letter contained a list of over a hundred incidents of beatings, shootings, hangings, tarring and feathering, and other violence against newly freed slaves in the area. This is why the army had been sent to Kentucky. We were here to show the people that racial crime and intimidation wouldn't be tolerated. Our role was to be visible and to support the marshals in their policing of the district.

For the next six months, we were camped at Bagdad. There isn't much more than a crossroads at Bagdad, but it was central, so it was a good place for us to establish a camp. Our camp was on the northern side of the town, on the Six Mile Creek. It was mostly farmland and countryside around us. The camp itself was in an open space a mile out of town. About fifty tents were erected to cater for the needs of the company. George and I were paired up to share a tent. Every soldier is issued a half a tent when they enlisted. Once paired up, troops would join their two half tents together with buttons and slung it over a rope that ran the length of the tent. Sometimes we'd tie it to a tree, other times a stick would suffice. Officers all had their own tents and there were tents for food and supplies. When we weren't in a fort, a tent and a blanket on the ground was our lot. It wasn't comfortable but after a long day on horseback, we could sleep anywhere. Beyond the tents, closer to the water, there was a corral for our horses.

It was obvious that we weren't welcome around Bagdad or in Kentucky broadly for that matter. The Ku Klux Klan were a secret organisation, they would conduct their business at night and while disguised. As we patrolled around, they weren't going to come up and tell us what they were doing. Having us visible did stop them from being blatant with their activity. Not long before we arrived, a white man murdered a negro man. He was arrested and put in jail where he was awaiting trial when, a mob of Ku Klux Klan members marched into the sheriff's office and released him. There was nothing that the sheriff was able to do. That sort of activity stopped while we were there, but it didn't stop everything.

We would get called out at night to deal with the scene of one of the KKK's crimes. Usually they would ride up to someone's house in the nighttime about midnight. They would have reason to be there, it would be the home of either a white person who was supporting the Republican Party or a coloured person who was standing up for their newly won rights. While the group waited outside, the victim would be summonsed out. If they didn't come out the house would be shot up or set on fire. If they did go out, they would be kidnapped, beaten, shot, or hung. By the time we got there, there was usually nothing we could do. The damage would have been done and the bandits would have disappeared into the night.

One night we were called out after there had been a shoot-out. The Ku Klux Klan rode into a township which was all negroes. They ordered all of them to leave the county within ten days or they would come back, kill them all and burn their houses. They shot an old man to prove they were serious. One of the negroes returned fire and in the shoot-out a member of the Klan was shot and killed. The rest of the raiders rode off and left their hooded colleague behind. We arrived about twenty minutes later. Some of the men were sent off to search for the raiders. George and I were among those that stayed at the scene. We tried to calm down the victims and reassured them that they wouldn't be arrested. They were worried about the Ku Klux Klan returning for vengeance. When George got off his horse to tend to the disguised men who was lying dead on the ground, he removed the mask, and the man was identified as being the local schoolteacher, a man with a wife and two children.

Another example of the kind of thing that we were trying to stop was the attack on Jordan Mosby. Jordan was a negro farmer. He lived in a small cabin with his family, on land owned by a Mr W.M Bourne. One night the Ku Kux Klan arrived outside the cabin and demanded to talk to Mr Mosby. He and his eighteen-year-old son went out onto their front porch to talk to the raiders. The Klansmen alleged that Mr Mosby had attacked a white girl in the nearby town. Mr Mosby said he did no such thing and protested his innocence. The Klan members approached him and his son and took them into custody. Then they asked Mr Mosby would he like his son to be shot or castrated. It was no choice really. The men then took a knife and cut the boys testicles off while he screamed in pain and his father watched on helplessly. After the deed was complete, they said to Mr Mosby that they wanted him to know that he would have no grand-children before he died. Then they shot Mr Mosby dead and left his son bleeding to death and his wife sobbing. There was nothing we could do when we arrived. It made us all angry when no arrests were made for vicious attacks like these.

Occasionally, we would search the house of someone who was suspected of being a member of the Ku Klux Klan and a few times we found their outlandish disguises or a copy of their newspaper; Kaleidoscope. That was about the extent of our success other than being visible and a deterrent.

After six months at Bagdad, at the end of September, we were moved to the town of Shelbyville which was about ten miles closer to Louisville. We packed up our camp and were there in a few hours. Shelbyville was a bigger town than Bagdad. We hadn't moved far but we were happy with the change. We established our camp on the north side of town on Clear Creek and went about our business as usual. Our activities and the areas we covered were much the same as they had been in Bagdad, but we had the advantage of being in a bigger town.

While I was stationed at Shelbyville in October of 1872, I received a letter from home. I always loved getting letters. They were rare but when I got them, I really cherished them. My mother wrote to say thank you for the money I had sent. She was always apprecia-tive of my continued support from my wages. She updated me on all the family occurrences and told me that my father's health had deteriorated badly. They were concerned that he might lose his leg if something didn't change. She also gave me the wonderful news that she had given birth to the baby. I had a new little sister that they had called Katherine or Kate, as my mother had called her in the letter. She had been born in August and my mother said she was beautiful and resembled my grandmother back in Adare. I was delighted and looked forward to getting to meet her once I got leave from the army.

After two months as Shelbyville, we were ordered back to Lebanon for the winter. This move was about fifty miles south, but we were also moving away from Ku Klux Klan policing for a few months which was good.

On the ride back to Lebanon, I rode close to Captain Keogh. He rode with such presence and authority; it was very impressive. I spent most of the fifty-mile march, studying Keogh and how he managed his horse, looking for ways to improve my own riding. I had really grown to admire him for the way he carried himself and how he treated the men. He was riding a beautiful gelding, Comanche. A tall horse of maybe fifteen hands, his coat was a beautiful bay colour that was unblemished apart from a scar on his hindquarters where he had been hit by an arrow a few years earlier. He was a beautiful horse, but I was more than happy with Sarsfield with whom I had already built a strong bond. In the cavalry, the bond between trooper and horse is really important.

### 1872

After a two-month winter stint in Lebanon, we returned to the Bluegrass and moved back up to Shelbyville. Our activities returned to the same as they had been the previous year. There was no let up in the unrest in the area and the crimes of the Ku Klux Klan continued unabated. By this point George and I had been a year in the army. I was really enjoying myself, but George wasn't happy.

He wasn't suited to such strict rules and was bored with policing Kentucky. He said he had expected more adventure and the chance to go out west in search of Indians. Over the course of a few weeks in April 1872, he became increasingly bothered by it and mentioned that he was thinking of leaving. I reminded him that we had enlisted for five years and that it wasn't easy to get out of that. He looked at me and shrugged his shoulders. I knew what he was thinking but we didn't discuss it any further.

On the night of 7th May, George and I were asleep in our tent. It was a hot night and neither of us slept well in the heat. I tossed and turned a lot but didn't wake. When the bugle call was sounded for reveille in the morning at 5AM, I stirred. A minute or two later, I had summoned the energy to wake and rise. When I turned over and faced where George was supposed to be laying, his bunk was empty. I knew he had slept in it because I had heard him in the night and his kit was there and was crumpled. It wasn't like George to be first one to respond to the bugle. I dressed and went to find him.

I wandered around the camp looking for signs of George but there was no sign of him. At 5.30 the bugle called for roll call. As we lined up, I still couldn't see him. When the corporal called his name there was silence. It was then I knew he had skipped camp and gone on "French leave" which is what we called desertion. Immediately after roll call it was drill time. As I saddled up Sarfield, I was deeply in thought. Desertion was common enough but if George was found, the punishment could be tough. Court martial, jailtime or worst case, being branded on the hip with the letter 'D'. I was worried for my friend.

That afternoon I rode with Private David Cooney and Private Archibald McIlharrgey. As we rode along, they quizzed me on what I knew. They couldn't believe that George hadn't let me in on his plan. I told them we hadn't discussed desertion but that it wasn't a surprise really because he had been unhappy and grumbling for a few weeks. I presumed that he was doing me a good deed by not implicating me in his plans. I might have been court-martialled if they could prove I had any knowledge and didn't report it. I never heard any more from George. It was good to have known him and I was very glad to have had his company in the first year I was in the army. I was established now and had a group of friends, but I was still sad he was gone.

During the summer we showed our presence around Kentucky as much as possible. There was a presidential election coming up in November and in the build-up, there was increased Klan activity. Threats and intimidation from the Ku Klux Klan became more common as they tried to control the outcome of the upcoming vote. As we had done the previous year, we patrolled around, made ourselves visible and attended the scene of various crimes. It was just after one of these patrols that I got my first glimpse of General George Armstrong Custer.

The Seventh Cavalry had been ordered to the southern states in January 1871 and its twelve companies had been spread across Kentucky and South Carolina. While we were at Bagdad and Shelbyville, the commander and his headquarters had been in Elizabethtown on the outskirts of Louisville, which was about fifty miles southwest of us. He had arrived there in September and set up residence with his wife Libby. Occasionally, Captain Keogh would ride off to report to him and spend time with the other officers. Word was that Custer was spending most of his time looking at racehorses, hunting and enjoying country life.

We were returning from an uneventful patrol out around the town of Frankfort. As we approached our camp, a runner rode out at speed to meet us. Captain Keogh called a halt to the line and spoke to the runner. After a moment, the captain spoke to Corporal Staples and then rode off at pace ahead to the camp. The corporal rode back along the line, telling us that General Custer was at the camp and that we should spruce up. We all dusted ourselves off, sat upright in our saddles and rode in strict formation into the camp. As we arrived, I was eager to see this man I had heard so much about. We dismounted at the corral and as I let Sarsfield free, I loitered by the fence where I could get a view of the captain's tent where I knew the officers would be talking, and there he was.

Sitting at a table outside the captain's tent was Captain Keogh and two other officers that I didn't recognise but one of them was unmistakeably Custer. Sipping on a cup of coffee, he was almost the opposite of Keogh. Keogh was dark haired, neat, and reserved. This man, who had to be Custer, was flamboyant looking with his long curly blond hair hanging in disarray on his shoulders. He was confident looking and had an air of authority about him. I could picture him riding bravely into battle at the head of a charging cavalry all right. I watched for a few minutes as the officers talked and laughed. It was clear there was no concern in their conversation. I then went about my business.

Lieutenant George Armstrong Custer -
Commander of Seventh Cavalry

As the 1872 US presidential election approached later in the year, tension and Ku Klux Klan activity heightened. President Ulysess Grant who had led the union army during the civil war and had been elected president in 1868, was standing for re-election representing the republican party. Horace Greeley was the democratic candidate. Another candidate on the ballot was Victoria Woodhull of the equal rights party. She was the first female presidential candidate and was running with ex-slave Fredrick Douglass as her vice-presidential candidate. As had been the case in the previous election, the southern states were rife with intimidation and threats to try and control the outcome. When the vote was taken, President Grant won in all but six states. In Kentucky, Horice Greeley had won by a small margin. Greeley died within weeks of the election, but the outcome was already decided anyway.

As we had done the previous year, we got orders in mid-December to return to the barracks in Lebanon for the winter. A week later we packed up camp and rode back. We were there in time for Christmas.

# IX

⚜

# US Canada Boundary Survey

## 1873

As well as suppressing the racial unrest, another reason we were in Kentucky was the illegal distillery trade. Before 1870 whiskey was sold directly from the barrel and there was no quality control. After the civil war, the government needed to raise money for the reconstruction of the country and they started to tax whiskey sales. Whiskey began to be sold by the bottle so the government could get their cut. This led to a surge in moonshine production in illegal distilleries, particularly in Kentucky. Whenever we found them, we were expected to destroy the distillery and to arrest the moonshiners.

On January 28th 1873, while we were still stationed at Lebanon, we were called out to tend to an illegal distillery that had been discovered and while we were there a gun fight broke out. I wasn't much involved myself but the moonshiners were all killed. In the crossfire, Captain Keogh's horse, Comanche, was wounded in the shoulder. Thankfully, Comanche was patched up and recovered quickly but that was to be the last action we saw in Kentucky.

After our second winter stationed at Lebanon, we received new orders in February 1873. The Seventh Cavalry was ordered to move to Texas. We were delighted to be going somewhere new after two years in Kentucky. Then at the last minute, our commander General Terry was re-assigned to be the new commander of the US forces in the Dakota Territory. He decided he wanted to bring the Seventh Cavalry with him, so our orders were changed. While most of the regiment would be going to Dakota with Terry and embarking on an expedition out to the Black Hills in Indian country, I company and D company were assigned to protect the North American Boundary Commission's survey of the border with Canada. Most of us were disgusted. Going out after the Indians was the more exciting assignment.

Way back in 1818, the border between the United States and British America was declared to run along the 49th Parallel of latitude from Lake of the Woods in Minnesota, across the north of that state, the Dakota Territory, Montana and on out to the Pacific Ocean. The 49th Parallel isn't visible so a survey party was sent out between 1857 and 1861 to mark it out. In the intervening years it had become evident that, in some areas, their work wasn't complete, leading to a need for clarification as to where the actual border ran in some locations. To resolve this issue, the British and US governments agreed to a joint survey with a team from each side, working in tandem, clarifying the line and establishing clear markers along its path. While the British decided to recruit local Metis Indians to be their guides and in so doing minimise the risk of unsettling the local Indian tribes, the US Border Commissioner asked for an armed escort for his party. Major Marcus Reno had been appointed to lead this escort and companies D and I of the Seventh Cavalry were assigned to accompany him in that mission.

Major Marcus Reno who led the expedition to protect the US Canada Boundary Survey

While most of us would have preferred the excitement of the Black Hills expedition, we were happy enough with the task. We all agreed that it would be interesting to see a new part of the country and we knew that along the border area there were different Indian tribes who we might get to interact with. We were also happy to be under Major Reno's command. Major Reno, Captain Keogh told us, was a strong leader who had served with distinction during the civil war. After the war he had spent some time teaching military tactics at West Point before joining the Seventh Cavalry a couple of years earlier. While we were stationed in Kentucky, Major Reno had been leading a similar mission in South Carolina. Captain Keogh had met him a few times and liked him. That was enough for us.

The previous year, the commission began the survey and had mapped out about a hundred and fifty miles of the border from Lake of the Woods, west as far as the Red River. In 1873, the task was to continue that work further west and survey as much of the remaining seven hundred and sixty miles from there to the Rocky Mountains in Montana as possible.

On March 3$^{rd}$, we packed up our kit and moved from the barracks in Lebanon to Louisville where the entire regiment spent a month preparing to move north into the Dakota Territory. We enjoyed being with the entire regiment. It was a very rare occurrence. In fact, this was the first time that all twelve companies of the Seventh Cavalry had all been together since the regiment was formed. There was great camaraderie amongst us all and I enjoyed seeing the senior officers, hearing the regimental band playing, and making a few friends with troops I met from some of the other companies.

From Louisville, we loaded onto steamboats which transported us along the Ohio River, south-west to the town of Cairo in Illinois. From Cairo we took trains as far as Sioux City, Iowa. From there the regiment headed on north to Fort Snelling in Minnesota. We finally arrived there on April 11th. We assembled camp and enjoyed the next four weeks of having the entire regiment together in one place. While we were there, we had some reinforcements join I Company. In May, we were joined by Corporal John Wild from Buffalo, New York and six new privates; Herbert Thomas a miner from Wales, Franz Braun a turner from Germany, George Haywood a saddler from Ontario, Gustave Korn a Polish clerk, Frederick Myers a labourer from Germany and Edward Driscoll who was a labourer from Waterford in Ireland. Of course, I made straight for Edward Driscoll and welcomed him to the company. He was a little older than me but we got on like a house on fire and from that point on we were always paired off on marches and in bunks.

Major Reno and Companies D and I left the rest of the regiment at Fort Snelling on June 3rd and we took the train north to Breckenridge which was on the Minnesota side of the Minnesota Dakota border. We arrived there two days later, on June 5th. The rest of the companies of the regiment went with General Custer up the Missouri River and on into Dakota Territory. We wouldn't all be together again until April 1875 when we would all be reassembled at Fort Abraham Lincoln.

From Breckenridge, we marched north along the Red River for about a hundred and ninety miles to Fort Abercrombie, Dakota

Territory. The river twists and turns as it goes north but the land was flat and featureless. It made for a dull ride.

Fort Abercrombie, on the western banks of the Red River, was a welcome sight when we finally got there. We were glad to be able to have a cooling swim in the river after the march in the heat and dust. The horses enjoyed it too. After the swim we went back inside the wooden perimeter fence of the fort and set up our camp beside the barrack buildings. We had hoped to sleep in the barracks which we thought would be more comfortable than the tents, but they were full of infantry men by the time we arrived. In hindsight, sleeping out in our tents was better for us anyway because of the June heat. We were also relieved not to have to do sentry duty at night as the infantry covered it, keeping an eye out from the two high wooden block houses at either end of the fort.

After a brief rest at Fort Abercrombie, we continued by train north to Fort Pembina and arrived there on June 22nd. Fort Pembina is just two miles short of the 49th parallel and was the headquarters of the boundary survey commission. This area was also home to the Chippewa and Assiniboine Indian tribes. The closer we got the more alert we were to possible attack. We need not have been concerned. Neither tribe were hostile to us. They were peaceful people who lived all around the area and they had no concern for the invisible border we were there to establish.

I had occasionally seen Indians over my lifetime. There were one or two in Savannah and after I joined the army and travelled through Kentucky, I saw more but as we travelled further and further north, they became an increasingly common sight. Fort Abercrombie was the first time I was within twenty feet of an Indian. He was an old man who, it seemed, lived near the fort and lived off trading with the soldiers who came and went. He had long greying hair hanging straight down but tied in place by a red bandana wrapped around his forehead. He had a big blanket over his shoulders and had it pulled around him. I stood for a few minutes looking at him. He seemed at peace with the world and without any trouble. I went about my business then and hoped that would be my experience with all the Indians I encountered.

At Fort Abercrombie we received our orders to move out to the Mouse River about two hundred and fifty miles west where the survey activity was under way. As we would be out in the wilderness for a few months, we were tasked with driving cattle out to the camp. It was fun riding out and keeping the cattle in check gave us something a little different to do as we went along. We arrived at Mouse River on August 3rd. The advance party had already set up a supply camp which we christened Camp Terry. Once we had corralled the cattle, we pitched our tents and made ourselves at home.

From Camp Terry we were to protect the surveyors who were, at that time, working in the Turtle Mountains nearby. We were now in Sioux and Cheyenne territory. They were more hostile than the Indians at Pembina so there was concern that they would harass the survey party. We kept a vigilant eye on them but nothing materialised from the Indians. At the end of August, we did see a party of Sioux Indians in the distance. We rode out to get a better look at them. This was my first interaction with "wild" Indians. There was about twenty of them. All armed with guns and they appeared to have white women amongst them. We were very curious but the women weren't in distress, and we were unable to get close enough to get proper interaction. After a couple of days of watching us from a distance they disappeared. This was a common occurrence over the time we were there. We were a curiosity for the local Indians and they would come and watch us from a distance. I guess once we weren't doing them any harm, they were content to leave us be.

As we kept a watchful eye, the work of the Boundary Commission got under way. They had all kinds of equipment with them and moved it around on wagons and pack mules. They were using astronomy to decide where the boundary was. I got talking to their Chief Astronomer, Captain Twining, one day and asked him to explain it to me. I didn't really understand how the alignment of the stars could decide where a line should be drawn down here on the earth. He tried to explain it to me but I still didn't understand. It was complicated stuff. With the line confirmed, the surveyors built a six-foot-high mound with a stake on tip of it. On the southern side of the mound, they etched the letters "US" and on the northern side "GB". These markers were about a mile apart. If the boundary line was in a wooded area, they cleared a path thirty feet wide along it. They were also drawing maps and they had a veterinarian with them who was examining animal life along the path of the border. We were interested in their activities for a while but soon got bored with it and found other ways to keep ourselves occupied.

Commission workers constructing one of the Boundary Markers
during the North American Boundary Commission Survey
Expedition

While the surveyors did their work, we kept a watchful eye on them but mostly it was quiet. Occasionally, we would be asked to escort members of the party on trips between the US commission's camp and the Canadian side's camp. During most of the first few months, I really enjoyed this expedition and life around the camp. The weather was mostly nice. From September on though, it started to get cold in the evenings and it could be difficult to sleep at night when it got really cold but the rest of the year, the weather was perfect. Our days were spent out watching the surveyors or doing errands around the camp. There was always a need to bring in firewood or water for food and heat. When we had down time, we would arrange horse races or other competitions to keep us occupied. In the evenings we'd sit around the campfire and talk, or someone might sing a song or play a guitar or a fiddle.

One of the biggest challenges we had on the expedition was getting fresh water. In some places, like at Camp Terry, we had access to fresh river water flowing from the Rocky Mountains. However, when we ventured out to watch over the survey, we often found ourselves without fresh water. Out on the plains, buffalo seek out any source of water both to drink and to get relief from flies and pests by rolling in it. It was common for them to just stand or to lie in the water and in doing so, they would contaminate it with their urine or waste. On occasion we had no other choice but to drink it but wherever possible we avoided it.

We were extremely far north and, as the autumn came in, the weather deteriorated badly. We were brutally cold. Through September the conditions were increasingly bothering us. Around the camp, morale was dropping, and everyone was complaining about having frozen ears and fingers. Then in late September we were hit by a storm. The Indian scouts pointed out to us that there were a lot of birds flying south so they knew it was coming. When it hit, it hit hard. It snowed continuously for several days with a furious gale blowing at the same time. The surveyors were forced to stop work and we holed up at Camp Terry waiting for it to pass. We got about ten inches of snow during that storm. It was incredible that we didn't lose our horses and cattle in the conditions. We had to try and keep warm in our little canvas tents with just a blanket, an overcoat, and whatever spare clothes we could lay our hands on. We'd only venture out to do camp chores or to tend the horses.

Marking out the border during the US Canada Boundary Survey

After discussions between the surveyors and Major Reno, it was agreed that the winter was now imminent, and it would be wise to suspend the survey and to go to Fort Totten where we were to spend the winter. There was delight amongst the troops when we heard, and we began to pack up the camp. The boundary surveyors had successfully mapped over four hundred miles of the border in those months. They seemed happy with their progress. It was a four day, one-hundred-and-twenty-mile march from Camp Terry to Fort Stevenson. After a short break there, we continued the two-hundred-and-sixty-mile march from there to Fort Totten. It was hard going as the weather continued to deteriorate but we finally got there on October 22nd.

None of us had been to Fort Totten before and we were all more than a little disappointed when we got there. It was isolated and there wasn't anything around to entertain us. The fort had been built just a few years before we arrived, on the south shores of Devil's Lake. We all said we knew why it was called the Devil's Lake, because it was so isolated and cold. We were about a hundred miles southwest of Fort Pembina. We agreed that it would be worth the hundred-mile march in the cold for the better surroundings we would have there but our orders were our orders.

The fort had barracks to house three companies. We were two companies so we had a little space, but it was still small and isolated. The fort was built around a parade ground which in winter was too cold to use. On the west side of the grounds was the officers' quarters. Directly opposite that were the enlisted men's barracks. On the northern side was the surgeon's quarters and the quarter-master's store. Opposite that, on the south side was the bake house and other buildings. That was it. For the next six months, this was our home.

Winter at Fort Totten was a difficult experience. It was probably the most challenging time because of the cold and because of the boredom. Temperatures dropped well below freezing and stayed there for months. When we weren't doing camp related chores like

fetching firewood or tending the poor horses, we were cooped up
in the barracks. We got on well as men but during those months,
relationships were certainly tested and there was inevitable the odd
fight amongst the troops.

Fort Totten, North Dakota where Thomas Patrick Downing
spent the winters of 1874 and 1875

When the weather permitted us to go out, we would do whatever maintenance was required around the fort and ensure that the
horses were protected as much as possible by building shields to
protect them from the wind. We did have some lighter moments
when we got to enjoy dogsled races or even tobogganing, but these
lighter moments were few and far between.

One of the good things about coming back into the fort was that
we were joined by some new recruits. In September, we had six new
additions to I Company. It was always good to have fresh faces join
us and I always sought out any Irish who joined to make sure they
felt welcome. That September we had a new Sergeant named Michael Caddle join us. He was from Dublin. Normally, we would be
a little reserved around the officers, but the Irish connection always
seemed to trump that. I already had a good personal relationship

with Captain Keogh, so I wasn't concerned about interacting with the new captain. He seemed like a nice fellow. We also had a new corporal join us; Corporal Joseph McCall was from Pennsylvania but also had Irish connections. Also joining us that month were Privates Felix Pitter a grocer from Hampshire in England, Joseph Broadhurst a weaver from Philadelphia, William Whaley a farmer from Kentucky, and Edward Lloyd an engineer from Gloucester in England. We welcomed them and showed them the ropes over the winter at Fort Totten.

## 1874

Having survived the long, frigid winter at Fort Totten, we were eager to get moving. We knew that we were destined to spend the spring and summer out protecting the boundary commission surveyors again. While that wasn't as exciting as chasing Indians around the Black Hills like the rest of the regiment were doing, it would be better than being cooped up in the cold, small, isolated fort. Occasionally, we would receive word that Custer and the boys had encountered and skirmished with Sioux and Cheyenne war parties which sounded like a thrill. We also heard that they had discovered gold in the Black Hills. We wondered how plentiful it was and were our regimental colleagues now wealthy because of it. We pictured them picking up gold nuggets freely from the ground. It felt like they had the better assignment.

Our departure from Fort Totten was delayed because the government couldn't agree to fund the survey team. That annoyed us but we kept ourselves busy around the fort. In April, Captain Keogh got word that his aunt had died back in Ireland. Her name was Mary Blanchfield and she had left him a lot of money in her will. He asked for and was granted six months leave of absence to go and sort out his affairs. We were sad to see him off but knew he would be back in time to lead us on whatever our next assignment would be. He was a single man and now a very wealthy one, some of the men wondered if he would come back at all.

On 30$^{th}$ May we finally got word that the government funding issue had been resolved and we were to depart to meet up with the boundary commission team again. We packed up from Fort Totten and set off on a monumental ride of fourteen hundred miles as far as the Sweet Grass Hills about halfway across Montana Territory. This is where the boundary commission's activities would be centred that summer. It was a very long ride to get out there. We first retraced out tracks from the previous autumn to Fort Stevenson and then on to where Camp Terry had been. This was wide open plains country. You could see for miles. Some scenery would have broken up the ride, but we passed the time telling stories to the troops around us in the column. Eventually we could see the three peaks of the Sweet Grass Hills on the horizon and knew we were almost there. We were all saddle sore from sitting on our horses day after day. Thankfully, Sarsfield was a fit horse and gave me no trouble along the way. Some of the other troops lost their horses along the way and had to be assigned new ones. Getting a new horse meant that you had to get to know them and that could take months. With Sarsfield, I didn't have to direct him. It seemed like he knew what I was thinking.

Sweet Grass Hills was the middle of Blackfoot Indian territory. The hills themselves were sacred to the Blackfoot tribe, and they lived and hunted in all the surrounding lands. They were known to be one of the strongest and most aggressive tribes on the north-western Plains. Two years before we arrived the Blackfoot had attacked some trackers who were trapping wolves and coyotes so we knew they could cause us trouble if they wanted to. The Blackfoot also had no concept of the boundary we were out here to survey. Their land was vast and was on both sides of this invisible border. Without understanding what a border is, they would naturally be suspicious of us.

In July, Major Reno received word that his wife Mary had passed away of kidney disease. He left the camp immediately to travel to his family in Pennsylvania and sent word requesting leave to attend her funeral. He returned to the camp within days, and we were all shocked that General Terry had denied his request for leave. It seemed like such a heartless decision. Major Reno was disconsolate and furious that his leave was refused, however, there was nothing he could do. In the army, orders are orders.

For the next few months, we returned to the same routine as the previous summer. We watched the surveyors do their work and occasionally a party of Indians would watch us as we did ours. Thankfully through the time we were there, they didn't cause us any real concern. The weather during that time was fine and the nights were clear so the astronomical work of the surveyors was able to be conducted without interruption. We were happy when we heard in September that they were finishing ahead of schedule, and we would be returning to Fort Totten for the winter season. We packed up our camp for the winter and started the long ride back to Fort Totten. We finally arrived back at our winter post on 14th September and got ready for another isolated winter season.

En route back to Fort Totten, we stopped briefly at Fort Stevenson. While we were there, Sergeant Larner from D Company accidentally shot himself in his own left hand, blowing it to smithereens. He was in another company so I didn't know him but we had a camaraderie amongst us that meant we were sorry for him. The poor fella was in a lot of pain as we left him behind. He had to be discharged from the army once he recovered because his hand was no longer of any use to him or the army.

Our spirits were lifted in November when Captain Keogh returned from Ireland. I spoke to him about home, and he told me that he was still too young to retire at just thirty-four years old, so he had signed over his inheritance in Ireland to his sister Margaret.

He said he was glad to be back in America and was looking forward to leading us on our next assignment, but first we had to survive the cold winter at Fort Totten.

## 1875

Once the worst of the winter of 1874 had passed, we received orders that we were to move to Fort Abraham Lincoln where we would rejoin the rest of the regiment after their expedition to the Black Hills. As always, we were happy to be on the move and we were delighted that we would be back with the rest of the Seventh Cavalry. In April, we rode west a hundred and thirty miles to Fort Stevenson and from there south along the Missouri River to Fort Abraham Lincoln.

It had been two years since the regiment was all in one location and we had a great reunion with our colleagues and listened enviously as they recounted their experiences from the Black Hills. They definitely had the more interesting mission. They had had a number of brushes with the Sioux Indians out there while our Indian interaction was always at a distance. We also learned that gold was indeed discovered but that none of the soldiers were even a penny richer because of it.

It was great to be amongst the rest of the regiment. When we weren't on duty, we were able to mix and meet the other soldiers. There must have been close to eight hundred men in the regiment but in all my interactions, I never met anyone from Georgia or the other confederate states. I guess that was because they were confederate and didn't want to be in what was the union army. I did meet some Limerick men; Andrew Conner from A company, Ed Davern from F company, John McKenna from E company and William Ryan from H company. It was good to have something in common with a few of the other troops and we'd look out for each other if we were out serving together on a patrol. I got to know Thomas O'Brien from B company best. He was a leather currier before he joined the army and just a little older than me.

This was my first time at Fort Abraham Lincoln. It was a new fort that had been built to protect the advancing railroad. It was across the river from the town of Bismarck which is where the Northern Pacific Railroad terminated at that stage. Further expansion of the railroad west had paused because the NPR ran out of money but Bismarck had started to blossom as an important frontier town by that stage. The fort was initially built in 1872 and was named Fort McKeen. Strategically it was in a particularly important spot, where the Missouri and Heart Rivers connected. Fort McKeen was built as an infantry fort. The infantry built their position high on a hill not far to the west of the river. It quickly became obvious to the military that this wasn't a good idea and the infantry, on foot, were not suited to fighting with the local Indian tribes on their ponies. It was decided that a second fort be constructed for cavalry and the combination of the two posts was renamed to Fort Abraham Lincoln.

By the time we got there in 1875, it had the capacity to garrison nine companies or over six hundred men. Compared to the other forts we'd been to, this was huge. It was a mile long and more than a mile wide. It was almost like a small city. At the north end of the fort was the infantry post. It had its own parade grounds and barracks. High on a hill, it also had four tall look out towers. At the southern end and on much lower ground was the cavalry post. This is where we were housed. Like most cavalry posts, it was rectangular in shape with buildings wrapped around a large parade ground.

A couple of days after we arrived at the fort, I caught sight of General Custer. He was out playing with his dogs on the parade ground. He always had dogs around the fort or camp. He sometimes had six or seven at a time. He played most with Tuck and Cardigan who seemed to be his favourites and they followed him around as he walked around the fort. When I saw him again after two years, he was thinner than I remembered but he still had the unruly curly golden locks. He looked well and I was glad to see him again. The fort had been home to General Custer and his wife Libbie for the last few years. When Custer led out the expedition to the Black Hills, Libbie had stayed behind at the fort with some of his dogs, awaiting his return. They had a house to themselves on the western side of the cavalry parade ground. It had just been rebuilt having burned down the previous February. The house was also home to the general's pet racoon, Dixie. He had all kinds of animals. At one point he even kept a cougar in the basement of the house but had to give it up when his cook, Mary Adams, refused to go into the food store that was down there for fear of being attacked.

Either side of the Custers' house were three duplex houses which served as the officer quarters. Each company commander and his family, if he was married, lived in these houses. At either end of the parade ground was a grain store, the quartermasters office, a laundry and various other buildings. There must have been about a hundred buildings in all scattered around the fort, all made of wood, and all built just a little off the ground to make sure they didn't suffer from rot.

Directly at the other side of the parade ground from Custer's house were three blocks of barracks for us troops. Each block housed two companies. Each company had a big dormitory with wooden bunks down the side walls. We had a little space to ourselves but not much. Down the centre of the dormitory on pillars spaced about ten feet apart were gun racks where we kept our rifles. They needed to be ready to access in the event of an attack. There were heaters at either end of the dormitory which were much needed in the winter. Depending on your seniority, you were allocated a bunk closer or further from the heaters. Off the back of each dormitory was a kitchen and canteen where we would eat our meals.

The inside of the troops' barracks at Fort Abraham Lincoln

The fort was on the edge of the Missouri River so had a steady water supply. Our horses drank ten gallons of water each day, so a steady supply of water was always important. Unfortunately, the Missouri River isn't the freshest so when we drank the water it was often cloudy, but we got used to it and it didn't make us sick. The food at the fort, though still scarce, was better than we'd had at Fort Totten. For breakfast we'd have coffee and bread or hominy. If we were lucky, we might get a little hash too. Around midday we'd get boiled bacon, beans, potatoes, or hardtack. Then for supper in the evening it was coffee and bread again. Sometimes there might have been an expedition and we might get buffalo or deer instead of the bacon. In the summer we might get some vegetables but, in winter there was nowhere to grow them, so we did without. When we got hungry, we could get something from the many traders who hung around the fort. Some of them were Indians, others poor immigrants like myself, trying to make a few dollars. They could get you anything you wanted, food or other supplies like clothing. We were only paid every two months so sometimes we had to ask for credit or else go without until pay day came around. I tried to limit what I bought from the traders. It was particularly important to me that I sent as much money home to my mother each month as I could. The longer I was away, the worse my father's health seemed to be getting and he was almost completely off work by this stage because of the ulcers in his leg.

Through the summer, things were relatively quiet, and we remained at Fort Abraham Lincoln. It was good for our horses to get a good rest and for us to have some downtime but at times it was unbearably hot. If we got a chance, we would ride the horses down to the river to let them cool off in the cold Missouri River. While on duty we had to wear our wool tunic and there were often times when men passed out from the heat in the peak summer months.

Some of the officers of the regiment took the opportunity to take some leave during the summer. Captain Keogh went to Louisville, Kentucky for a month, General Custer had taken five months off, and Major Reno was on a sabbatical after the death of his wife. Because he was refused leave to go and bury his wife, he took the first opportunity he could and took his children on a trip to Europe.

The one big thing that did happen at Fort Abraham Lincoln during the summer of 1875 was the signing of a treaty between the Sioux tribes from Standing Rock Reservation and the Berthold Reservation tribes. These groups had been sworn enemies since the start of the century and were continually waring with each other over territory. Now that both were on reservations, an agreement was reached over their grievances. The treaty was signed on 29th May. For a few days before that, they converged on the fort. At the time there were about six hundred troops at Fort Abraham Lincoln and over a thousand Indians came to witness and celebrate the treaty. We were all ordered to be on alert just in case.

About four hundred Sioux from the Yanktonai, Hunkpapa and Blackfoot tribes came from Standing Rock and set up camp outside the fort to the northwest close to the infantry post. Then an even bigger group came from the Berthold reservation with Arikara, Hidatsa and Mandan tribes all represented. They set up camp to the southwest, a little south of the cavalry post. These two sets of sworn enemies were no more than a couple of miles apart. Because of its size, Fort Abraham Lincoln didn't have a perimeter fence like other forts. The pure scale of it and the number of soldiers there at any point in time was enough of a deterrent to keep it from being attacked. Surrounded by these Indians, we waited and watched the comings and goings with interest. We were all on edge that week.

The night before the treaty was signed, there was drumming and singing coming from both camps. It was quite an experience for us. We didn't know if they were singing war songs or songs of peace. For all we knew, the two sets of Indians could combine and overwhelm us. We were thankful that one of the fort's scouts, a seven-foot tall Hunkpapa Lakota Indian named Long Soldier was able to reassure us that they were songs of peace and we could rest easy. As the sun set, I walked out and up a small hill near the post. I could see the distinct silhouette of tepees in the distance against the red sky of the setting sun. I listened to the drums and could make out the wailing sound of the Indians singing. Their way of life was so different to ours. I wondered if we could coexist and live side by side or if there would always be conflict between them and us white men.

In the lead up to the signing of the treaty, there was a lot of posturing with the Mandan initially refusing to sign because they were unhappy that the US Government kept sending expeditions out onto the plains and they were driving the buffalo herd further west. The Sioux were also protesting that they hadn't been invited to send a representative to meet the 'Great Father' in Washington when a delegation was sent a few months earlier. It was all settled by the morning of the signing though.

On the day the treaty was signed, there was a lot of pomp

and ceremony. General Cartlin oversaw proceedings as General Custer was still on vacation back east. Cartlin witnessed the treaty on behalf of the US government. Colonel Burke, the agent from Standing Rock reservation witnessed the treaty on behalf of the Indian Department. Also in attendance was Major Sperry who was the agent from the Berthold reservation. After a few speeches, the Indian Chiefs came forward and signed. Son of the Stars and White Shield signed on behalf of the Arikara, Crow Breast and Lean Wolf for the Gros Ventre, Bad Gun and The Lance for the Mandan, Two Bears, Bad Bear and Bull's Ghost on behalf of the Lower Yanktonai, Running Antelope, Bear's Rib, Thunder Hawk, Long Soldier, and Slave for Hunkpapa and Grass, Big Head and Sitting Crow for the Blackfoot. Finally, Wolf's Necklace, Fire Heart and Blackeye came forward and signed for the Upper Yanktonai. It was fascinating to watch. These chiefs sat in their two clusters, cross legged on the ground. All refused the chairs they had been offered. Then, in turn, these men come forward and put their mark on the treaty. None of them could read or write so a simple 'x' gave their consent. As they came forward, we admired their different hairstyles, dress and they were each adorned with different jewellery made from beads, skins and bits of carved bone. Some carried what looked like weapons but we were assured they were coup sticks representing their bravery. It was an amazing sight to witness.

After the treaty was signed General Cartlin gave each tribe a pair of oxen and then all parties returned to their camps where they sang and ate until late in the night. The signing had passed off without incident and again we looked out from the fort at sunset, listening to the celebrations, relieved that there hadn't been any trouble.

The following day when the Indians were leaving there was a little bit of an incident. The Sioux headed west with clear land ahead of them. The Berthold Indians on the other hand, had to cross back over the Missouri River and there wasn't enough transport to get them across it. Bloody Knife, an Arikara scout and several others were left behind. When they tried to get on board the last boat, they were ordered off because of a lack of space. Tensions rose, not helped by the difficulty in communication between English and the different Indian languages. Bloody Knife who wasn't happy that he couldn't board, pulled his rifle out and let off a gunshot randomly into the boat. Immediately, Sergeant Connolly pulled his revolver. Bloody Knife fired two more random shots but they both missed anything. After some mediation, tensions were calmed down, but we were all on alert around the fort in case it escalated further.

While this treaty was agreed between the two sets of waring Indians, tensions continued to rise between the US and the Indians. More and more prospectors were flooding to the Black Hills in search of gold and their numbers were such that there was nothing the army could do to stem the tide. The Indians were becoming increasingly agitated. This was in violation of the agreed treaties and the Black Hills were sacred to the Sioux. Towards the end of June, word reached Fort Abraham Lincoln that about a hundred lodges of Sioux Indians had left Standing Rock reservation, had gone on the war path, and were threatening to attack the fort in retaliation to these transgressions. We were sceptical that they would attack the fort but had to be prepared for anything, so we stepped up our drilling and doubled our scouting missions to keep an eye out. Nothing eventuated.

It was during this summer that we adopted a little dog into I Company. There were plenty of dogs around the fort and we felt that, if it was ok for Lieutenant Colonel Custer to have them, we should be allowed too. Anyway, this little fella started to hang around us in the camp. He used to beg for food and sit with us if there was a campfire going. He was yellow in colour and a mongrel cross between a terrier and a bulldog. We all enjoyed him because he distracted us from the boredom of being in camp. One of the troops decided that he had to be given a name if he was to be part of our company and before long, he had been named Private Joe Bush. If we were going anywhere around the fort or just outside the fort, Joe would often follow us, and we would bring him on all our future expeditions. He would sit up on the pack wagon and loved being part of the team. Sometimes he would sniff around Custer's dogs, but they were all a lot bigger than he was, so he was soon run off and always returned to us with his tail between his legs.

Through that summer we temporarily lost Captain Keogh to ill health. The captain had had two accidents in the previous years that occasionally caught up with him or at least that is what we were told. On Valentine's Day 1868, while he happened to be on his way to a wedding, Captain Keogh slipped on an icy pavement in Boston. In the fall he broke his right ankle and badly tore ligaments. It took him months to recover. The second accident was in 1870. The Seventh Cavalry were stationed at Fort Leavenworth and as they often would to pass the time, the officers were taking part in a horse race. The captain's horse tripped at the second hurdle of a steeplechase, threw him and subsequently kicked him in the face, knocking him unconscious for almost ten minutes.

From July until October of 1875, Captain Keogh was mostly bedridden with what the surgeons at the fort diagnosed as "remittent fever and severe nervous prostration". We all knew that Captain Keogh was prone to bouts of melancholy and drank to medicate himself. We presumed that this was one of those bouts and looked forward to having him back in the saddle with us.

That August, while Captain Keogh was bedridden, my friend Ed Driscoll got himself into some bother. He was on stable guard which we all had to do from time to time. He got into an argument with 1st Sergeant Varden who was supervising the work. Ed's temper got the better of him and the next thing you know, Ed had given Varden a right slap. It's never a clever idea to assault a superior officer, even though Ed would never have agreed that Varden was superior to him in any way. For his trouble, Ed was court martialled and was sentenced to two weeks confinement with hard labour and for the next six months he would have ten dollars docked from his pay. That was nearly all his salary. Ed was livid, protesting to me that Varden had it coming to him which in fairness, I agreed with. Varden was one of those guys who let his rank give him a big head. He was the opposite to Captain Keogh, who was always approachable and friendly. Varden, a thirty-year-old from Yarmouth in Maine, thought he was better than everyone else and verbally berated us if we did the slightest thing wrong. With Captain Keogh absent, Varden was even more of a brute than he usually was. I didn't see Ed for a few weeks while he was doing his time. It was quiet around without him as he was the one I spent most of my time with.

On September 1st there was a national day honouring ex-president Andrew Johnson. He had been taken over as president when Abraham Lincoln had been assassinated in 1865. He had died of a stroke at the start of August. To mark his passing it was agreed that from sunrise until sunset at forts across the country, a gun salute would be sounded every thirty minutes. For the early part of the day, it was a sombre thing but by the end of the day, we were all tired of the noise and looked forward to sunset when it would all stop.

More new additions to the company arrived in September 1875. Sergeant James Bustard was another Irishman to join the officers. He was from Donegal. Private George Post was a saddler from Michigan and Private John Barry from Waterford in Ireland. They both became good friends of mine, and we would often pair up on whatever expeditions were going on. John McShane, a cooper from Montreal, Andrew Grimes a labourer from Pennsylvania and Francis Kennedy a labourer from Missouri also joined us. The last two to join us were two barbers, Private Adam Hetesimer from Ohio, and Private Mark Lee from Maine. Hetesimer and Lee were busy boys as soon as people realised that they could get a cheap haircut from them. As they were new and trying to make friends, they obliged and even the officers commented that we were the finest looking company in the regiment when we were all spruced up.

In late September, the rising tensions with the Indians came into sharp view when John Wright was murdered. Wright, along with George Lewis were out herding cattle, just across the river, outside of Bismarck. Once the herd had reached a creek ten miles from town, Wright and Lewis split up and rode on either side of the herd. They were about two miles apart. About 10AM, Lewis heard a gunshot but didn't think much of it. Late that evening, when they were due to come back together, he found that Wright was missing. He searched through the night to no avail. Next morning while he continued to search, he sent word with a passerby that his colleague was missing. A search party was sent out from town and Wright's body was found in the early afternoon. An examination of the body showed a gunshot wound to the head, from the rear, passing through the neck just below the right ear. Another bullet had passed through the head coming out at the left temple. Wright's head had been split open with a tomahawk and the forehead crushed with a blunt object. There were also three knife wounds where scalping had been attempted. Near the body a coup stick was found, left by the Indian attackers, presumably to taunt the locals. The body was taken back into town and buried. Word reached the fort and two search parties were sent out. One, led by Captain Yates, went out and followed the tracks from the scene which led towards Standing Rock Reservation. The other, which I joined, was led by Captain Weir. We followed the same track but on the opposite side of the river. After a full day of riding there was no sign of any Indians and it was presumed that they had made it back to Standing Rock reservation. It was clear that the Sioux and Cheyenne at Standing

Rock were getting agitated by the continued trespass on their lands and were making it known that they would retaliate if necessary.

As the winter approached our regiment was split again. Half of the companies were moved to Fort Stevenson. Companies C, D, F, and I, remained at Fort Abraham Lincoln. Having spent the two previous winters at cold and isolated Ford Totten, I was happy to be spending this winter at Fort Lincoln. It was still going to be a very cold winter but there were more people and activity around Fort Lincoln.

Winter at Fort Abraham Lincoln was tough. It was freezing for months on end. Custer didn't drink so he ordered that the fort be dry except for a very occasional drink that the officers were allowed. The men were expected to remain alcohol free. A few men signed up for temperance societies, in fact, most of H company didn't drink. Others couldn't resist the delights that lay just across the river in the towns of Bismarck and Edmonton. Occasionally, men would sneak out during the night, make their way across the river for a night of revelry with drink and women easy to access. During the winter this had its dangers. In May 1875, one of the civilian workers on the fort, a man named Jack Sweeney, had a night out in Edmonton. Drunk with the delights he had experienced, he was swimming back across the freezing waters and drowned. On another occasion one of the infantry troops, Patrick Cunningham, was making his way back, walking across the iced river, he slipped, banged his head knocking himself unconscious. He was found frozen to death the following morning. Both of these men were buried in the fort's graveyard up on the hill near the infantry post.

# X

# Ultimatum

The year 1876 was a landmark year for the United States. It marked the centenary of the signing of the Declaration of Independence from the British and festivals were planned across the country to celebrate. It was also looking likely to be a landmark year in relations between the US government and the Indians. Through the last few years, the matter of the Indian treaties had been prominent but now it was all starting to come to a head.

For generations, the Plains Indians had lived a nomadic life. In the summer months they followed the buffalo herd that provided most of their sustenance and clothing. Then in winter, they would scratch out an existence on whatever wasn't frozen or covered in snow. By spring they and their horses would be half starved, and they would start the cycle again. The arrival of the white man from the east and then the railroad, pushed them westward causing various tribes to overlap on their traditional territories. There were constant wars between the tribes as they fought for their territory and survival.

In 1851, the US government had signed the Fort Laramie Treaty with nine of the tribes including the big ones, the Cheyenne, Arapaho, Crow, and Sioux. Under this treaty all territorial claims between these tribes were settled and agreed. It was hoped that this would lead to peace in the west. As part of the treaty, the US government recognised that all the land in question was Indian land and agreed not to claim it or to try and settle it with farmers. In return, the Indian tribes agreed that white people travelling through their lands would be allowed to pass without harassment. This treaty was almost immediately broken. All of the tribes ignored the agreed territory alignments and started raiding each other's territory and fighting with each other. The US army continued to kill Indians and the Sioux chief, Red Cloud, attacked any US troops who strayed too close to Sioux lands.

Through the civil war, various infractions occurred but the US was otherwise distracted from the Indian problem. When the civil war ended, thousands of ex-troops fresh from the war, headed to the frontier to prospect for gold or to start a new life and problems started to occur again.

A second treaty was agreed in 1868. This one was between the US government and the Sioux tribes. Under this treaty, the Great Sioux Reservation was established and importantly, the sacred Black Hills in Dakota Territory were granted exclusively to the Sioux. By 1876, it was clear that this second treaty was also failing. General Custer had found gold in the Black Hills on his 1874 expedition while we were on the Canadian border, the railroad was continuing to advance west into Indian lands and there had been a rush of prospectors to the Black Hills looking to get rich on the gold to be found on this sacred Indian site.

In September of 1875, the US Government offered to buy the Black Hills from the Sioux but the offer was refused. In the meantime, conditions for the settled Indians on the Great Sioux

Reservation were deteriorating. The US government wasn't providing sufficient supplies for the Indians living there, western illnesses were rife, and many of the Indians longed for a return to their old nomadic lifestyle. In summer, many of the reservation Indians would leave and live the summer months out on the plains. As conditions deteriorated on the reservation, the number of Indians who returned to the plains increased. By November 1875, the US Government had decided that the only way to deal with the 'Indian question' was through a war against the Sioux.

On December 3rd, the US government issued an ultimatum to all the Indians who were not on the reservation. It gave them two months to comply and return to the reservation. Any Indian not on a reservation by 31st January 1876 would be deemed "hostile" and would be treated accordingly. It was a particularly chilly winter that year and the couriers who were sent out with the ultimatum didn't even make it to the Indian villages by the time the deadline expired. So, the deadline passed and the Indians, led by Sitting Bull, Crazy Horse, and Gall, were seen to have ignored it.

At Fort Abraham Lincoln, we listened to the updates on what was happening with interest. We all knew that if the US government declared war on the hostile Indians, that it would be us who would be sent out to deal with them. Through the first few months of 1876, we waited with a mix of anticipation and excitement. We all wondered what might happen. I company was probably a little more excited by the prospect of an expedition out into Indian territory. We had missed the earlier expedition to the Black Hills and the anticipation of a battle with hostile Indians appealed to many of the troops.

General Custer, our commanding officer, had left Fort Abraham Lincoln in November to travel to the eastern states. Major Reno was put in command in his absence. He had just returned from his year of travelling in Europe. I liked Major Reno and knew him well from our time on the boundary survey. He was stern but he and Captain Keogh, always kept us informed on developments as they occurred.

A day after the deadline had passed, the US Secretary for the Interior, Zachariah Chandler, handed over the Indian problem to the Secretary of War William Belknap, telling him that the army should do "as they may deem proper". There was only ever going to be one plan from that point on; war was inevitable. Within a week, the army generals were building their strategy. By the start of March, word had reached us at Fort Abraham Lincoln that there was going to be a campaign against the Sioux, and we were put on standby. Our excitement began to rise and the newer members of the regiment, or those like myself who hadn't been on the expedition to the Black Hills, began asking questions about what to expect. I took the opportunity to talk to Captain Keogh about it as I had not had any real engagement with Indians in battle. Captain Keogh said not to worry, that there were so few of them and so many of us, it wouldn't be an issue but he also said that the Indians were a brave and crafty people who use guerrilla tactics so we needed to be prepared for anything out there. The truth was that even though Captain Keogh had vast battle experience, he had never actually been in a battle against Indians. We also heard in March that one of the local Indian scouts, Bloody Knife, had been hired as a civilian scout for the upcoming campaign. He had previously led Custer on the expedition to the Black Hills.

Bloody Knife was well known around Fort Abraham Lincoln, and I had seen him around a fair bit. He was the guy who fired the gunshot into the boat after the signing of the treaty between the Indian tribes. He was in his mid-thirties and half Sioux and half Arikara. Because of his mixed heritage, he had been picked on by his fellow Sioux. He and his brothers moved away from their Sioux village to live with their mother's tribe before Bloody Knife then found work with a fur trader and moved away. Two of his brothers were later killed by the Sioux during a raid on his mother's village. Bloody Knife hated the Sioux and was happy to help the US army track them down. I never fully trusted any Indian scouts. Maybe it was because Captain Keogh had told me that Indians were a crafty people. I always had a feeling that they were just looking for an opportunity to lead us into trouble. I am sure I was wrong to think that way, but I did.

Early in the spring, Major Reno had ordered all the troops to step up drilling exercises in preparation for a campaign. There was a little extra gusto in the drilling as we were all keen to be as prepared as possible. In March we also had a daily one-hour target practice session. I had learned to shoot fairly good by this time but the extra target practice was still good to do because there were lots of new recruits. There had been a shortage of bullets after the war and so the opportunity to do target practice was rare and some of the new recruits really had no opportunity to learn to shoot straight. All cavalrymen were issued a Springfield Trapdoor carbine rifle. The carbine was shorter than the full rifle that the infantry had, so it was easier for us to manoeuvre on horseback. Most of the older troops loved having the trapdoor. Just a few years previous, all the rifles were muzzle loaded so an expert shooter could get off just two or three shots a minute. With the trapdoor a good marksman could get ten shots off in a minute. It made an enormous difference in battle. The only problem with them was that they sometimes didn't eject the spent cartridge and would jam up. That could be deadly if it happened at the wrong time. We all also carried brand new six shot Colt revolvers. When we had arrived at Fort Abraham Lincoln from the US Canada Boundary Survey, we were each issued with these new revolvers. These new Colt six shot revolvers were nice guns, but they took some time to get used to.

No one knew where the hostile Indian village was exactly and no one know how many Indians were out there. So, a plan was developed that involved three different columns departing from three different forts, with all of them converging on the general area around the Rosebud River where it was believed the village was roughly located. Colonel John Gibbon would lead the Montana Column east, departing from Fort Ellis, General Terry would lead the Dakota Colum west, departing from Fort Abraham Lincoln and General George Crook would lead the Wyoming Colum north, departing from Fort Fetterman. We would of course, be part of the Dakota Column.

Through January and February there was no sign of General Custer. Major Reno continued to lead us, but we all knew that there was no way that we would go out on a major expedition against the Indians like this one without our commanding officer. In the second week of March there was a blizzard. In the middle of this raging snowstorm, a sleigh being led by the General's brother Tom Custer, arrived at the fort and on the back of the sleigh, covered in snow, was George Custer himself. There was a big cheer from the men when they saw him returning. We knew now that things were going to heat up. Then, a couple of weeks later at the end of March, the general unexpectedly left the fort again to go to Washington. Major Reno was back in command. It turned out that the general was called to testify in a court case and that there was a doubt as to whether he would be back in time to lead us out or not.

As April progressed, we continued our preparations for the campaign under Major Reno. Major Reno had never been in a fight with the Indians so some of the men were concerned that we might be led into battle by a less than ideal commanding officer. At the end of the first week of May, word came through that we were to finalise our preparations and that General Terry, Custer's superior officer and commander of forces in the Dakota Territory, would be the one to lead the column. There was still no clarity on what was happening with General Custer. When we asked Captain Keogh, he told us that Custer, in his evidence to court in Washington, had implicated the brother of President Grant in army corruption. As a result, the president had ordered that Custer not lead such a prominent campaign and that was why General Terry was leading us out. It all seemed very complicated and political so we tried to stay focused on getting prepared.

General Terry - Commander of forces in Dakota Territory

On the 10th of May, after seven weeks away from the fort, General Custer arrived back. He was a little subdued on his return, lacking the presence of someone who normally commanded the stage wherever he went. This made sense when we were told that General Terry would indeed lead the Dakota Column and that General Custer was only to lead the Seventh Cavalry component of it. General Custer might not have been happy but we were thrilled. He was the most experienced army officer in tracking and fighting the Indians. We all felt safer with him as our leader in the field. We also knew that General Terry would defer to Custer in any big decisions.

It was announced that we would depart for Indian country on May 15th. In that last week before we departed, the plan became a lot clearer for us. The column was going to be huge. All twelve companies of the Seventh Cavalry would be going. Also, three companies of infantry, a battery of gatling guns, thirty scouts, five doctors, hundreds of cattle and mules, plus a convoy of supply wagons.

Our rough path would take us due west of Fort Abraham Lincoln. For the first one hundred and fifty miles or so, the terrain would be gentle rolling hills and open prairie. Then we would cross the Badlands with its rougher ground, rocky valleys, and hills. At any point from there on, we could come across the Indians. Further north from where we were at Fort Abraham Lincoln, the Missouri River met with the Yellowstone River. The Yellowstone ran in a curve from that point around in front of us as we looked west. We would keep going west until we got to the Yellowstone. From there we would travel southwest following its course. It was felt that the most likely place the Indians would be found was along one of the rivers that emptied into the Yellowstone. We would scout the Powder River, the Tongue River, Rosebud Creek, and the Bighorn River as we travelled southwest.

For the expedition, each company of approximately fifty men would have a wagon to carry some of their food and supplies. The rest we would have to carry with us on our horses. We had a light blue woollen saddle blanket with an orange trim to go under our saddle to protect the horse. For ourselves we carried an overcoat, blanket, ground cloth and some extra clothes. We'd carry five days rations, oats to feed the horses, a spare set of horseshoes, a horse brush, and our mess kit. Each of us had our Springfield Carbine rifle, a revolver and we'd carry a hundred rounds of ammunition. It was quite a weight for the horses. Tents and other supplies would be carried in the company's supply wagon.

## May 15th, 1876

Reveille sounded at 4AM on Monday May 15th. This was it. Today we head out into the wilderness in search of the hostile Indians. I roused from my sleep even though I hadn't been able to sleep much with excitement. After a moment, I turned to where my partner Ed Driscoll was lying.

*"Hey, Ed. You awake?"*, I asked in a croaky voice.
*"Kind of"*, was Ed's weary reply.

*"This is it. This is the day we finally get to go on a real expedition"*, I said eagerly.

*"mmm"*, was all Ed could muster in response.

*"Come on Ed. We've been waiting for this."*, I said trying to raise him a little. Ed wasn't much of a morning guy, but I was surprised he didn't have more enthusiasm this particular morning.

*"I hope you are faster to rise if we find ourselves under attack"*, I scolded him.

We climbed out of our bunks and started to get ourselves ready. I looked outside and the weather was absolutely miserable. It was raining heavily. I groaned and started a feel a little more like Ed. It was going to be an awful ride in these conditions. There was a lot of activity around the camp as we got ourselves moving. All kinds of loading and unloading of wagons, people waking and stretching, others already shaving in their little handheld mirrors. I could smell the coffee from the mess tent so we went there first before it got too crowded. Breakfast was the usual hardtack and a few strips of bacon. No special treat for the day that was in it, we all joked. Over breakfast, we complained about the weather, talked about what to expect and wondered how far we would march that day.

At 6AM, the bugle sounded for roll call. We lined up and waited to be counted. It was tedious to be doing this in the rain. It took twenty minutes and by the time we were dismissed, we were all soaked through to the skin. At 6.30 the order came to get the horses ready and saddle up. By 7AM we were all saddled up and sitting in the rain waiting for our orders to move out. Sarsfield didn't seem to mind the wet. I was lucky he was such a placid horse. I could see some of the other men wrestling to keep their horses in check while we waited. While we waited the officers were gathered on the verandah of Custer's house. We could see there was a problem or a discussion going on but we waited patiently. Between us we were placing bets on what it was. Most were betting the weather was a problem. Ed jokingly said he wondered if Custer was delayed getting his hair done.

After a while, the officers all went their separate ways back to their troops. Captain Keogh came over to us and said, *"Gentlemen, Stand down. The weather is too bad. Our horses and wagons will get bogged down in the mud. Its better we wait a day or two for the rain to pass"*. The men all groaned and complained about getting wet for no reason but I know most were happy that we wouldn't be riding all day in this rain. We unpacked and unsaddled the horses and then we all went to build fires so we could warm up and dry our clothes. We had the rest of the day to ourselves. We spent most of it around the fire talking. Some of the men took the opportunity to write a letter home before we left.

The following day, the rain had cleared but the decision was made to hold off for another day to allow the ground to soak up the rain. We were kept busy around the fort in the meantime. In the evening, we were again warming ourselves around the fire when the word came that we would definitely be going in the morning. We were all happy with that. The weather was better, and we were tired of waiting around. At least now we would be moving. I was excited and found it difficult to get good sleep. My bunk mate, Ed, had no such trouble. He was snoring before the bugle played 'Taps'.

# XI

❦

# Hunting Hostiles

**May 17th, 1876**

As it had done two mornings previously, reveille sounded at 4AM. Again, we roused ourselves and set about preparing for the march. Because it had been so wet for the last few days, it was too hard to light fires, so breakfast was just hardtack and water. Not a good start to our campaign and we all moaned about it. As usual, breakfast was followed by roll call. At 5AM the bugle sounded to pack up. We did that in the cold and misty dawn. By 7AM we were mounted and in formation ready to move out.

Even at dawn, we were an incredible sight. Hundreds of horses, wagons, infantry all gathered and lined up ready to move. It was quite a sound too; the murmur of low conversations, the shouting of orders, the sound of horses neighing and of bridles clinking. Out at the front of the line was General Custer with his regimental staff. He had two horses, both fabulous beasts that he had bought while we were all serving in Kentucky. On this morning, he was riding Vic. Short for Victory, Vic was a striking thoroughbred. Chestnut in colour with a flash of white across his nose and three white socks. Custer probably rode him that day because he really stood out against the other horses. Custer loved being the centre of attention. His second horse, a stronger looking, deep brown thoroughbred called Dandy, was being led along by his personal orderly, Private John Burkman from the regimental staff.

Along with the general was his wife Libbie and the wives of one or two other senior officers. Behind them was the regimental band. All resplendently turned out on their white horses and playing music to keep everyone's spirits up. Following the band were the twelve companies of the Seventh Cavalry, each with our colour coded horses. We were in the forward part of the column, maybe a hundred feet behind General Custer. Behind us were three other companies before there was a break for the artillery. We were bringing four gatling guns on this expedition. They were being pulled by horse teams and were accompanied by a team of thirty-four specially trained infantry men. Then, after the artillery, came the remainder of the cavalry companies.

As we lined up at the parade ground, the Indian scouts were off to the side. They lived in encampments outside and around the fort but had come in early that morning to prepare for the march. They were banging on their drums and singing their melancholic native songs. They were surrounded by the other Indians and their families. They would join in behind us as we marched out of the fort, before moving to the front alongside the general when we were out on the trail.

The supply wagons had already started their journey and were on the move ahead on the trail. A little after 7AM we got the order to move and we marched in procession, around the parade ground and then passed General Terry and his staff who were perched on a viewing stand. Even though General Terry was leading us on this expedition, tradition was that he would inspect the troops before joining the column himself.

I company were led out by Captain Keogh on his horse Comanche, and we sat up in our saddles with our shoulders back to contribute to the spectacle. First, we passed the married soldiers' quarters. Married soldiers were allowed to live on the grounds of the fort with their wives and families. Their wives would do laundry work around the fort and so their barracks were called "Suds Row". As we proceeded passed them, their wives and children were outside waving them off. It was a sad sight; their families were all crying, and the men turned in their saddles to try and console them through eye contact or perhaps to get a last glimpse. I was a little sad that there wasn't someone there to see me off and hoped that one day I would have a wife and child to wave me off like this. Some of the children marched along beside us pretending to be playing drums. For a moment, I had flashbacks to when myself and Tim marched behind the Georgia militia as they passed through Savannah at the start of the civil war.

Then, with the band playing our regimental song, Garryowen, we passed the viewing stand where General Terry was applauding the passing soldiers. Sitting upright and pulling the horses' reins tight to keep them in step, we were ordered to "Eyes Right" as we passed him. All the drill work on the parade ground paid off. We were in perfect synchronisation. After we'd passed the stand, Captain Keogh, yelled *"Well done boys"*. We continued proudly on out to the trail. We were facing west and the prairie rose in a slight hill ahead of us. In the distance we could see the supply train already a mile out. When the entire column was outside the cavalry post, the general called a halt. We all stopped as directed. There was a pause for a moment, and we waited with just the sound of the horses and bridles clinking before word came back along the line that married men could dismount and go back to say goodbye to their wives and children. Quickly, they dismounted and dashed back, their horses being held in position by their neighbour in the column. I looked back towards the fort. I could make out the Missouri River and the outline of the barracks but the rising sun was too strong, so I couldn't see the men say their farewells. After five minutes waiting, the married men all rejoined the column and were back in the saddle before the order came to "forward march" and off we went. We marched on proudly, all the while wondering what lay in store for us. Each company marching in fours, up the hill while the band played "*The Girl I Left Behind*". There were chuckles from the troops as we recognised what song the band were playing. For a fleeting second, I thought of Miss Grace from Chattanooga. She is the closest I had to leaving a girl behind.

The entire column must have been nearly two miles long. After we got out onto the trail, the infantry joined the column at the rear. In all there were over a thousand men, seventeen hundred horses and mules and of course the wagons and cattle that we needed to supply the whole lot. Once we were out on the prairie, we moved into our march formation which created a perimeter around the central supply train. General Custer, the scouts and a company of the cavalry rode out in front. With the supply train and the cattle herd in the middle, we split into two wings, one on either side. We were part of the right wing so would travel on the right-hand side of the train. The right wing was commanded by Major Reno and had our I company along with B and C companies. The left wing was being led by Captain Benteen and then a rear guard travelled behind the train along with the infantry. We were to stay within five hundred yards of the train, and we had a rolling system where one of the three companies of the wing would ride ahead about a mile, dismount and let the horses graze while the train caught up and then passed by. They would then join the rear of the right wing and another company would ride ahead. It was a safe way to give the horses a break and allowed us all to stay alongside the slower moving wagons and infantry who were on foot.

It was nice to catch a glimpse of my fellow Limerickman Ed Davern from F company who had been reassigned to be Major Reno's orderly and so was marching with the right wing. As we were serving on the same wing, our companies would set up camp alongside each other. We got to catch up in the evenings from time to time along the way. Ed was about ten years older than me and had a lot of army experience. It was always good to get his views on things because, as Reno's orderly, he was privy to more information than the rest of us.

The first day we had to cover some really hilly terrain before we got onto open prairie. The ground was damp because it had been raining so much. That, along with the hills, made for exceptionally slow progress on the first day. The column was so large it was never going to be fast. As we rode along, I was usually in the middle of the line of four. Ed Driscoll was on my left, John Barry on my right and outside him was 'Postie' as we called George Post. We all got on well, so we talked and joked to pass the time. We had the luxury of being on horseback but many of the column were marching so for every hour we rode, we took a ten-minute break to allow people to rest. Horses walk about four miles an hour. They trot at eight miles an hour. When we travelled without infantry the routine was one hour of walking followed by ten minutes rest, then another hour of walking followed by a twenty-minute rest. We'd then do a twenty-minute trot and twenty minutes' walk. Someone in the army had analysed the most effective way for a column to travel and that was it. We could travel thirty-five miles a day in good weather using that routine without wearing out our horses.

We continued through the day until around mid-afternoon when we reached the Heart River. We'd covered about fourteen miles in eight hours. It was much slower than if we were just the cavalry. We all joked that we'd never be able to sneak up on the Indians at this pace. We knew their scouts would see us ten miles off and we had a fair idea that they would be watching us as we progressed along the trail.

The Seventh Cavalry on the move

Once the order to halt came, we knew we would be setting up camp. It was a suitable location as it was on the river with plenty of water for the horses. It was in a dip in a valley and surrounded on three sides by hills. We would position the wagons between the open prairie and the camp to form a blockade. Each night about fifteen men would be on patrol to keep us secure. This first night, as we were getting ready to set up camp, a rattlesnake was found so we all spent twenty minutes having a scout around for more. About a dozen were found and disposed of before we were ready to make our camp. A corral was built for the horses, we watered them first and then tied them in the corral. One member of each company would stay with the horses, taking care of them and keeping them secure. Each company had their own wagon with supplies. Our cook started to prepare food and as we waited, we paired off and put up our tents. As always, I was sharing with Ed.

After dinner, we were sitting around the campfires when the bugle sounded for payday. We were called in turn by company and went to pick up our wages from the paymaster who had set up a desk under a tree just on the edge of the camp. We hadn't been paid for a few months and the general was smart to hold off on paying us until we were out of the fort. If we'd been paid a few days earlier, we'd have struggled to get all the men into their saddles and the day after pay day was also notorious for desertions. I joined the line and when I got to the paymaster, he handed me three months wages less deductions, $30. The monthly salary for a private in the army was $13. The government kept one dollar to contribute towards a pension for us. Another dollar was subtracted for laundry when we were in a fort. For me, there was also a tobacco deduction. Because we hadn't been paid, most of us had debts to pay so we then lined up to pay off our loans from the post sutler who had come along to ensure everything was settled before we strayed too far out on our expedition. Close to half of my pay was handed over to him. The other half wouldn't be much use to me on the trail so, like I always did, I handed it straight back to him and asked that he forward it on to my mother.

That evening, we just sat around the campfire. The regimental band played a concert for the officers and wives. We were out of hearing range, so we had to make do with conversation. Around seven o clock, there were some shouts from the edge of camp as the soldiers on picket duty noticed that he prairie a couple of hundred yards out from the camp had caught fire. A bunch of the troops went out to quench it. We spent the rest of the evening discussing how the fire might have started. Captain Keogh reckoned that it had been started by Sioux scouts sent out to watch us and they were letting us know that they were there. It felt a little scary that we were one day out of the fort and already the Indians were watching us, but we didn't know where they were.

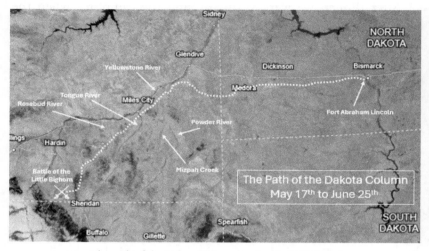

The path of the Dakota Column to the Little Bighorn

## May 18th, 1876

I was deeply asleep at 3AM when the reveille was played on the bugle. This was an early start. It was still dark but this was to be the standard reveille time from now on. It was a nice clear morning but cold. We got dressed, took down the tents and loaded them onto the company supply wagon. They were still damp from the morning dew but they would dry once the sun rose. After breakfast we got ready for another day in the saddle. The routine was usually that we would break camp two hours after morning reveille so we would be departing just as the sun was rising at around 5AM. While we were preparing the horses to saddle up, we watched as General Custer's wife Libbie and the paymaster packed up and started their journey back to Fort Abraham Lincoln. They were escorted by a handful of troops. They were only with us for the first night and my wages were now safely on the way back to the fort.

Once they were out of sight, we got ourselves into formation and the order came to move out at 5AM. We had to cross over the Heart River and with the column being as long as it was, this took hours. It was about 8:30 by the time we all got across. That task completed, we continued for another eleven miles. We were following the twists and turns of Sweetbriar Creek. It was open prairie country, so we were using the creek for guidance in the absence of any major landmarks. With the going slow and eleven miles covered, the general called a halt at 2PM and we made camp for the night on the edge of Sweetbriar Creek.

A lightning storm came in during the late afternoon. We had to run for cover and spent most of the afternoon in our tents as torrential rains came down. It cleared a little in the evening and we hoped that it would stay that way. The heavy rain would cause mud and with all the wagons, mud would be a problem for us.

While we were in our tent that evening, Ed and I got to talking about the Indians. I had told Ed about my father being a strong abolitionist. Ed had lived in Illinois before he enlisted so he had a northern state perspective and was also anti-slavery. I told Ed that I wondered why we were treating the Indians differently than we had the slaves.

"Surely a man is a man and should be given the freedom that the constitution gave him", I positioned.

"If the union army had fought to defend the rights of the negroes, why were we doing the opposite for the Indians?", I pondered.

"I agree", Ed said.

"But the negroes weren't sitting on land that was full of golden nuggets.", he added.

"Its about land and money Thomas. Land and money. We are in the army now and an order is an order. You better make peace with killing Indians because that is what we are out here to do.", he told me.

He was right. We were going to be the oppressors. Those poor Indians had no option once the US government had decided that they needed to be herded from their land and even though I felt bad about it, I was going to be part of it. I thought back to the words my father had said to me when Abraham Lincoln emancipated the slaves.

*"Son, there is injustice in the world, and you will at times be a victim of that injustice but remember, that doesn't mean you should be part of the injustice. Always do the right thing."*

I tossed and turned that night trying to find a way to settle my conscience between my army orders and the advice my father had given me. I couldn't sleep and I couldn't find a way to be true to both.

## May 19th, 1876

When we woke to reveille at 4AM, there hadn't been too much rain during the night. The clouds were dark though, so things were looking ominous. We struck camp and began marching a little after 5AM. Sweetbriar Creek was swollen from the previous evening's rain. It was about fifty feet across and ten feet deep in places which made it difficult for us to cross. We rode up and down looking for a safe crossing point. We tried a few spots, but the mud was treacherous and there was no way we could safely get the wagons across. The clouds suggested that the weather was going to deteriorate so, at around noon, the general changed the plan. Rather than cross Sweetbriar Creek, we would move further along to Buzzard's Roost Butte and camp there.

We rode ahead of the wagons and, within an hour of the change of plan, we had arrived at Buzzard's Roost Butte and began to set up our camp. We could only get so far without the wagons, and they were terribly slow to arrive. Some of them had been completely mired in the mud and needed ten or twelve mules to drag them out, others had to be abandoned altogether. While we waited, we were hit with a horrendous hailstorm and were all completely soaked through. We were all swearing at the wagons and the mud and wondered if this was a bad omen for our expedition. Thankfully, the sun broke through in the late afternoon and a bit later the wagons arrived, but it was too late, we were absolutely soaked and frozen. We had a miserable evening and night in the cold and because of the dampness there was no way to light a fire, so cooking was out of the question. Dinner was hardtack and water.

## May 20th, 1876

None of us slept that night. We were hungry. We were wet and we were uncomfortable. When reveille sounded at 5AM, I didn't know if it was good thing or a bad thing. At least waking up meant we could get moving and hopefully dry off. There wasn't much conversation amongst us as we got started. Everyone was keeping their thoughts to themselves and trying to stay positive. It was hard going.

We started the march at about 8AM. There was another river to cross a couple of miles out, so an advance party had been sent out to find a crossing point. It was still raining and we all knew it was going to be another tough day. After about five miles we came to a creek. By the time we reached it, not only were we cold and miserable, but we were also starting to chaff. Our damp woollen trousers being rubbed up and down the inside of our leg meant that we were all red raw around the inner thigh and crotch area. Trying to avoid the rubbing was impossible because the horse's movement was so hard to predict. Once we'd crossed over the river, the general, sensing the low mood, gave us all a rest for an hour. After we'd reset and eaten, we saddled up again and continued along the track. Most of us had tried in vain to dry out our trousers a little during the stop but it was useless.

It was terribly slow going. We would get a hundred yards and one of the wagons would get stuck. That would back up the ones behind and one by one they would all get stuck. Through the day we only managed to travel seven miles. When we reached the Muddy River and met up with the advance party. They hadn't found anywhere easy to cross so the general ordered a bridge be built and we set up camp for the night.

The evening weather was bad and it rained again for most of the evening and night. There was little firewood available and what was there was reserved for cooking. Without a fire near our tents, it was very cold and there was no way to dry our trousers properly. Most of us had torn up our inner thigh and were red raw. We were at a low ebb and it was only a couple of days into the expedition. We grumbled amongst ourselves but put on a cheerful outlook whenever an officer was around. We were already thinking that if the weather didn't improve, we would be forced back to Fort Abraham Lincoln.

## May 21ˢᵗ, 1876

Overnight, despite the wintry weather, I slept without my long-johns on. They were damp and I needed to find some relief from the chaffing. I lay in my blanket with my legs wide apart to stop further rubbing between my thighs and to let some air at my raw wounds. It gave me a little relief but I knew once I was on the saddle again, I would be rubbed raw within minutes.

I hadn't slept much before reveille was sounded at 3AM. We emerged out of our tents tentative about what the weather was like. It was dark and gloomy but thankfully it was not raining. We were a little slower to get started this morning because the officers were discussing our route. Eventually we set off at 6.30AM. Overnight the engineers had built a pontoon bridge across the Muddy River so we crossed that with relative ease. Progress continued to be slow until around noon when the sun came out and blasted some much-needed heat onto our bones. We had had a tough couple of days and it was beginning to show in the morale of the troops. Some of the mules were also feeling the strain. One had to be shot to put it out of its misery, another we decided it was best to cut it loose and leave it behind. Maybe it would survive and find a way home or maybe not.

The terrain improved as we got into the afternoon. We got to open prairie again which made passage much easier for all of us. Through the afternoon, conversation amongst the troops started again, whereas for the previous few days it had been very muted. In the mid-afternoon the engineers had to bridge another stream, but we passed it fairly quickly. Then about 3.30PM, we were ordered to halt for the night. We had travelled thirteen miles and it was still slow going.

This camp was a lot more pleasant thankfully. The ground was a little rocky so was firm under foot. There was plenty of grass for the horses and water for bathing and cooking. We had to go on horseback to gather wood but it wasn't too bad. The mood being lifted meant that there was an appetite for a song in the evening as we warmed ourselves and dried out our trousers and our groins.

## May 22nd, 1876

The mood the next morning was completely transformed. We were warmer, we were dryer and we had had a chance to socialise the previous night around the campfire. Reveille sounded at 3AM and it was easier to get moving because the weather was brisk but clear. With no dampness and plenty of fire to be had, the cooks were at it early and we all enjoyed the smell of bacon as we packed up camp. A warm breakfast with coffee was almost a luxury after the difficult few days we'd been through.

We broke camp before 5AM and made timely progress in the morning. Dew on the ground kept the dust down and the ground was firm enough for the wagons to pass without getting stuck. The only real obstacle we had to get over was a dry riverbed and that was only because it had steep banks. We lost one wagon in the process after it overturned, and everything came crashing out of it. We were able to carry its load on the other wagons.

In all, we covered about fifteen miles before the general picked a spot for us to camp on the edge of the Knife River. We were in camp by mid-afternoon. To cap off a really good day, when the mail call was sounded on the bugle after we went into camp, I received a letter from home. It is one of the best feelings when your name is called for a letter. There were a thousand men out on this trail and each day about twenty got called for a letter. When I heard my name being called out, a shiver ran down my spine as if a bolt of love had arrived with the letter and hit me. It was such a nice feeling. In anticipation, I rushed forward to collect it. I knew it was going to be from my mother. She was the only one who wrote to me. She would always send regards from the rest of the family, but she was the only one who took the time to write. I took the letter back to my camp and lay down outside the tent, leaning back on my saddle. I would always smell any letter I received, to see if I could get a trace of my mother or the house. The envelope wouldn't have anything but almost always I could get a little bit of something from the letter inside that would bring me home and, for a brief moment, make me feel like I was sitting at the dinner table with my family. I loved it. This letter had something a little extra. After a page of the usual pleasantries and updates on my father and siblings, I read that my mother had given birth to a little girl. Analastasia, they had named her. It meant "she who shall rise up again". I had never heard the name, but it was beautiful, and I am sure she is too. Whenever one of us received a letter, there would be great chat and debate afterwards around the campfire. We'd sometimes share the letter around. Some men never got letters and so in a way they felt like they had an adopted mother and family by reading the others' letters. Some men couldn't read and so one of us would read letters to them. We got to know each other's families well because of the letters from home.

The day had been a good one and the general, seeing that there was a slight rise in spirits, decided to keep the momentum going and asked the regiment band to play a concert for the men that evening. We always enjoyed these welcome events.

## May 23rd, 1876

After another good night in camp, reveille sounded at 5AM. We were happy that it was a little later than it had been in previous mornings. We broke camp and started marching into another cool and clear morning. The terrain continued to be easy going as it was still mostly prairie or low hills and the ground was dry.

In the afternoon, an elk was spotted a hundred yards out. The general decided to chase and hunt it, as he had done with other wildlife on previous days. His dogs were sent off in hot pursuit, but the elk got away. While he was out there, Custer came upon an abandoned Indian camp with the fire still burning. They were close and probably tracking our progress. It was an eerie feeling to march through their camp. Just an hour or so before, it was likely that an Indian war party had been there. I wondered what tribe they were from, Sioux? Cheyenne? There were three lodges, so the estimate was that there were about fifteen of them. We had no indication as to whether they were peaceful families or a scouting war party but we presumed the latter.

Custer sent out his scouts to see if they could track them down. The land was flat so we were all scanning the horizon to see if we could see anything. It was no good. These Indians were masters in this landscape. While the land looked flat, there were gentle valleys and blind spots all over the place. They could have been fifty feet away and we would have had difficulty seeing them. We marched on, still scanning the horizon and some of the troops kept their revolvers drawn just in case.

In the late morning, we passed the grave of Sergeant Henry Stempker. He had been part of the 1874 expedition into the Black Hills but had died of dysentery on the way back to Fort Abraham Lincoln. Captain Benteen had arranged for him to be buried where he died. As we passed, we bowed our heads and some of us said a quiet prayer. Some of his friends were given permission to break from the column, to visit his grave to pay their respects properly. Passing Henry's grave got me thinking about the reality of what lay ahead of us. He was on an expedition just like this, he had skirmished with Indians on that trip and had survived but his gut got him. There was no room for sentiment out on the plains. If anything happened to me, I would be buried out here somewhere with no family to lower my coffin. The best I could hope for would be my mother getting a telegram to inform her a few months after I had been buried and maybe, if troops happened to pass my grave, I'd get a prayer like the one I said for poor Henry. At least in the two years he had been buried out here, no one had done any damage to his wooden grave marker which we were all happy about. As we marched on, I made a pact with Ed that we would personally ride to each other's mother's home to tell her what had happened if one of us was to fall out here. We would remember where the grave was and offer to escort the other's mother to visit it, if they wanted to.

After only a few hours march and with eight miles covered, the decision was made to set up camp for the night, to scout the area for Indians and to rest ahead of a possible longer march tomorrow. We were all thrilled with the news and were in our camp before noon.

Having been in camp early, there was a nice long stretch of the afternoon to rest and take care of the horses. When it was getting close to dusk, we spotted a party of about twenty Indians out on the horizon. This was my first time seeing a hostile Indian party. There was a nervous energy shooting through me as I watched their silhouettes move across the horizon. There was no doubt they were the Indians from the camp we had found earlier. They were too far off to chase down so we let them be. Seeing them made the expedition real. That is what we were out here for. To be on the safe side, a double picket was placed on the guard around the camp that night in case there were more around.

As we were trying to get to sleep, myself and Ed talked about the Indians and the camp we had discovered. We agreed that there was no doubt they were watching us. We were both excited that we were getting closer to them. We wondered how much further their village might be. From that night on, we both slept with our guns close by, fully loaded and ready to go in case we were attacked.

Custer on expedition. Scout Bloody Knife is kneeling to his right pointing at the map

**May 24th, 1876**

After a week on the trail, things were looking a little brighter. The weather had improved so morale was up, and we had started to see signs of Indian life. We were awoken to another bright and sunny day, and we were expecting a long march having broken for camp early the previous day. We were on the move a little after 4AM and made good progress through the day. We covered nineteen miles before we reached the Green River where, in mid-afternoon, we set up camp. We were now just over a hundred miles out from Fort Abraham Lincoln. We were moving much slower than I had expected but the officers seemed content with our progress.

The Green River was a good spot for us to stop and camp. Our cook spent a few hours fishing and managed to catch a few fish. When shared amongst the fifty or so men of our company, there wasn't much to go around but it was nice to have a different taste for a change. The river also gave us all a chance to wash ourselves and because the weather was a lot warmer, we were able to wash our long-johns and have them dry before we went to sleep. A week is a long time in one pair of long-johns especially when you have been chaffing at the crotch. There had been no signs of any Indians this day. We wondered if it might have been a one off the previous day or maybe they were just hiding well.

Every other day since we left the fort, scouts would be sent back to deliver mail and field updates from General Terry. When they returned after a day or two, the reverse happened, letters would come for troops and the latest updates from the other columns arrived. There was going to be a mail run back to Fort Abraham Lincoln that evening so many of us wrote letters home. I wrote my mother a couple of pages to let her know where I was and what my experiences had been that week. I didn't like to worry her, so I kept it high level and upbeat. As darkness fell, two of our Arikara scouts took off back to the fort with our mail and a field report from the general. I wondered how long it would take for my letter to reach my mother. That night I dreamed that I was knocking on her door hand delivering it to her. It was comforting to know that I could let her know I was safe.

## May 25th, 1876

Another day of steady progress. We set off from our camp at 4.45AM. The weather was clear and warm, and the terrain was still mostly flat prairie. In some areas the grass was long which was ok for us on the horses, but the wagons started to struggle a little in it. We covered about twenty miles and in the mid-afternoon the general picked a spot at Crow Ridge for us to establish camp. It had been a relatively good day and again there was no further sign of Indians.

As we rode that day, we started to talk about the Indians we were out here to find. None of us were fully sure of how many of them were out there or what tribes we might encounter. In fact, it was pretty clear that we didn't know much about them at all. One of the scouts rode along with us and explained a little about them.

The Sioux didn't refer to themselves as Sioux. That was a name given to them by the white man. They had their own tribal names. There were seven different 'Sioux' tribes. The Dakota Sioux were made up of the Sisseton, the Wahpeton, the Mdewakantons and the Wahpekute. The Nakota Sioux were the Yanktons and the Yanktonais. The last of the seven tribes were the Lakota Sioux or Tetons. There were then seven different Lakota bands; Brulé, Oglala, Hunkpapa, Minniconjou, Blackfeet, Two Kettle and Sans Arc. All of these Sioux groups spoke the same language and they were all woodland Indians. They were nomadic and hunted their primary food source, the buffalo, until we forced them from the land.

We were able to name a few of the Indian chiefs that we had heard were hostiles. Sitting Bull was known to be the ring leader. He was from the Hunkpapa Lakota band of the Sioux. He was in his mid fifties and had already built a reputation for ferociousness. He had led a number of war parties fighting under Red Cloud during the 1860s. Crazy Horse was another well known Indian warrior who had left the reservation. He was from the Oglala band of the Sioux and came to prominence after he took part in the Fetterman massacre in which eighty US troops were killed in an Indian ambush. He was younger than Sitting Bull, about forty and he wasn't a chief. He was a war leader. The last Indian we could all name was Gall. Like Crazy Horse, Gall was a war leader, not a chief. He was from the Hunkpapa Sioux like Sitting Bull. Word was that he got his name when he ate the blood soaked gallbladder of a freshly killed buffalo. He sounded savage. We were also told to expect other non-Sioux Indians. The Northern Cheyenne were strong allies of the Sioux and were known to have left the reservations in numbers and some Arapaho Indians could also be out there.

## May 26th, 1876

Another early start and as we were breaking camp, a small group of Arikara scouts came riding into our camp. Anytime horses approached the camps at speed, there was a moment of hesitation as we double checked who it was. This time it was just the mail run from the fort. For a few minutes I wondered if there might be a letter for me, but it was too soon since I'd written. It was nice to think of home for a brief moment anyway.

We continued our march westward and we were glad to see a slight change in the landscape. After ten days of prairies, we were starting to hit a rockier terrain. This meant we were approaching the Badlands of the Missouri. The landscape got more striking the further we went. The prairies were replaced with rocks and the smaller hills we had been seeing since we left the fort were replaced by rugged reddish slopes with hardly any vegetation on them. The centuries of harsh weather wouldn't allow grass to grow here.

We continued and crossed a few streams. At each one we took the opportunity to rest and water the horses. The weather was getting a lot warmer now. Camp was called in the middle of the afternoon. We had covered only twelve miles. In another sign that things were changing, we were swarmed by mosquitoes in the camp that night. Heavy rain came in late in the evening and cleared them off but not before they had eaten me alive and taken up residence in our tent. All through the night, I would just be falling asleep when I would hear a buzzing sound in my ear. In my semi-conscious state, I would wave the attacker away only for it to return a few minutes later. It didn't seem to bother Ed, he snored through it all.

## May 27th, 1876

The 3AM reveille woke us to a damp morning. Before I even moved, I knew that I had been feasted on by the mosquitoes. My ear and neck were on fire with an itch that I couldn't quench. The rain had cleared off during the night but there was a lot of fog around. We broke camp at 4.30AM and set off. Due to the fog and the twilight of the dawn, we found it difficult to find our way at first but around noon the fog burned off and it became easier. Thanks to the overnight rain, there wasn't much dust today which made the going a little easier but there was nothing I could do about the itch in my ear. All day I scratched but that just seemed to make things worse.

In the afternoon we entered the valley of Davis Creek and then about an hour later and a mile up the valley, we called a halt for the night. Because of the rocky terrain, the wagons found it difficult to get into the valley and they were delayed in getting to the camp. Some didn't arrive until close to midnight. We had covered another seventeen miles without any more trace of Indians. We were now a hundred and fifty miles out from Fort Abraham Lincoln. We were ten days into the trail and still no real sign of any major Indian activity.

This was a poor camp site. The water was foul from alkaline and because of the changing terrain, there was limited grass for the horses. To compensate a little, the general got the band to play for the troops in the evening.

## May 28th, 1876

Now that we were in the Badlands, we were expecting that we would start to pick up the trail of the Indians. The general had received intelligence that they were in this general area. Nothing was said amongst the troops but you could feel that there was a little more trepidation and excitement amongst us all. Camp duties like establishing the corral and picket duty were being taken just a little more seriously and I noticed around camp people were cleaning their guns a lot more.

We broke camp at 4.30AM and started our march. There was a lot of activity at the front of the column as scouting parties came and went, each returning to give General Custer an update on what they had seen or found out ahead of the column. The scouts were doing two things. Firstly, they were looking for landmarks that we could use to navigate by. General Custer was following the same path as the earlier expedition to the Black Hills and was using sketches from that trip to stay on the right path. Of course the second thing the scouts were doing was looking for signs of the Indians.

As we marched through the canyons of the Badlands, the temperature rose significantly. There was no breeze to cool us and the walls of the canyons seemed to reflect and amplify the heat. It was a busy day for the engineers too, they had to construct eight bridges to allow us to cross the various creeks we encountered along the way. Each time we got to take a break and water our horses while construction was underway. The engineers were efficient at what they were doing. So long as there was ample wood, they could build a pontoon bridge over a creek in less than an hour. Just as well as there were a lot of bridges needed on that day. A little after noon we established camp. Slowed down by the need for engineering works, we had only covered seven miles. The camp site wasn't ideal either. We had wood and grass for the horses but there was no fresh water for us to drink or for cooking.

**May 29th, 1876**

As usual we had 3AM reveille and we were in the saddle from 4.45AM. We continued through the Badlands to the Little Missouri River. The general had gone ahead and selected a site on the edge of the river for us to set up camp. We had travelled just over six miles and were in camp by 11AM. We were happy because without water at the previous camp our horses weren't properly hydrated, and we hadn't been able to cook. Early camp on this day allowed us all to recover.

We were under orders not to discharge any firearms as we were now in an area where Indians had been scouted. We didn't want to attract any attention but we all knew we were being watched anyway. As we were establishing our camp, we heard a roar from behind one of the tents just a little over from us. It was Private Francis Kennedy shouting and jumping up and down holding his hand. We ran over to see what the problem was.

*"It's a rattler. Bit me straight on the finger"*, he said.
*"I thought it would be an Indian that would get me out here. Now it looks like a rattler has killed me"*, he added.

Kennedy had been reaching down to pull up a tent tether pin and was bitten on his trigger finger by a rattlesnake that had coiled around the pin. I ran to get the surgeon, Dr Williams. In the meantime, the other men killed the snake and tossed it outside the camp. Within a couple of minutes, I was back with Williams. We gave him space while he inspected the wound. After a minute or two, he produced a bottle of whisky and poured a dab on Kennedy's finger. Then he made him drink half the bottle of the whisky straight and told him that it would cure him. We all stood around wondering if the doctor was getting him drunk so he wouldn't know he was dying or if it was a magic cure for snake bites. I am sure some of the boys were thinking that they should pretend to be bitten to see if we could get some whisky for themselves. Within twenty minutes, Kennedy was as drunk as a mule and he started vomiting. Then he was passed out for the rest of the evening.

We were delighted that evening when orders came through that we would not be marching the next day. A big cheer went up across our company. It was probably louder than the gunshots we had been ordered not to fire. The following day, the general was going to go on a scouting expedition up the Little Missouri River and was taking four companies with him, but we weren't amongst them so had the day off. An easy day around the camp was just what we needed. It would also give Private Kennedy a chance to sober up, if he didn't die during the night.

## May 30th, 1876

When reveille was blown the following morning, we still had to rise. However, after the general and companies C, D, F and M, and their scouts rode out of camp at 5AM, we were able to go back to our tents and rest. We checked up on Private Kennedy. He was still alive. He was in a lot of pain from his hangover, but the snake bite hadn't taken him. The Indians would still get their chance, we joked with him.

The rest that afternoon was just what we needed. It gave us a chance to wash, and I wrote another letter home. Being out here on the trail, I was active and excited about what might happen, so

I didn't have as much time to think about home but when I did, I liked to write them a letter.

In the late afternoon, the general and the scouting party returned to the camp. They had travelled about fifty miles through the canyons that surrounded the Davis Creek. They hadn't encountered any sign of Indians.

## May 31st, 1876

It had rained all night long and things were soaked when we were awoken by the bugle. The bad start to the day was compounded by the fact that it was too damp to light fires for a cooked breakfast, so it was hardtack and raw bacon washed down with water. We broke camp at 8AM and started out on the trail.

Our first task was to cross over the Little Missouri River. Thankfully, it wasn't too deep, and it had a gravel bed so it wasn't too difficult to cross. Climbing the bank on the far side was the only really challenging part, as it was quite slippery and muddy. In all it took us about an hour to get everything across.

It was misty morning and there was a cool breeze blowing so we had good conditions for the horses. As we marched, we kept an eye on some dark clouds that were threatening our advance. After we had travelled about six miles beyond the river crossing, we came to Andrews Creek and the general decided to set up camp. In the evening at about seven, a freezing rain came in, then it turned to sleet and by midnight it was snowing heavily. We were wrapped in our overcoats and blankets trying to keep ourselves warm in the tents, but it was a very wintry night and none of us slept well.

## June 1st and 2nd, 1876

Right through the night it had snowed, and the outside of our tent was covered with it. By around 1AM the tent was like a refrigerator. Huddled up inside, we tried to keep as warm as possible, but it was hard to sleep in the cold. Reveille didn't sound at the normal time but we were probably awake anyway because of the cold. It eventually sounded a six and we knew that there would be no movement that day because of the weather. With the damp and cold, there was no fires for breakfast, so it was hardtack and water. Then we returned to our tents and did our very best to keep warm. By lunchtime, the weather had thawed a little and we were able to light fires but there was no movement and there was still snow falling.

After a second freezing night, we again awoke to falling snow and again orders were to stay where we were. We stayed in our tents again for most of the day as there was about three inches of snow on the ground. The only exception being the time we were tending our poor horses.

## June 3rd, 1876

After two days cooped up in our tents in the freezing cold, we were happy to wake this morning to the order to break camp. We were packed up and on the trail at 5AM. There was still snow on the ground as we set off but it melted away quickly as the sun came up and by the afternoon, we had a complete turnaround with the sun baking down on us.

A little after 10AM we spotted three riders approaching from the northwest, on the right-hand side of the column. The riders were riding at a gallop. One of the scouts Charley Reynolds rode out to meet them and it turned out they were couriers coming in with dispatches from the Gibbon's Montana Column. They reported that Gibbon had spotted Sioux east of the Rosebud and south of the Yellowstone. This put the Indians further to the west from where we were and explained why we hadn't seen much sign of them.

After about six miles of marching the column emerged from the Badlands back into beautiful rolling prairies. We continued our march for another nineteen miles making this the longest march so far. We found a campsite at the junction of Beaver Creek and Duck Creek and set up camp at about 4PM. Beaver Creek was about thirty feet wide and was cold and clear, so it was a good spot for watering our horses. Unfortunately, there were also a lot of mosquitoes at the site, so we tried our best to keep them out of the tents and to cover as much of our skin as possible. It was pointless though. Again, I was eaten alive.

## June 4th, 1876

The following morning, covered in mosquito bites, we continued our march south along the eastern bank of the Beaver Creek. At 7AM we came to a ravine that needed the engineers to build a bridge for, so we took a break while they worked. We were on the move again at 10AM.

A little after 2PM, some of the Arikara scouts rode back to the column and reported that they had found an Indian camp that was about a week old. The camp had three Indian lodges in it and the leaves used in the camp were still green. That is how the scouts were able to distinguish how old it was. The general, feeling like we had made enough progress in covering eighteen miles, decided that was where we should camp for the night. The creek gave us plenty of fresh water and there was ample wood and grazing for the horses.

## June 5th, 1876

A couple of miles out from camp this morning we caught sight of an Indian out on the horizon. We were riding in the right wing of the column as usual, along with B and C companies. B column were out in front of us when word came back that the first sergeant had spotted something. Captain Keogh rode up to where he was stopped a little out from the column. We could see them conferring and pointing at the distance. We looked but couldn't make out what they were pointing at. Captain Keogh had a looking glass and was using it. After a few minutes, the captain returned to the column and five troops from B company rode off at pace in the direction they had been pointing. Captain Keogh told us that they had spotted an Indian and that he was probably scouting us. After about an hour the troops returned. They couldn't track him down.

We continued our march southwest. We passed over a divide between the Beaver Creek and Cabin Creek. The ground was quite sandy for a little while afterwards which made it hard going for the horses and wagons. We also started to see signs of a buffalo herd. They travel in such numbers it's hard to miss the signs. Vast tracks and distinctive poo made it obvious that we were in buffalo country. We went into camp in the late afternoon having travelled twenty-one miles. The horses needed a break, so we made sure to take loving care of them that evening.

That night two men from Captain Benteen's H company went out at dusk to do some hunting. This was a common enough occurrence. Out here there was plenty of wildlife and with rations being a little on the small side, some of the troops would find ways to get a little extra food. These two went off into the darkness hoping to find some prairie dogs or a rabbit but they didn't come back.

## June 6th, 1876

After reveille when roll call was being done, it became clear that the two members of H company, who had gone off hunting after dark the previous night, hadn't returned. There was a scouting party sent out to see if they could be found but shortly after, they returned with no sign of them. It was presumed that the Sioux had taken them and that they had had a horrible death. I was a little surprised how short the search for them had been. It was no more than forty-five minutes. I suppose the scouts knew the land and the Indian ways.

There wasn't much talk that morning as we broke camp and set out on the trail. The disappearance of the two made this all very real. If the Sioux had taken them, then they must have been within a hundred yards of our camp. We were all a little spooked by that thought. We had been lulled into a false sense of security by not having had a serious encounter with them. We would have to keep our guard up or we could be next to disappear.

At about 10AM, we saw two riders approaching the column. They looked like soldiers. As they got closer it became clear that it was the two missing soldiers from H company. As their identity was confirmed, a great big cheer went up along the column to welcome them back. It was like they had returned from the dead. It turned out that they hadn't been taken by the Sioux but had lost their way in the darkness. We were happy to have them back and I am sure they were happy to have found us and safety. I think the scare we all got, thinking it was the Sioux that took them, was probably a good thing anyway. It made us more focused.

After we had welcomed back the prodigal pair, we were ordered to remount to continue our march when a shot rang out. We were all a little stunned. What was it? Where did it come from? Was this a surprise Indian attack? We all immediately jumped for cover and tried to pull our horses into some form of shelter. After a minute of confusion there had been no more shots and there was some yelling from the area H company had been using for their rest. Slowly word reached us that one of the soldiers in H company, Private McWilliams, had accidentally shot himself when throwing his leg over his horse. His pistol had gone off and he managed to shoot himself down through his shin. The bullet had come out the back of his ankle. There was a twenty-five-minute delay as he was seen to by Dr de Wolf but with the bullet already out, all he got was some whisky to clean the wound and a mouthful to dull his pain. For the rest of the day, he was the laughingstock of the regiment. Amongst us we were warning each other to be careful anytime someone was mounting. It was silly but fun for a while. Private McWilliams was sent to the Powder River hospital that evening along with Private Lepper from L company who had developed an abscess in his hand and Private Kane from C company who had developed a chest problem. The three of them were sent off with an escort and all three would miss the action. They didn't know it at the time but they were lucky souls.

I rode alongside Captain Keogh for a while that day and we got to talking about Dr de Wolf. Captain Keogh didn't seem too fond of him and when I asked why, Keogh told me that when he left Ireland in 1860, he went to Italy. He was one of the Irish St Patrick's Battalion who went to defend Pope Pius IX in the Papal Wars. The army of Garibaldi was trying to unify the Italian states and was encroaching on land owned by the Catholic church. Captain Keogh fought alongside six thousand French, Swiss, Australian and Irish Catholic soldiers in the defence of the Adriatic port of Ancona on the east coast of Italy. Garibaldi's army first put the coastal city under siege and then unleashed a severe battering by artillery until the city was forced to surrender. Afterwards, Keogh and his colleagues were put in prison in Genoa for six months. Conditions were bad and the prisoners suffered a lot. He then explained to me that Dr de Wolf was in Garibaldi's army, as was Private Giovanni Martini one of the trumpeters. It was then I understood why there was tension between them. It was interesting to hear the captain's story first hand. My admiration for him continued to grow the more I knew him. I particularly enjoyed the fact that he didn't allow formality between himself and the men. Many officers wouldn't be so approachable.

A few miles into on the trail this day and the signs of buffalo we had been seeing the previous day became a reality. We summited a small hill and as we came over the crest, we came into a valley that was filled with them. Hundreds. A big black mass against the green prairie grass. Most of them were in a herd together but there were others who had strayed away a little from the cohort. This was my first sighting of a herd of buffalo, and they were majestic. Unbothered by us, the grazed away. They were a wonderful sight. I could immediately understand why they were so revered by the Indians. A group from the general's party at the front shot off in pursuit of one of them and before long there was a stampeding scatter as the herd realised there was danger. A shot rang out and one of them came crashing down maybe a hundred yards from where I was. The rest of the herd just kept on running without a care for their fallen friend. The general and his party had buffalo steak for dinner that night, no doubt. The only female on the expedition was Mary Adams, Custer's personal cook. A freed slave, Adams was paid an annual salary of two hundred and fifty dollars, almost double a soldier's wage. This always annoyed Ed so I made sure to mention it often.

As we were now in open country with little, if anything, to block the wind, we were riding directly into a gust all day. It made for a hard ride. While I rode with my handkerchief up over my nose and face, my lips and nostrils were completely dried out. With my lips cracked from the hot wind, it was difficult to talk and for a lot of the day we were all pretty quiet. The short relief of a swig from my canteen would last ten minutes and I'd be parched again. At about 4PM and with about twenty-two miles covered, the general called camp. We were delighted. The wind had made it a particularly difficult ride and we were all exhausted. After what had happened the previous night with the late-night hunters, we were all a little more guarded. No one went in search of extra food that night.

## June 7th, 1876

The camp the previous night was two hundred and fifty miles from Fort Abraham Lincoln. It had taken us three weeks to get this far. We knew we were getting closer to our target, but we were all a little frustrated by the slow progress.

We broke camp just before five in the morning and started what would become a long march that day. Our target was to get to the Powder River and General Terry felt we could get there before three in the afternoon. It was a stop start march with us having to stop for engineers to bridge a ravine at one point. Along the way we passed numerous buffalo carcasses, the remnants of Indian feeding. There was a half a dozen of them which meant a large group of Indians were there recently.

We finally made it to our destination three hours later than scheduled. We had covered thirty-two miles, and everyone was exhausted when we fell into camp. The last of the wagons didn't arrive until 9PM.

Our location was now on the Powder River just twenty miles south of where it intersected with the Yellowstone River. All the intelligence we had received was that the Indians were camped along one of the four rivers that ran into the Yellowstone. The Powder River was the first, then the Tongue River, the Rosebud and finally the Bighorn. While we had felt that we were getting close, we knew now that we were in their territory and at any moment we could stumble on their village or be subjected to a surprise attack.

## June 8th, 1876

We were delighted to have a day in camp. We had been on the trail for over three weeks and were all tired and particularly so after the marathon march the previous day. I was starting to get a little concerned about Sarsfield's energy so when we learned that we wouldn't be in the saddle today, I went down to the corral, gave him a good grooming, and made sure he had plenty of water. I managed to get some extra oats for him too.

In the early afternoon, we were lazing around our tents when we saw General Terry and two companies riding out of the camp. They were riding ahead of the rest of us to meet up with the Far West which had sailed up the Yellowstone with supplies and was waiting where the Yellowstone and Powder Rivers met. The Far West was a steamboat that was used up and down the Missouri River and had been commandeered to support expeditions such as this one. She would ferry troops or officers up and down the rivers and was used to supply depots along our route. I never had a chance to go aboard but it was a fine vessel with two big, tall black chimneys and a big paddle wheel at the back. The deck was mostly available for cargo and above that was a cabin where officers would meet or stay while they were onboard. The ship captain was in a cockpit above that again. The later it got before General Terry returned, the more confident we were that we wouldn't be moving early the next morning. Most of the men felt certain we wouldn't move the next day as they went off to sleep.

The Far West

## June 9th, 1876

No 3AM reveille was expected but as usual, our natural sleep cycle had us awake anyway. We were able to relax until 5AM when it eventually sounded. General Terry still hadn't returned so we spent the day around camp. The weather was clear until the afternoon when heavy rain came into the camp, and we were confined to our tents for the evening. Late in the evening General Terry returned. He'd brought Mitch Bouyer with him.

Scout Mitch Bouyer

Mitch Bouyer was the chief scout on Colonel Gibbon's Montana column. We speculated what was happening when we saw them return. Captain Keogh went off to meet with them to find out. After an hour he returned and let us know that we would be going on a scout the next day and that Bouyer would be going with us.

After a couple of days resting in camp, and with our horses well recovered, we were happy enough to have a scouting expedition to look forward to. We knew we were getting close to where the Indians must be so perhaps, we'd be the first to encounter them.

# XII

⌘

# Scouting the Rosebud

**June 10th, 1876**

At this stage we had been on the trail for three weeks and had been getting tired. Those few days at the camp on the Powder River had given us a chance to recover slightly and more importantly to rest the horses. There was a lot of coming and going on the Far West as the officers conferred and built their plans. In the meantime, we relaxed while we could and did the work that needed to be done around the camp. There was light rain most of the morning, but it cleared before noon. In midmorning, Captain Keogh came to us and told us to get prepared as we had been assigned to go on a scouting mission with Major Reno.

The Indian village had to be on one of the rivers and creeks around this area. We didn't know which one. There were four main rivers as we headed east from our location on the Powder River. The first was the Powder River, then the Tongue River, the Rosebud and finally the Bighorn. Our scouting mission would cover about two hundred miles of rivers in the hope that we would locate the

192 ~ DES RYAN

Indians. Our orders were to travel south following the Powder River upstream for about a hundred miles. Then we were to turn west and cut over as far as the Mizpah Creek. Once we found that, we were to follow it north back as far as where it intersected with the Powder River. From there we were to again travel west as far as the Pumkin Creek. Once we found that we were to follow it north to where it joined the Yellowstone River. At the Yellowstone we would be met by the rest of the regiment. We were basically rolling out an Indian presence on the Powder River and the creeks around it.

It was going to be a big column on this scout. We were expecting to be gone for about ten days. Major Reno had been assigned six companies: Captain McDougall's B company of forty-six men, Lieutenant Harrington's C company of fifty-two men, Lieutenant Smith's E company of fifty-one men, Captain Yates' F company of fifty men, Lieutenant Calhoun's L company of fifty-nine men, along with our forty-eight from I company. On top of that we were bringing a gatling gun and some scouts. Each company had eleven pack mules to carry enough supplies to last for twelve days.

Our lead scout Mitch Bouyer was about forty years old. His father was a French fur trader and his mother was Santee Sioux. He knew the lands around here well and was a good addition to our group. I was happy that the group was going to be so large. We knew we were getting closer to where the Indian village was going to be and there was every likelihood that we would stumble across them on this scouting mission. At least with over three hundred men, we had enough soldiers to defend ourselves if we were suddenly attacked.

We were all packed up and ready to depart at three in the afternoon. Led off by the scouts, we made slow progress which was to be expected with the size of the scouting party. We managed to travel eight miles in the first day before stopping for the night and setting up camp on the eastern side of the Powder River. Bringing the gatling gun with us had pros and cons. The pro was that if we were in a battle, we could wipe out the attacker with its automatic fire. The con was that it was very heavy and awkward to carry in some of the terrain we were covering. Numerous times over the course of the scout, we had to dismount the gun from its cart and carry it by hand over gullies or streams. It definitely slowed us down but it was reassuring to have it with us at the same time.

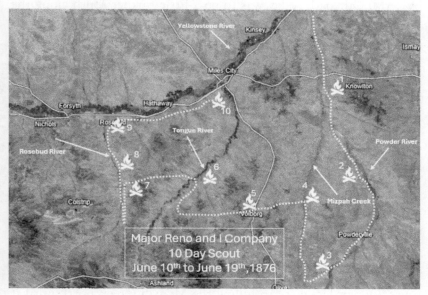

The path of the Reno scout - June 10th - June 19th

# June 12th, 1876

On 12th June we continued our scout for another twenty-four miles around the bend of the Powder River. Staying on the western bank, we marched until it was time to establish camp. It had been a fair day and visibility was good. At about 2PM we came across an Indian camp that was about a week old. A trail led west from the camp and it looked like about thirty families were travelling together so it was a big enough group. Major Reno decided that this would be a good place to camp so we stopped for the day. At dusk, an Indian pony strayed up to the corral where our horses were resting. These were real signs that we were getting closer. That night we slept with our guns loaded and nearby. That Indian pony spooked us.

## June 13th, 1876

Early start with reveille at 3AM and as usual we were on the trail by 5AM. Our path today was to go a little further south along the Powder River before turning west and crossing over to the Mizpah Creek. From there we headed north along the Mizpah Creek for a few miles before establishing our camp for the night. It was a hot but uneventful day. From camp, scouts were sent further north along the Mizpah Creek to look for signs of Indians. They returned late and had found nothing.

## June 14th, 1876

On the 14th of June we deviated from the orders we were given at the start of the scouting expedition. When the scouts returned the previous night from their travel further north along the Mizpah Creek, and reported no signs of Indian life, Major Reno decided it would be a waste of time to bring the entire party along the same route. Our orders were to follow the Mizpah Creek north until it met with the Powder River. Instead, Major Reno decided to cross over the Mizpah Creek and continue west to Pumpkin Creek. No one challenged this change and the Indian scouts with us, who called Major Reno "Man with a dark face", were happy to change route. Had we followed our orders, we would be covering dead ground and we already knew there was nothing to be found there.

We crossed over the Mizpah Creek and continued about twenty miles until we reached Pumpkin Creek. There we turned north and marched a few miles until we met Little Pumpkin Creek. At this point, the Major called for camp to be established. Again, we had no sign of any Indian activity.

## June 15th, 1876

Had we followed our original orders we would have hit Pumpkin Creek about twenty miles north of where we now were, and we would have marched south ending up where we were. Major Reno sent a scout north along the Pumpkin to make sure we hadn't missed anything by deviating from our orders. He then ordered us to continue west along the Little Pumpkin and we would then turn north once we reached the Tongue River.

The scouting party that went north along the Pumpkin Creek returned with no sign of Indians, so we marched on for about twenty-five miles as far as the Tongue River. It was a difficult march. The terrain wasn't suitable for a column like ours and in places the trail was so narrow that even a single horse would struggle to pass it. We also had the gatling guns to contend with. In several places that day, we had to take them from their wagon and physically carry them through parts of the trail.

Once we had established camp, the chief scout, Mitch Bouyer, took Major Reno a little bit south of our camp to show him the remains of a large Indian camp. It was a few months old, but it was large, and it was clear from the trail, that the Indians had moved further west. Because of this discovery, Major Reno again decided to deviate from official orders. We would follow the trail west. The Indians must be on the Rosebud.

## June 16th, 1876

As usual reveille sounded at 3AM and we were on the trail by 5AM. With the change of plan, we first marched north along the Tongue River to find a place where we could safely cross over. After about eight miles, we came to an abandoned Indian village.

It was big. It looked like it had about four hundred lodges, but it was an old camp. It was clear that these Indians had travelled west and crossed the Tongue River in the direction of the Rosebud. Excitement and anticipation was continuing to rise. These were big Indian villages and we could see the direction they were moving. We were getting very close. We were well off of our original route though. If anything went wrong now, we would have to fend for ourselves no matter how large the Indian camp was.

We found a crossing point on the Tongue River and were soon on the path even further west towards the Rosebud. As we marched along there were plenty of signs of Indians having been there with buffalo corpses and the like, but all the signs were more than a week old. After twenty-seven miles we started to approach the Rosebud. As we passed more and more rivers going west, the likelihood of us encountering the Indians was getting a lot higher. We called a halt to our march about four miles short of the Rosebud and rested there while scouts went forward into the valley of the Rosebud to see if the Indians could be found or if we were safe to continue. After a six hour wait, the scouts returned. They had found more Indian camps, but again, they were not recent ones. It was safe for us to continue and establish camp on the Rosebud for the night. We got there at about 9PM and built our camp on the same site as the Indians had camped. It had been another long day.

We were now very much in the area where the Indians would be. Major Reno ordered that no bugles were to be blown, no gunshots to be fired, and no shouting was to be done while we were on the Rosebud. He also ordered double pickets to be put on the camp around the clock. We had been sleeping with our guns loaded and nearby for a few weeks now, but we started to sleep with them by our blankets now. At any moment we might have to defend ourselves.

**June 17th, 1876**

As we had arrived late the previous night, reveille wasn't called until 6AM to allow us to recover a little. As ordered, there was no bugle call so the captain and orderly went around the tents waking the troops. We awoke to the one-month anniversary of being on this expedition. As we ate our breakfast, Captain Keogh was in conference with Major Reno about the plan. The captain was a little concerned about going against the orders we had been given by General Terry. If we continued to follow the Indian trail, we were likely to encounter them and we didn't know what to expect. Eventually, they agreed that the march that day would be south along the Rosebud for about six miles to see if there was any sign of Indians. If not, we would then turn around and backtrack to where we were camped. From there we would continue north along the Rosebud towards the Yellowstone River where we could align with the tail end of our original orders and return to where General Terry and the rest of the regiment were camped.

We broke camp at 8AM and marched south along the Rosebud for a couple of hours. At 10AM we came to another abandoned Indian camp. There was nothing much to report here. It was the same as the others; large but the Indians were long gone. We took a break for a few hours and scouts were sent further south along the Rosebud. While the scouts were gone, Captain Keogh told us that one of the scouts named Forked Horn, had told him *"If the Dakotas see us, the sun will not move very far before we are all killed"*. If the scouts were on edge, they knew we were close. They estimated we were within a day's ride of the village. We just didn't know which direction it was.

The scouts returned and reported that the Indian village was headed west towards the Little Bighorn River. With that information, Major Reno decided it was best to travel back to update General Terry. In the mid-afternoon we began to march north, covering some of the same ground we had covered that morning but headed in the opposite direction. We passed the point where we had camped the previous night and continued further north. We established our camp at 8PM. While our scouting mission had been fruitless, we now knew that the Indians were headed towards the Litle Bighorn. Major Reno was excited to update General Terry and Custer.

## June 18ᵗʰ, 1876

With the information that the Indians were almost certainly on the Little Bighorn River, it was important that we report back to General Terry as soon as possible. Our original orders had us reporting back to General Terry who would be camped on the Yellowstone River where it intersected with the Tongue River. We broke camp at 5AM and marched north along the Rosebud until it reached the Yellowstone River. When we reached the Yellowstone, we turned east and began marching along the southern bank of the Yellowstone.

After an hour, we came to a point where Colonel Gibbon's Montana column was camped on the far side of the river. When the plan was originally put together, three columns were to march out of three different forts and converge around the area where it was thought the Indians would be camped. While General Terry led us west from Fort Abraham Lincoln, General George Crook was marching north from Forth Fetterman in Wyoming Territory and Colonel Gibbon was marching east from Fort Ellis in Montana Territory. This was the first time that the columns had connected. We established camp across the river from the Montana Column.

While we were there it was important that we update each other's command on what the current state of the mission was. Major Reno and Colonel Gibbon tried to shout across the river at each other, but it was difficult. They looked for a crossing point, but the river was just too wide. In the end Private Willheit of I Company of Colonel Gibbon's column was enlisted to deliver dispatches back and forth between the two. It was difficult because the river was high and with a strong current. Willheit decided to try and float across the river on a log. We all got a good laugh from watching his progress. In the end, he was successful and managed to courier messages back and forth and he also gave Major Reno a message for General Terry which Reno arranged to be delivered along with his next field update.

## June 19th, 1876

On the final day of our scouting expedition, we were on the trail early, breaking camp at 4AM. We waved across the river to Colonel Gibbon's men and marched thirty-three miles east along the southern bank of the Yellowstone until we were about eight miles short of the agreed rendezvous point with General Terry. As we'd been marching for twelve hours, Major Reno decided to stop, establish camp and to send a report along with Colonel Gibbon's message on to General Terry. Once we had set up camp, Major Reno sent Mitch Bouyer to General Terry carrying a message. It read:

*"I'm in camp eight miles above you. I started this morning to reach your camp, but the country from the Rosebud here is simply awful. I enclose you a note from Gibbon, whom I saw yesterday. I can tell you where the Indians are not and much more information when I see you in the morning. My animals are leg weary and need shoeing. We have marched near to two hundred and fifty miles".*

We awaited a response. In the meantime, it had been an exceptionally long march that day, so we took the opportunity to rest ourselves and our horses.

# XIII

❦

# Closing In

**Tuesday June 20<sup>th</sup>, 1876**

It was good to be back in camp and close to the rest of the regiment. While it had been exciting to go on the scout over the previous ten days and have the thrill of getting closer to the Indians, it felt safer to be back with the entire column. We didn't march in the morning. Major Reno was waiting for word back on the message that Mitch Bouyer had brought to General Terry. While we waited, we caught up on personal grooming and other things that it was impossible to do while we were out on the scout. I took the opportunity to reshoe Sarsfield. The terrain we had been covering was rough and his hoofs took a bit of a pounding so it needed to be done. I also gave him a good grooming. He loved the attention and I could tell that he felt better when I was finished. I also took the opportunity to have a nice cool swim for myself in the Yellowstone River. We didn't have much chance to bathe while on the scout and this was a particularly sweltering day, so a few of us took to the cool water for a swim. We just had to be careful where we swam. A little further upstream there had been an Indian camp. They must have been there for a while because there were a few of their graves there. The Indians built these stilt graves where they would 'bury' their dead up on a platform. I think it was supposed to keep them up off the ground and clear of any animals who might desecrate the grave. Some of the troops decided that they didn't want to camp near the graves so they took them down and threw the bodies in the river. The graves also had offerings for the dead to take to the next word, like beads, weapons, and extra clothes. They were all plundered as souvenirs by the troops.

In the late morning, General Custer arrived at our camp with the rest of the Seventh Cavalry and he immediately went to Major Reno's tent. He and General Terry had obviously received Major Reno's message. We were about fifty yards away but we could easily hear a major disagreement between the two officers. General Custer was furious that we had disobeyed our orders and he was shouting that, even though we did in the hope of pinpointing where the Indians were, we were still unable to say exactly where they were or how many of them there were. To be able to overhear the shouting between two officers was a little embarrassing. Ed and I looked at each other and both agreed we were glad we were a little distance away. Had we been closer, it would have been very awkward. Here, at least, we could let on we weren't listening in.

Shortly after General Custer arrived, and in the middle of the argument, the Far West arrived and moored on the riverbank. General Terry came ashore, and he also went straight to Major Reno's tent. Things calmed a little once General Terry joined in but the officers stayed in conference for a good hour.

At lunchtime, the order came around that our sabres would not be needed on the final part of the expedition so they were all collected up and stored on one of the wagons. None of us were concerned about this. We didn't expect to be having close enough contact with the Indians to need sabres anyway. Our carbine rifles and revolvers would be more than enough for any fight and the sabres were sometimes a nuisance dangling down the side of our saddles.

After General Terry emerged from his meeting with Major Reno and General Custer, he reboarded the Far West and sailed further west towards the Rosebud. Shortly afterward, we were ordered to prepare to break camp and at about five o' clock we joined the rest of the Seventh Cavalry and followed General Custer on an eleven-mile march west along the Yellowstone where we joined the camp of Colonel Gibbon about four miles short of the Rosebud. We were glad the march was in the late afternoon because it had been a sweltering day, and it would have been a really hard march in the midday heat.

We spent the evening in camp discussing the officers' argument from earlier in the day. It was clear that General Custer was annoyed by the tone of Major Reno's note, and he let him know he wasn't impressed. Major Reno in his defence had managed to get a better result out of the scout by not following orders. Had we done as we were directed, we would not have been able to identify where the Indians were now almost certain to be. We would have marched up and down the various rivers and encountered nothing of note to report back.

### Wednesday June 21st, 1876

After spending most of the previous day in camp, watching the comings and goings of the officers at Major Reno's tent, we had a 6AM wake and by 8AM the entire Seventh Cavalry was on the move again. Headed by General Custer, we were moving just a few miles further west along the Yellowstone. When we reached the mouth of the Rosebud, we established camp again. It had been a short enough march of just a few hours.

Once we were back in camp at the Rosebud, the Far West arrived, and all the senior officers spent the afternoon on board discussing the plans. The rest of us watched and waited for word on what the plan would be. We asked Captain Keogh if he knew what was happening and he said he didn't but that we were so close to the Indians now that we should take every opportunity to rest. We were happy enough with that. In the five weeks we had been out of the fort, we had been marching almost every day and on the few days we didn't march we had been snowbound. We were all feeling the effects of the trip and, with the weather warming up, any march would take more out of us. We worked out that in the thirty-six days we were on the trail, we had just five where we weren't on the move and that we had travelled on average sixteen miles a day. No wonder we were all exhausted. We were at risk of burning out our horses too.

At 4PM the officers call was sounded on the bugle and all the other officers joined the senior ones in General Custer's tent to be briefed on the plan. After an hour, Captain Keogh returned to give us an update. General Custer would take all twelve companies of the Seventh Cavalry, including us, and march south along the Rosebud Creek and from there cross over to the Little Bighorn where it was thought the Indian village was. Meanwhile, General Terry and Colonel Gibbon would take the remainder of the force and march further west along the Yellowstone, to the far side of the Little Bighorn and then turn back to form a pincer movement which it was hoped would trap the Indians between the two. It sounded like a good plan to us. Estimates were that there would be about eight hundred Indian warriors and the Seventh Cavalry alone was over six hundred. If we encountered the Indians ourselves, we would be more than enough for them. If we caught them in a pincer with over twelve hundred troops, they would be no match for us at all. Our official orders were as follows:

*Headquarters Department of Dakota, (In the Field,)*
*Camp at Mouth of Rosebud River, Montana, June 22, 1876*

*Colonel: The brigadier-general commanding directs that as soon as your regiment can be made ready for the march, you should proceed up the Rosebud in pursuit of the Indians whose trail was discovered by Major Reno a few days since. It is, of course, impossible to give you any definite instructions in regard to this movement; and were it not impossible to do so, the department commander places too much confidence in your zeal, energy, and ability to wish to impose upon you precise orders, which might hamper your action when nearly in contact with the enemy. He will, however, indicate to you his own views of what your action should be, and he desires that you should conform to them unless you shall see sufficient reason for departing from them. He thinks that you should proceed up the Rosebud until you ascertain definitely the direction in which the trail above spoken of leads. Should it be found (as it appears to be almost certain that it will be found) to turn towards the Little Horn, he thinks that you should still proceed southward, perhaps as far as the headwaters of the Tongue, and then turn towards the Little Horn, feeling constantly, however, to your left, so as to preclude the possibility of the escape of the Indians to the south or southeast by passing around your left flank.*

*The column of Colonel Gibbon is now in motion for the mouth of the Big Horn. As soon as it reaches that point it will cross the Yellowstone and move up at least as far as the forks of the Little and Big Horns. Of course, its future movements must be controlled by circumstances as they arise; but it is hoped that the Indians if upon the Little Horn, may be so nearly enclosed by the two columns that their escape will be impossible. The department commander desires that on your way up the Rosebud you should thoroughly examine the upper part of Tullock's Creek; and that you should endeavour to send a scout through to Colonel*

*Gibbon's column with information of the result of your examination. The lower part of this creek will be examined by a detachment from Colonel Gibbon's command.*

*The supply-steamer will be pushed up to Big Horn as far as the forks, if the river is found to be navigable for that distance; and the department commander (who will accompany the column of Colonel Gibbon) desires you to report to him there not later than the expiration of the time for which your troops are rationed, unless in the mean time you receive further orders.*

*Very respectfully, your obedient servant,*

*Ed. W. Smith*

*Captain, Eighteenth Infantry, A.A.A.G.*

At seven in the evening a thunderstorm hit us. It was quite a deluge but thankfully only it lasted for an hour. As we huddled in the tent, Ed and I talked about whether it was a bad omen that as soon as the plan was announced, the thunderstorm hit. He was pessimistic but I reminded him about our numbers and how the Indians were no match for us. I am not sure I convinced him.

After the storm passed, we sat around the campfire and had a sing song. It was a dark night. With clouds in the sky it was hard to see the moon and stars but the light of the campfire kept things visible. All the old reliable songs were sung. A few Irish ballads thrown in for good measure. We all loved a good song in the evening. While we were singing, the officers all played poker in General Custer's tent. Captain Keogh came over to join us as we sang *'Follow me up to Carlow'* and then returned to the poker game. They were still playing at two in the morning, but I had turned in at midnight, mindful of what Captain Keogh had said about taking rest when it was on offer.

## Thursday June 22nd, 1876

I was glad I took an early night when reveille sounded at four. Sunrise was shortly afterwards while we were having our breakfast. Our orders were that we would move out at noon, so the morning was spent getting ourselves ready to move out as a column.

Under General Custer would be the thirty-one officers of the Seventh Cavalry, five hundred and seventy-six troops spread across the twelve companies. Five lead scouts and quartermaster employees; Mitch Bouyer, George Herendeen, Charie Reynolds, Bloody Knife and General Custer's youngest brother, Boston Custer. Two interpreters; Isaiah Dornan and Fred Gerard, twenty-three other scouts. We had seven civilians with us which included newspaper reporter Mark Kellogg, Custer's nephew Autie Reed and five civilian packers. It was a big column and enough for any Indian battle.

We were carrying fifteen days of rations and twenty-four thousand rounds of reserve ammunition. They would be carried on a mule train of one hundred and eighty-five mules. Each man was issued one hundred rounds of carbine rifle ammunition and twenty-four rounds of pistol ammunition. We also carried on each of us twelve pounds of oats for our horses and we were issued some salt in case we had to resort to eating our horses. God forbid I would have to shoot Sarsfield and eat him.

After speaking to Major Reno about the difficulty we had in bringing the gatling gun on the scouting mission, General Custer decided not to take any of the gatling guns with us. They would all go with General Terry and Colonel Gibbon. We felt that there was enough of us anyway so didn't think much of this decision. In hindsight, they would have been very useful.

Before we left camp, we heard that two of the regiment would not be coming with us and would return down the Yellowstone River having come down sick. Private Mark E Lee from our I Company wasn't well enough to continue. He was joined in leaving the camp by a Private Ackerson from E company who had severe constipation. They would miss the exciting part of the expedition. We knew Mark well so were sorry to see him go. He was a barber before he joined the army so was popular amongst the men because he would cut their hair. A little before noon we waved him off and said our goodbyes. We told him to have his scissors sharpened and ready for us when we got back to Fort Abraham Lincoln. He laughed and said he would.

At noon, we were ready to move. Before the regiment split off from General Terry and Colonel Gibbon, General Custer led us on a makeshift parade before them. With our bugles playing Garryowen, we marched passed and saluted the officers. Colonel Gibbon's men were cheering and wishing us well as we rode by. As each company passed by Terry, the officer in command of that company would ride up to General Terry, salute and he would wish each one well on this trip. I am not sure what message he had for Captain Keogh, but he blushed and said 'thank you' before re-joining us in the column. All twelve companies then split off and followed General Custer south along the edge of the Rosebud.

We marched out for about an hour. The Rosebud Creek wasn't very wide, maybe three feet. The water was crystal clear and you could see the riverbed as we passed over it. We crossed back and forth depending on which side of the creek had the easier terrain for the column. Even though we had just come back from our scout along the Rosebud we sent scouts out in front of the column to map the way and watch for signs of Indians. Each day, one of the companies would be allocated to the rear guard and they would ride behind the mule pack.

After marching about twelve miles, General Custer decided to establish camp for the night. It was about four in the afternoon. As we rested in camp in the evening, the general summonsed all his officers to his tent. They talked for about twenty minutes after which each officer returned to their company to relay the orders. From this point forward there would be no more bugle calls. The guards who were on duty overnight watching the horse corral, would wake the troops at three in the morning. Custer told them that we were within a day's ride of the Indian village and that the intelligence was that there were about three thousand Indians there with somewhere between eight hundred and fifteen hundred braves. He was confident that this mission would be over in a couple of days and that we would be back at Fort Abraham Lincoln to enjoy the centenary celebrations.

### Friday June 23rd, 1876

As directed by the general, there was no bugle call in the morning to wake us. The night guards woke the company commanders at three in the morning and they in turn woke their troops. To keep the smoke down, small fires were lit by each company for breakfast. The fires were dug into hollows in the ground, and we were all strictly warned about the amount of smoke to create. The fire was enough for us to make coffee and fry some bacon but that was it. As quickly as possible the fires were extinguished.

At five we broke camp and started our march further along the Rosebud. As always, the general led the way, marching under two flags: one his personal flag, the other the red and white flag of the Seventh Cavalry. It was another really hot day and we rode under trees as much as we could to keep our horses shaded a little. As we marched along, we came across increased evidence of Indians having been here recently. Bones from dead animals, abandoned camps and their trails. The further we went, the larger their trails became. It was as if more and more Indians had been joining them, swelling the size of their herd. Despite the heat, we managed to cover thirty miles before we called camp at 4.30PM. The pack train took another three hours to finally catch up and make it to the camp site.

### Saturday June 24th, 1876

As we had been the previous morning, we were awoken by Captain Keogh at three. Today was our turn to provide the rear guard so we had a few extra minutes over our breakfast. At 5AM the column took off but, by the time the pack mules had left the camp it was 5.30 and then we followed on behind them.

From the back of the column it was hard to see what was going on up front. Every now and then the column would halt and we would catch up, but we were so far back at times we couldn't even see the main column.

About an hour after we set off, we reached a really big Indian camp. The rest of the regiment had been there for close to an hour by the time we reached it. Word reached us that the scalp of a soldier had been found tied to a stick. They couldn't tell for sure but they thought it might belong to Private Stocker, one of Colonel Gibbon's men who had been killed a few days earlier. It was quite confronting to see it. I knew it was their custom to take the scalp of their enemy, but I hadn't seen one and I couldn't fathom why it was necessary to desecrate the body of someone who was already dead.

This camp was big and there were lots of lodges and implements left lying around the place. The lodges were arranged in a circular formation. At the centre was a lodge that looked like extra work had gone into its creation. One of the scouts said he thought it was a Sun Dance lodge. The Sun Dance is a spiritual festival where the Sioux seek the blessing of Wakan Tanka, the Great Spirit. The chief would emerge from a sweat lodge and dance all day until he fell into a trance and had a vision of what lay in store for the tribe. The scout said it meant that they knew we were coming and were preparing for war and that Sitting Bull, the Lakota Sioux chief had probably been the one to lead the Sun Dance.

As we waited in the camp, the general's personal flag had been planted in the ground in the middle of the camp. For no apparent reason, the flag fell over. Lieutenant Godfrey from K company rushed forward and replanted it firmly in the ground only for it to fall over again a few minutes later. The Indian scouts said that that was a bad omen for General Custer. We didn't think too much about it and passed it off as Indian superstition.

We continued for a few more hours before we called a halt at about 1PM. We broke for some coffee, some food, and a rest while the scouts continued further along the trail to see if they could find which direction the Indian trail went. They were gone for three hours and we enjoyed a rest. When they returned, we were ordered to saddle up again and prepare to move on.

We continued the trail for another couple of hours. There was a lot of dust, so we had to spread out a little to not kick up too much. If we went at our normal pace and in strict column, the dust would have been easily visible to any nearby Indians. As we went, we continued to see indications of Indians, their trail was getting larger and at one point we could see that it was almost a mile wide because the vegetation was all torn up by their pony herd.

We covered twenty-eight miles before we pulled into camp at 7PM. We, being at the very back of the line didn't arrive until nearly 9PM. Captain Keogh went immediately to the general's tent to catch up on events. He came back shortly after to tell us not to get too comfortable because we were probably going to do a night march. He told us that the scouts had told the general that there was a lookout point called Crow's Nest further along the trail where it was possible to see into the valley of the Little Bighorn. They would be going ahead this evening to see what they could see from there.

At a little after 9PM, the scouts rode out of the camp. Captain

Keogh told us that six Arikara scouts; Crooked Horn, Black Fox, Strikes the Lodge, Red Star, Bull, and Foolish Red Bear, along with four Crow Scouts; Big Belly, Comes Leading, Curly Head and Strikes Enemy were going. The Crow Indians knew this territory best because we were now in Crow country so they would be the best guides for the Arikara. They brought along an interpreter and were led by Lieutenant Varnum and Charlie Reynolds. If they were not back by 11PM, we would begin marching towards them.

Barely an hour after we had arrived in the camp, we were told to assemble and be ready for an 11PM march. The other companies had all had a good rest because they arrived in camp earlier than us. We barely had a chance to water our horses. Nonetheless, the column marched at 11PM and we were again on the rear guard. A little after we started, we came to a mud creek which we had difficulty getting the mule train across. We spent a good hour and a half navigating across while the rest of the regiment waited on the far bank. It was a really dark night and it was really hard to even see the horse in front of you. The only way we could navigate was by listening for the jangle of the horse bridles, or the murmur of the men talking quietly. We continued to march until 1.30AM when we found a spot to camp. We were ordered to lie down and if possible, sleep. We didn't have to be told twice. By this point we were all exhausted. We had been forty days out from Fort Abraham Lincoln. In those forty days, I company had only had five where we weren't on the march. We had marched the last sixteen days straight and were covering an average of sixteen miles a day. We took our chance to rest. We tied up our horses and found whatever space we could to throw down our saddles. As we lay down, leaning back against our saddles, some of the men, mostly those who had experienced a battle before, found sleep. My mind was racing. What lay ahead of me? How would I react to battle? Could I kill a man? Were we right to chase the Indians from their land? I wasn't afraid of what was in store, it was more nervous anticipation.

## Morning. Sunday, June 25th, 1876

We rested for six hours before we were woken for another day. As usual we made coffee and stretched our weary limbs after a tough night sleeping rough. We packed up our things and were tending our horses when there was some commotion on the edge of the camp. Always curious, I walked towards it to see what was happening.

One of the Arikara scouts, Red Star, rode up. As he approached the sentries on the picket at the edge of the camp, he zig-zagged his horse which was a sign that he was a friendly and they had found the enemy. He shouted the call that the sentries were expecting to hear and so they let him gallop passed. He then galloped passed another Arikara scout named Stabbed, who shouted to him *"My son, this is no small thing you have done"*. He was proud that it was an Arikara scout and not a Crow who was carrying this important message to General Custer.

Red Star pulled up by the officers' tent, jumped off his pony and tied it up. Bloody Knife went to meet him. They spoke for a minute. There was excitement in their voices so we knew it was a message to say they had found the Indian village. We watched on with interest as General Custer and his interpreter, Fred Gerard, walked over to join them. Custer kneeled on one knee and spoke to the scout. As they were talking a small crowd gathered around them including the General's brother, Tom Custer. I strolled towards them to see if I could pick anything up. As I did so, I heard the general say *"We are going back to where his party are on the hill"*. Then, General Custer, Red Star along with Tom Custer, Bloody Knife and two other scouts Bob-tailed Bull and Little Brave, jumped on their horses and bolted out of the camp in the same direction that Red Star had come from. Custer was going to see for himself.

A murmur spread across the camp within seconds. This was it. We'd found them. Men started to get themselves ready. We just had to wait now for Custer to return and issue our orders. A few minutes after the Custer and the scouts rode out of the camp, another Arikara scout rode in. It was Bull, and he had been with Red Star on the way to pass the message that the village had been found, but he had fallen behind and was only now arriving in the camp. Of course, he was quickly interrogated by the other scouts as to what it was they had found, how many of them were there and what was happening.

I immediately went and told the other troops what I'd seen and heard. There was a little bit of a buzz around the camp over the next hour as we waited for the general to return. In the meantime, we packed up our stuff and prepared the horses. I went to Sarsfield, gave him a good brush down, watered him and gave him a feed of oats. After I had saddled him up, I paused for a minute to gather my thoughts. It was a Sunday so, with my left hand holding the horn of the saddle and with my forehead bowed forward touching the leather of the seat, I took my mother's crucifix in my right hand and said a prayer. I prayed that the Lord would protect me and Sarsfield in this our first battle. I left it at that.

Soon after, General Custer returned and rode around to each of the company commanders and told them to have the men ready to march as soon as possible. He then assembled the scouts and rode back out to Crow's Nest where they were able to see the Indian village. Not long after the general rode out, we set out to follow him. Riding at a pace, we travelled for about two hours before we found a ravine that was thought to be a good place to hide ahead of a surprise attack on the village. Custer's plan was to hide out here overnight and then launch a surprise attack from here at first light.

While on this march, some of the pack mules dropped some packages from their loads which were left behind on the trail. After we had halted, Sergeant Curtis of F company reported to Captain Keogh that some things had been dropped. The sergeant was ordered to take four men and to go back to pick up the lost items and return as quickly as possible.

At a little after 9AM, while we were waiting in the ravine, Sergeant Curtis returned and said that they had found the missing items, but that Indians had found them and had been rummaging through them. The troops had successfully chased them off and recovered everything, but the Indians had gotten away and might report our whereabouts. This was a problem. If we were discovered, our plan would be sprung.

Shortly afterward, General Custer returned again from the look-out point. When he was told that it was likely that we had been discovered, he had a decision to make. He called his officers together. We watched on as they discussed the situation. When Captain Keogh returned to us a few minutes later, he told us that we had no choice but to attack the village now. The plan had been to hide out, rest the horses and attack the next day. If the Indians knew we were there, they would split up and the general was concerned we would spend months chasing down small bands of them. If we attacked now, we could get this sorted out for once and for all. The captain told us that we were about fifteen miles from the village, and we still couldn't be sure how many warriors we would meet but we expected a thousand or so which we could easily manage.

Captain Keogh then returned to where the officers were gathered to get specific orders for our troop. There, it was agreed that Captain Benteen would take companies D, H and K and scout off to the left-hand side of the valley where the village was located. General Custer had seen some trees and scrub out in that direction and didn't want to be surprised by any Indians coming from there and attacking our rear. Captain Benteen was to go down there, attack anything he found and if there was nothing, to return and rejoin him in the attack. Once we were down in the valley, Major Reno was to take companies A, G and M and ride down the left bank of the Little Bighorn. That was the side of the river that the village was on. They would full frontal attack the village and drive the Indians back. At the same time, the scouts were to try and round up or drive off as many of the Indian's ponies as they could to prevent them escaping. Meanwhile, General Custer would take companies C, E, F, L and our I company, ride down the right bank of the Little Bighorn, they would go beyond the village before crossing over and coming back at it from the opposite side to Major Reno. We would catch them in a pincer movement and they would have no chance to escape. Captain McDougall and B company would ride with the pack train. They would follow us on.

To help protect the pack train, each of the twelve companies were ordered to assign one officer and some troops to stay with them. Captain Keogh picked Sergeant Delacy to be the officer from I company and told him to pick some troops to go with him. My heart sank when I heard this. I was the youngest in the company and I had never been in a battle before, I was sure that he would pick me. I backed Sarsfield up a little and tried to stay out of Delacy's eyeline. He started to call out names; Charles Ramsey, then my friend David Cooney from Cork, Gustave Korn. Eugene Owens and James McNally were called together. They were friends from back home in Kildare. Franz Braun. There was a pause between each name being called as Delacy scanned the faces to decide who to choose. Henry Jones. I quietly waited with my head down, hoping that no more would be called out. Francis Kennedy. As each name was called out, the selected man would groan their disappointment. We had all been out here a long time and this was going to be the climax of the whole trip. No one wanted to miss out. John McShane. Then he stopped. I kept my head down as he ordered those men to move out. I needed a few more seconds to pass before I was certain but I was elated. I was in. My first Indian skirmish. While I was nervous about what lay ahead, it would have been awful to miss the action after all the effort to get here.

Where we were located was on the edge of Wolf Mountain overlooking the Little Bighorn Valley. After a few more minutes of preparation, we set off. I was looking forward to seeing the village once we reached the look out point from where it had been spotted.

It took us about an hour to get there. As we came to the edge of the mountain and the valley came into view below us, I could see nothing that would indicate an Indian village. We didn't have the looking glass that Custer had or the time to stop and look properly but we each scanned the valley below and none of us could see it. The village was still fifteen miles off so it wasn't surprising that we couldn't see it.

We continued on down the small creek that led from this high point, down into the valley below. The descent into the valley wasn't steep. It was a gradual slope that eased down into the valley over a couple of miles. The further down the slope we went, the landscape became clearer with pine trees scattered across the ground. As soon as we reached a little bit of a clearing, Captain Benteen and his troops split off to the left to scout the left flank as ordered. The rest of us continued.

We were traveling at a fast walk and as the creek widened, we followed General Custer on the right-hand side of the creek while Major Reno and his troops travelled on the left. It didn't take long for the pack train to fall behind and out of sight. As we continued, and as usual, the scouts would ride out in front, riding back and forth to keep General Custer aware of what they were seeing out ahead. There were plenty of spots along the route where we would descend into a gully and then come up over a hill so it was important that the scouts kept an eye. We could easily encounter a party of Indians who were hidden from view.

After about two miles, the General ordered a halt at a point where there was good water for us to give the horses a drink. It was now early afternoon, and the heat was really rising. While we were stopped, I took off the woollen tunic that we all wore as part of our uniform. Most of the men stripped back their clothing and abandoned any excess weight in preparation for a battle. While we were stopped, one of the scouts rode back to the general and told him that there was a party of about fifty Indians riding not too far ahead of us. They were headed in the direction of the Indian village. Were they the ones who had found the dropped supplies? Were they going to report our presence to the village? The general rode up onto a small hill and looked ahead towards where the village was. It was still way off in the distance.

We rode on and soon came across an abandoned Indian camp. There were two lodges in it. One was partially knocked down. There were ashes in the fires that were still smoking in the centre of the camp. It looked like the fifty Indians the scout had just seen had left this camp. As we waited for orders to continue again, one of the men shouted that there was a dead Indian in the lodge. Sure enough, when it was torn down, there was a scaffold inside with dead Sans Arc warrior on it. The general ordered that the two lodges be torched. Within seconds the bone-dry grass was alight, and the remains of the Indian burial scaffold was in flames.

Again, we continued. Major Reno was leading his command of about one hundred and seventy men further along the creek. After about another three miles or so, the creek we were following joined the Little Bighorn River. The Bighorn River was about thirty feet wide but not too deep, so Major Reno's men crossed over. Once across, they paused, and we could see that his troops had dismounted for a minute to adjust their bridles and to take a quick rest. They were preparing for a charge on the village which was still about five miles north. Meanwhile, we followed behind and then turned north before we reached the Little Bighorn.

We were now poised. Major Reno and his men would charge the village along the flat open ground that was on the far, western bank of the river. We would ride along the eastern side, over the hilly ground, with the intent of flanking the Indians and coming at them from the far side. Captain Benteen would complete his scout to the west and then join the battle and the pack train would follow along with ammunition and reserves should we need them. This was it.

Tatanka Iyotake (Sitting Bull)
Hunkpapa Lakota Chief

1831-1890

# XIV

❧

# The Little Bighorn

**Afternoon. Sunday, June 25ᵗʰ, 1876**

After forty days in the saddle, we were finally going to see some action. I had been in the army for close to five years and this would be my first battle. I had never even shot my gun in anger. I looked around the other members of I company. Half of them had joined after I had enlisted, and we had all been on the same expeditions so half of us were going into this as our first Indian fight. The thirty or so others, who predated my enlistment, were a mixed bag. I would wager that no more than twelve of these men had seen a battle against Indians. We were novices. Despite his vast experience, even Captain Keogh had never been in a battle against Indians.

I looked at Captain Keogh. He was quiet and sullen most of the time but he looked confident and so I decided that I should be too, even though I wasn't. Ed turned to me and told me he was nervous. I didn't like to say it, but my stomach was playing up. It felt like there was an animal in there running around. I was nervous too.

Looking around the other troops, you could see we were all in the same position. Everyone was nervously shifting in their saddles.

Hunkpapa Sioux War Chief Rain In The Face who fought at the Little Bighorn

With a gesture of his hat towards Major Reno across the river, General Custer called *"Move Out"* and we started up the right-hand bank of the river. Slowly at first but then we started to trot. The side of the river that Reno was on was flat but on our side, as you got closer to where the village was it was very hilly. The river ran along the bottom of some very steep bluffs and in between the bluffs there was a series of gullies and ravines.

After about half a mile, General Custer called a halt. Once we had all stopped, he rode up onto a hill where he could get a better view of the surroundings. While we were stopped, we could see and hear Major Reno's men on our left flank, starting to accelerate towards the Indian village but they weren't charging it yet. We couldn't really see the village at this stage as it was behind a ridge and some brush. Custer returned after a couple of minutes and we continued our fast trot north.

What we didn't know at this stage was that the Indian village was the largest ever assembly of Indians on the plains. In the village were Indians from several different tribes. The Hunkpapa Sioux, Santee, Yankton, Brule, Miniconjou, Oglala, and the Cheyenne were all there. We still didn't know how many warriors were in the village, but estimates are more than two thousand and they were being led by Sitting Bull, Chief of the Lakota Sioux, Two Moons, Chief of the

Cheyenne, Crazy Horse, war leader of the Oglala Sioux and Gall of the Hunkpapa.

As we were progressing along, the excitement in the troop grew and the horses picked up on the excitement. Sarsfield was trotting along with his ears pricked and pointed forward. Captain Keogh was riding to our left and was yelling encouragement and guidance as we went. *"Hold your reins tight boys. Don't let your horse get over excited"*, *"Keep your mind clear boys"*, he was saying. For someone young like myself, riding into my first battle, Captain Keogh was exactly the kind of leader that I needed. He knew that half of us were novices and was gently guiding us along, giving us confidence and keeping us calm.

Hunkpapa Sioux War Leader Gall who fought at the Little Bighorn

Up ahead, General Custer was also giving instructions. *"Boys, hold your horses. There are plenty of them down there for us all"*, he roared. He was excited about the battle but he had been through lots of them. For him it was just another day of excitement on the plains.

As we got closer to the village, we rode up a really steep bluff. The incline was a good fifty feet or more. We paused again as we rode over the peak of a hill. General Custer surveyed the surrounds again. As we waited, we watched events unfolding across the river. We could see our Arikara scouts had ridden out wide around the back of the Indian's pony herd and they were trying to round them up. Indians from the village had seen them and were rushing out to fight them off. We watched Major Reno's men too as they charged the village. At first, they were riding at full charge. From our vantage point, high above them looking down from the bluff across the river, it looked like M and A companies were leading the charge with G company being held back slightly. The cavalry in full charge is an amazing sight. In a charge the horses get up to sixteen miles an hour. They are whipped up into a frenzy by excited troops roaring threats and encouraging their mounts. Then suddenly, as we watched from across the river, the leading companies of the charge pulled up and dismounted to form a skirmish line. We wondered if that was the plan, but we could see a dry riverbed just ahead of them and so presumed there was something there that was just too much of a leap for the horses. We still couldn't see the village but we could see the Indians riding out to meet the advancing troops head on. Then, we could see G company move up in line with the other two of Major Reno's companies, extending their skirmish line. All the while, more and more Indians were coming out of their lodges, mounting horses, and riding out to meet the challenge. A serious battle was raging over there. The noise of the guns reverberated around the valley. A swirl of dust was kicked up by the Indians who were growing in number. It looked like they were purposely kicking up the dirt to obscure the village so their women and children could get away. *"Come on boys"*, we all muttered to ourselves as we watched on. We all knew fellows in those companies. I was worried about two of my Limerick friends Andrew Connor of A company and Ed Davern of F company who was an orderly to Major Reno. Somewhere in that battle, they were both involved.

General Custer, having looked around and seen what was happening across the river, called forward Sergeant Kanipe, gave him a note, and sent him back where we had come from. It was a note for Captain Benteen, and it read *"Benteen, Come on. Big Village, be quick, bring packs. P.S. Bring pacs".* We needed Benteen's men and we needed any spare ammunition we could get our hands on. This was going to be a big fight.

Custer then motioned for us to continue forward along the high ridge traveling north. After another half a mile or so, we reached another high point with good visibility, so he stopped the column again. *"Courage boys, we've got them. We'll finish them up and then go home to our station",* he roared out to us. We all responded with a big cheer. I wondered though if this was going to plan or not. The battle across the river didn't seem to be going well. The skirmish line had started to splinter, and we could see some of the men retreating into the

Cheyenne Chief Two Moons who fought at the Little Bighorn

trees along the side of the river. On top of that, from this high vantage point we could now get a proper look at the Indian village. It was absolutely massive. It must have been two miles long with maybe a thousand lodges. This was much bigger than we were led to believe. The eight hundred and fifty to a thousand warriors estimate was very wrong. There were Indians pouring out of the village and swarming around Major Reno. With every second that passed, more and more Indian warriors were coming out of the lodges and joining the fight. The noise was getting louder and louder. It was mayhem over there.

Custer looked on. It looked like Major Reno was in trouble. We needed a plan. He saw the Indian women and children streaming

226 ~ DES RYAN

from the northern end of the village. These noncombatants were escaping to safety. If we could round some of those up, we could force the warriors to surrender. Increasingly, we could see Reno's men were retreating from the skirmish line into the line of trees along the river and some were even starting to cross the river as the number of Indians continued to swell. We could see they were suffering casualties. The gatling guns or even one of them would have been very useful to the men down in the valley but, of course, we didn't bring them.

Custer looked back to see where Captain Benteen might be. He could see a dust cloud about four miles back. That must be Captain Benteen, he thought. It would take about forty-five minutes for them to reach the point where we were now. Too slow. We needed to do something now to support Reno's men.

Custer called Captain Yates and Captain Keogh forward for a quick conference. After a couple of minutes, Captain Keogh rode back to tell us what the plan was. We needed to stall for Captain Benteen to arrive and we needed to draw some of the Indians away from Major Reno. Captain Yates would take two companies (E and F) and ride down the hill to the edge of the river. They would try and draw attention to themselves and hopefully bring some relief for Reno's men. Meanwhile, General Custer and Captain Keogh would keep companies C, L and I and stay up on the ridge so that Captain Benteen knew where to go. When the time was right, we would fire some shots in the air to signal to Yates to retreat back up the hill to us. Once that was done, we would continue and round up some of the non-combatants.

So far, we had had an easy enough ride. None of us had had to fire our weapons. We were away from the main action, which was with Major Reno, but we knew that over all we were on the back foot and that anything could happen. Captain Yates gave the order and companies E and F moved out down the hill towards the river and towards the battle. I caught sight of John McKenna with E company as they marched off. I gave him a salute and shouted, "*Go get them John*". He smiled nervously back at me and rode on.

Cheyenne warrior Wooden Leg who fought at the Little Bighorn.

Captain Yates and his men were only gone for a minute or two before we came under fire up on the hill. Suddenly, we were in the action ourselves. It was the first time I had been shot at and my instinct was to duck, but I was on a horse, so it was impossible to drop out of sight. It took me a couple of seconds to find my bearings and to understand what was happening. Coming from the north, a band of about fifty Cheyenne Indians had spotted us and were firing at us. With three cavalry companies, we outnumbered them very significantly. General Custer ordered us to dismount from our horses and to fire back at them. I jumped off Sarsfield and left his reigns to Postie (George Post) to hold. I drew my carbine rifle from the saddle and walked forward to the skirmish line. I kneeled with my right knee up, rested my right elbow on my knee, rose my rifle to my cheek and started looking for a target. The Indians were a few hundred yards away. They were within shooting distance, but it would be a hard shot. I took aim at one individual. Took a deep breath and without thinking too deeply about it, I pulled my trigger. My shot missed. All along the line, troops were taking their first shot at a human being. I cracked open my carbine, the spent cartridge ejected as it was supposed to do, and I popped another one in the chamber. Again, I put the gun to my shoulder and took aim. I could hear Captain Keogh behind me

saying "*Keep calm boys. Aim low*". I found another target. A wild looking fellow with hair spiked up and with white streaks of war paint
on his cheeks. I took a breath, held steady, aimed low and pulled the
trigger again. The Indian I was targeting fell. He was hit! I had no
idea if it was my shot or someone else, but he took a bullet in the
shoulder, and it knocked him back on his back. I couldn't believe it.
I had shot someone. I started to wonder if he was dead. Excited by
my success, again I popped open the rifle and the spent cartridge
ejected. Again, I loaded a bullet in the chamber and looked to take
aim. This time I couldn't see any targets. They were gone. These were
typical Indian tactics. Get close, attack, fade away. After a moment
Captain Keogh, realising that they were gone, called "*Cease fire*" and
we all stopped.

My heart was racing. In my excitement, I turned to Private
Darwin Symms beside me in the line.

"*I got one. I got one!*", I blurted out.
"*Good man. I only got one shot off. My damn gun jammed. Don't think I
hit anything*", he replied.


We remounted our horses but my mind was in a blur. I couldn't
believe I had not only fired my rifle at a human being but that I
might have actually killed one. While I was distracted, battle hard-
ened Captain Keogh and General Custer were immediately looking
for progress from Captain Benteen and watching Captain Yates
down by the river. There didn't seem to be any movement closer
from Captain Benteen. Captain Yates and the men of E and F companies had pulled up short of the river and were skirmishing with
some Indians down there. After fifteen minutes during which we
were under sustained attack from small groups of Indians, General
Custer decided to recall Yates and shot four rounds into the air.
Within seconds, Captain Yates and his men remounted and started

to retreat up the hill towards us and we let off some shots as covering fire to pin the Indians back while they pulled back.

Following Custer, we moved further north along the ridge, then
down a gully and back up onto another ridge further north. After
a couple of minutes, Captain Yates' men rejoined us on the ridge.
They had lost a handful of men and were being pursued by Indians.
From where we were, up on the ridge, they seemed to be coming
at us from all angles now. There were bullets flying passed us and
every few seconds an arrow would arc through the sky and land
amongst us. It was getting scary. We were ordered to fire at will so
any time we saw an Indian get too close, we let off a shot at them.
Some of our men started to get hit at this point and one or two
of them fell dead from their horses. It was getting tense and, in the
heat, and noise it was hard to think. While we continued to take
shots, General Custer called his officers together to decide what to
do next. We needed to do something quick, or we would be overrun.
After a moment, Captain Keogh returned to us with our orders. We
were to stay put. We were going to provide a rear guard for the
General who was going to push north to see if they could capture
non-combatants. Custer wanted us to stay on this high ground and
visible so that Captain Benteen knew where to go. I didn't like this
plan much. We were already under pressure and surrounded. Would
we be able to hold them off?

Custer and Captain Yates, rounded up their men and moved further north and then west, down the hill towards the river. As they
rode away, I looked at General Custer for the last time. I could tell
he loved the thrill of battle but he was also showing signs of stress.
We had bitten off more than we could chew. He rode off north,
with his long blonde curls flowing in the wind from under his hat.
He was riding his horse, Victory; the same one he rode when we left
Fort Abraham Lincoln. He had the reins in his left hand and in his
right, he was pointing the way forward with his revolver. He kicked

his heels into Victory and they rode off. That was my last sight of him. No sooner had they gone a hundred yards, than a band of Indians had climbed the hill and were following them down the bluff towards the river crossing at the north end of the Indian village.

As Custer rode away, Captain Keogh looked around and made his plan for the remaining troops under his command. We had three companies left with us. We had Indians coming at us from all directions. He needed to create a skirmish line, so the captain ordered Lieutenant Calhoun's L company to split into two groups, one led by Lieutenant Calhoun, the other by Lieutenant Crittenden. He ordered them to form two lines and to open fire on anything that was approaching. Lieutenant Cal-

Sioux warrior Short Bull who fought at the Little Bighorn

houn and Crittenden each stood behind their line of troops, passing orders and shooting at any Indian that came within view. The captain then ordered C company to line up behind Lieutenant Calhoun and Lieutenant Crittenden. C company were the least experienced of the troops in the regiment and were also without their commander, Tom Custer, who was gone with his brother, the general. Captain Keogh must not have wanted to expose them to direct attack until it was absolutely necessary. Our I company was held back a little further up the hill. Within moments of Lieutenant Calhoun and Crittenden forming their lines, they were under severe attack from their left flank, so Captain Keogh had no choice but to deploy C company on the left of Lieutenant Calhoun. He ordered that the three most senior officers of C company, Sergeant Bobo, Sergeant Finley, and Sergeant Finckle take positions at the extreme end where he knew the Indians would try to penetrate around the line. This worked for a few minutes, but the Indians reorganised and came back at them even more strongly. Quickly, the inexperienced C troops started to fall dead before about half of them were forced to retreat north, back in behind Lieutenant Calhoun's line which was also now under heavy attack. It was at this point that I knew we were in deep trouble. Up to this point, I had confidence that General Custer and Captain Keogh would be able to pull something out of the fire to turn the tide. It was only now that I started to feel fear. I had nervous anticipation before but was always confident that we had superiority over these savages. As things started to unravel around us that changed. I could feel my heart starting to pound in my chest and I was increasingly finding it difficult to take in the enormity of what was happening around me. As I tried to reload by rifle, my trembling hand was taking a split second longer to find the chamber. Looking around I could see I wasn't alone. I could see fear creeping into the faces of those around me and I could hear anxiety in their voices as they shouted at each other.

From my position, a little further up the hill from the disintegrating skirmish line, I was doing my best to keep shooting. We had formed a secondary skirmish line behind L and C troops. The barrel of my gun was getting so hot, I could barely hold it and the spent cartridges started to get stuck in the chamber. I had to use my bayonet to dig them out after every shot. It was chaos and it was really hard to focus. In the distance, I noticed an Indian warrior riding at pace up from the river. He was clearly one of the leaders because he was being followed by a band of about fifty other warriors. He was a formidable sight. Riding so freely on his horse, it looked like he didn't even need to hold on. Wearing just a breechcloth, he was naked except for his distinctive warpaint. He wore a red neckerchief around his forehead keeping his long hair tight to his head. He had two feathers spiking up from the back of his head, kept in place by the neckerchief. His face was painted with a red lightning bolt and his horse had very distinctive dots painted all over its torso. It was Crazy Horse. I took aim at him. He was traveling fast but because of his incredible horsemanship he was still managing to get shots off from his rifle. I followed him, looking down the barrel of my rifle. Trying to stay calm and to breath normally, I wanted this shot so badly. Then, when I thought I had him, I let fly. I took the gun down from my cheek and watched, waiting to see him fall. For a moment, time stood still as I waited to see if I had hit him but he kept on riding. I had missed. I don't think I even came close to hitting the target.

With the line under so much pressure, the next order from Captain Keogh was that there was a need for more rifles in the line so, he ordered that the men holding the horses, every fourth man, should now join the line too. Each man would have to hold the reins of their own horse while also shooting at the Indians or make the decision to let their horse go free. It all disintegrated quickly. The horses started to get spooked. Some of them bolted and ran off to safety. One of the troops got his ankle caught in the reins of his bolting horse and was dragged off when his horse ran. The horse ran straight into a group of Indians, and we never saw that troop again.

It was all falling apart. What was left of L and C companies were retreating up to where we were. We were shooting at will at anything that moved. Completely surrounded, there wasn't enough of us to defend our position. I looked to my left and saw one trooper who had clearly decided that he didn't want to fall into the hands of the Indians. In the middle of the chaos, he stood up in the disintegrating skirmish line, took off his hat, put his revolver to his right temple and blew his own brains out. I watched on as he, almost in slow motion, slumped to the ground. There was so much mayhem at that point that no one flinched. We were each fighting our own battle within this battle.

Our only remaining hope was to try and get to where General Custer and his troops were. All of us together might stand a chance. I looked north and down towards the river to where General Custer was about a mile away. He hadn't been able to cross the river and was now retreating up onto a hill further north of us. He had already lost some of his eighty or so men. They were in trouble too.

Just then, a bullet hit Captain Keogh. He was on his horse Comanche, riding behind our line giving orders. He was just a few feet from where I was in the line. I looked around briefly and saw that the bullet had hit him in the knee, and he had fallen from his horse. Ed's old adversary, Sergeant Varden, was close by and ran to the captain's aid. I didn't have a chance to see how serious an injury it was. I had to keep shooting. I was starting to run low of bullets. We only had one hundred rounds for our rifle each. I was half way through mine. I started to think about what Private Rivers had told me once. He was an older soldier who had been in a good few battles with the Indians. He told me never to allow myself to be captured by the Indians. *"They would torture you in ways you couldn't imagine"*, he told me. *"It is better to keep your last bullet for yourself and kill yourself before they take you"*. That must have been what was going through the mind of the trooper who had shot himself a few minutes earlier.

I looked again at where General Custer was. He and his troops had taken refuge on a hill about a mile north of us. They had hundreds of Indians circling around them. From our distance, it looked like they had shot their horses and were using them as a defensive shield.

I kept firing. Private John Barry to my left was swearing and praying at the same time. Canadian Darwin Symms on my right was shouting for more bullets. My friend Ed was just beyond him.

I couldn't see or hear him and beyond Ed was Postie as we called him. We were all fighting for our lives now and it was starting to dawn on us that we were unlikely to get out of this alive. Poor John, Darwin and Postie had only been in the army for six months. Even though myself and Ed had been in the army for a few years by now, this was still our first battle. Such chaos.

Yanktonai Sioux warrior Iron Bear who fought at the Little Bighorn

The excitement amongst the Indians was rising. They were yelping with glee. They knew victory was theirs and they were starting to enjoy it. Some would ride around us, taking shots, almost willing us to shoot them. Meanwhile, others on foot would creep closer and closer. At one point two Indians on horseback, one of them being Crazy Horse who I had shot at and missed, rode straight at us, ignoring the bullets flying passed them. Having come within a few feet, they turned and rode away again. It was almost as if they were toying with us.

Again, and again, I let off shots, but they were getting closer. Some were as close as just a few yards now. Getting braver. Then a wave of them came charging at us. There must have been fifty, galloping towards us, screaming. As they got within a few feet, some of them leapt from their horses, jumping onto troops and attacking them with whatever weapon they were carrying. One of the ponies came straight at me and I had to dive out of the way as its rider, stooped down and took a swing at me. I managed to avoid the swipe but we were all awry. Our place on the high ground was gone as we stumbled and fell from the charge.

As I got back to my feet, I found a small group of troops who had rallied around Captain Keogh who was lying prone having been shot from his horse. I kneeled in with them and continued to shoot. At this stage I didn't know which way to look because they were everywhere. Then out of the corner of my eye, I saw something moving in the gun smoke. Before I could register if it were friend or foe, an almighty upward wallop cracked my right wrist. It was a wooden club and an Indian had hit me. I caught a glimpse of the club. It was about two feet long and had a big, rounded end on it. The handle was ornate and had a rabbit fur and leather wrapping. Boy did it give me a belt. The upward trajectory of the club took my wrist and rifle with it. My loaded gun flew out of my hands, spun, and landed on the grass to my left. My wrist followed the gun up, almost taking my shoulder out of its socket and the power of it lifted me backwards until I landed on my back. A little dazed and in a lot of pain from the wrist, it took me a second to catch my breath. Then with a pounce, he was on me. His left foot first pinning my right arm then his right knee pinning my shoulder as he squatted on my chest. This is it.

# XV

## Epilogue

All of Companies C, L and I, who had been left under Captain Myles Keogh's command at the Little Bighorn, were wiped out in the middle of the afternoon of 25<sup>th</sup> June 1876. There were no survivors other than Captain Keogh's horse, Comanche. The hill on which they fought is now known as Calhoun Hill. Just north of Calhoun Hill is the grave marker for Captain Keogh which is surrounded by a cluster of unnamed grave markers.

General Custer and Captain Yates, along with the men of E and F Companies, tried to cross the river north of the Indian village but could not get through. They retreated onto a hill which is now known as Last Stand Hill. There, they were all killed in what is referred to as Custer's Last Stand. In the dying moments of that part of the battle, a handful of men fled from Last Stand Hill in desperation but were all cut down by the Indians who pursued them. There were no survivors.

Major Reno and his command (Companies A, G and M) retreated from their charge on the Indian village. They fought a battle while they retreated through the trees and across the Little Bighorn River, losing at least thirty men and leaving others unaccounted for. Those who escaped took refuge on a hill on the east side of the river, now known as Reno Hill. There, they managed to hold off the Indian attacks that continued on into the evening of June 25th and through the following day. Captain Benteen and his men (Companies D, H and K) joined Major Reno and re-enforced that position when they caught up with the battle after completing their scouting mission. Captain McDougall and the pack train, which was following the rest of the column but at a much slower pace, eventually made it to where Reno and Benteen had fortified a position and they all remained there. From Reno Hill, the troops were unable to see what was happening a little over four miles from them on Calhoun Hill and Last Stand Hill.

In total, two hundred and sixty eight troops were killed at the Battle of the Little Bighorn. Another fifty five were injured. Of those, six died later of their wounds. Somewhere between thirty and three hundred Indian Warriors also died at the battle.

## The Aftermath

Major Reno, Captain Benteen and Captain McDougall held out overnight and through the day of 26th June until the Indians dispersed in the late afternoon. They remained entrenched overnight. On the morning of 27th June, a dust cloud was seen approaching from the distance. Unsure if it was the Indians returning or their own troops, they waited on Reno Hill as it approached. It was General Terry and his part of the column. It was only when Terry arrived, that an inspection of the battlefield took place and the disaster that had occurred became apparent.

On the morning of 28th June, the dead soldiers were buried on the battlefield where they had fallen. The injured troops were evacuated on the Far West and eventually made it back to Fort Abraham Lincoln.

OLD FORT MEADE OF 1886 IN BACKGROUND

"COMANCHE" 7th U.S. CAVALRY HORSE

Comanche - The sole survivor of the Battle of the Little Bighorn

## I Company

On 25th June 1876, there were sixty-eight members of I Company. Fourteen of them were not with Thomas Patrick Downing at the Little Bighorn. They were on detachment elsewhere and that undoubtedly saved their lives. Another six were on sick leave, also saving their lives. Private John Porter, a cooper from London, happened to be in confinement for a crime. Ironically, this crime saved his life.

The remaining forty-seven members of I Company were all at the Little Bighorn that day. Ten of them were split off to protect the pack train with Captain McDougall and that saved their lives. The remaining thirty-seven took part in the Battle of the Little Bighorn and all of them were killed.

According to official records, Thomas Patrick Downing was the youngest US soldier from I Company to die that day. He was twenty. The oldest member of I Company, fifty-one-year-old Private Henry Allen Bailey was also killed. He had been a blacksmith in Rhode Island before he enlisted four months before Downing did in October 1872.

The average age of the thirty-seven who died was twenty-nine. Twenty-two of them were born in the US, eight were born in Ireland, three were English, two Germans and one each from Switzerland and Canada.

Myles Keogh's original grave marker on the battlefield. Thomas Patrick Downing would have died within yards of this point.

From I Company, only Captain Myles Keogh's body was not mutilated by the Indians after the battle. Mutilation was their way of making sure that the bodies of the dead would be of no use to them in their afterlife. Captain Keogh's was also the only member of I Company to have his body recovered from the battlefield. The other thirty-six are still lying on the field.

## Sitting Bull

After the battle, the US Army increased their presence in the Dakota Territory and pursued the Indians. Many of them were forced to surrender and submit to life on the reservation. Sitting Bull refused to surrender and led his people north into Canada where they stayed for the next four years.

The colder winters in Canada and the sparce Buffalo herd eventually forced Sitting Bull and his followers to return to the United States. He finally surrendered at Fort Buford July 19th, 1881. As he surrendered he told the commanding officer at the fort, Major Brotherton, *"I wish it to be remembered that I was the last man of my tribe to surrender my rifle"*.

Sitting Bull and his family were transferred to Fort Yates near Standing Rock Reservation, then moved to Fort Randall before they were eventually allowed to settle at Standing Rock Reservation in 1883.

In December 1890, fearing that Sitting Bull was going to flee the reservation, an attempt was made to arrest him at his house. A dispute erupted during which Sitting Bull was shot and killed along with several of his supporters.

Sitting Bull was initially buried at Fort Yates but his body was later moved to a new gravesite overlooking the Missouri River on Standing Rock Reservation.

## Crazy Horse

After the Battle of the Little Bighorn, Crazy Horse and his followers stayed in the area and fought further battles against the increasing number of US troops sent to avenge the massacre. In May 1877, he decided to surrender and led his people to Fort Robinson in

Nebraska where they surrendered and were allowed settle at nearby Red Cloud Agency.

In September 1877, following an alleged threat to kill an officer, Crazy Horse was arrested and brought to Fort Robinson. Once there, a scuffle broke out and Crazy Horse was stabbed with a bayonet by one of the guards and was killed.

Despite his prominence as a Lakota War Leader, there is no verified photograph of Crazy Horse. His body was buried by his family but the gravesite is now known.

## Gall

After the Battle of the Little Bighorn, Gall went with Sitting Bull to Canada. With pressure mounting from the US Government for their return, a lack of food supply and tension with other Indian tribes, Gall split from Sitting Bull in November 1880.

With about three hundred other Indians they returned to the US in early 1881 and they camped at Poplar Agency in Montana. Following a short standoff with US soldiers, Gall and his band surrendered to Major Guido Ilges and was escorted to Fort Buford. He lived out his days as a farmer on Standing Rock Reservation and is buried there.

## The Battlefield

In 1877, General Custer's body was exhumed from the battlefield and moved to West Point Military Academy where he was re-interred. Also in 1877, Captain Myles Keogh's body was exhumed and moved to Fort Hill Cemetery in Auburn, New York.

In 1879 the battlefield was named a National Cemetery and a temporary monument was erected at the site. Two years later in 1881, the current marble obelisk was installed. While this was underway, the bodies of the soldiers were all exhumed and moved to Last Stand Hill where they were reburied under the obelisk.

Markers were placed where the original burial sites had been and in 1890, these markers were replaced by the current marble block gravestones.

In 1946, the site was re-designated as the Custer Battlefield National Monument but was further renamed in 1991 to the Little Bighorn Battlefield National Monument, reflecting the two cultures that collided at the site.

The memorial obelisk at the Little Bighorn. Thomas Patrick
Downing is shown on the bottom left.
*Copyright © Des Ryan*

## Other Troops Mentioned

**John Barry**

Born in Waterford, Ireland in 1849. He enlisted on September 21st, 1875, and was assigned to I Company of 7th Cavalry alongside Thomas Patrick Downing. Prior to enlisting he had worked as a labourer.

John Barry was killed in the battle on the afternoon of 25th June 1876. He is buried on the battlefield with his colleagues.

**Andrew Connor**

Born in Limerick, Ireland in 1842. He enlisted on November 8th, 1872, in Lowell, Massachusetts and was assigned to A Company of 7th Cavalry under Captain Myles Moylan. Prior to enlisting he had worked as a moulder.

Andrew Connor was with Major Reno during the battle. He took part in the charge on the village, the retreat across the river and defence on the hilltop.

Andrew Connor survived the battle and was discharged from the army at the end of his term on November 8th, 1877, at Fort Rice, Dakota Territory.

**David Cooney**

Born in County Cork, Ireland in 1848. He enlisted on December 16th, 1872, in Preston, Massachusetts and was assigned to I Company of 7th Cavalry alongside Thomas Patrick Downing. Prior to enlisting he had worked as a labourer.

All of Company I who were at the battle, were killed with Thomas Patrick Downing. However, David Cooney had been assigned as an escort for the supply train and so was not with his colleagues. The supply train arrived last in the afternoon and joined Major Reno and Captain Benteen on the hilltop, so Cooney was in that part of the battle. He was wounded in the right hip but survived.

He was transported back to Fort Abraham Lincoln on board the Far West and arrived there on July 5th however, his condition deteriorated, and he died of a blood stream infection on July 20th, 1876.

David Cooney was initially buried at Fort Abraham Lincoln but was reinterred at Custer National Cemetery at Crow Agency in Montana.

### Edward Davern

Born in Limerick, Ireland in 1844. He first enlisted on August 12th, 1867, and was discharged at the end of his five-year term on August 12th, 1872, at Louisville, Kentucky. He immediately re-enlisted and was assigned to Company F of 7th Cavalry under Captain George Yates.

All of Company F who were at the battle, were killed with Custer on Last Stand Hill. However, Edward Davern was assigned as an orderly to Major Reno during the battle. During the battle, his horse was shot out from under him during the retreat after Major Reno charged the village. He survived the battle, although wounded and completed his second term. He was discharged on August 12th, 1877, at Camp Buell in Minnesota.

Edward Davern went on to serve two further terms before he finally exited the army on August 30th, 1887, at Fort Meade, Dakota Territory. By that time, he had been promoted to corporal.

After he retired, he moved to Washinton D.C where he died on August 10th, 1896. He is buried at Arlington National Cemetery in Washington.

### Edward Driscoll

Born in Waterford, Ireland in 1850. He enlisted on May 19th, 1873, in Chicago, Illinois and was assigned to I Company of 7th Cavalry alongside Thomas Patrick Downing. Prior to enlisting he had worked as a labourer.

Edward Driscoll was killed in the battle on the afternoon of 25th June 1876. He is buried on the battlefield with his colleagues.

### Francis Kennedy aka Francis Johnson

Born in Pacific, Missouri in 1854. He enlisted on September 27th, 1875, and was assigned to I Company of 7th Cavalry alongside Thomas Patrick Downing. Prior to enlisting he had worked as a labourer.

All of Company I who were at the battle, were killed with Thomas Patrick Downing. However, because of his rattlesnake bite, Francis Kennedy had been assigned as an escort for the supply train and so was not with his colleagues. The supply train arrived last in the afternoon and joined Major Reno and Captain Benteen on the hilltop, so Kennedy was in that part of the battle but survived.

Francis Kennedy moved to St Paul after he was discharged and worked for the department of public works for ten years. He died following a short illness on January 9th, 1924, in St Paul, Minnesota.

### Archibald McIlhargey

Born in County Antrim, Ireland in 1845. He enlisted on November 19th, 1872, in Shelbyville, Kentucky and was assigned to I Company of 7th Cavalry alongside Thomas Patrick Downing. Prior to enlisting he had worked as a labourer.

All of Company I who were at the battle, were killed with Thomas Patrick Downing. However, Archibald McIlhargey had been assigned as a striker to Major Reno during the battle. After Major Reno's men charged the village and then retreated across the river, Major Reno sent Archibald McIlhargey to carry a message to Custer. Having done as ordered, McIlhargey stayed with Custer and was killed on Last Stand Hill.

McIlhargey was married and left his wife Josie and two children

Roselia and Archibald. They received his pension of $10 a month after his death.

## John McKenna

Born in Limerick, Ireland in 1843. He enlisted on December 19th, 1874, in Boston, Massachusetts and was assigned to E Company of 7th Cavalry under Lieutenant Algernon Smith.

All of Company E who were at the battle, were killed with Custer on Last Stand Hill. However, John McKenna had been assigned as an escort for the supply train and so was not with his colleagues. The supply train arrived last in the afternoon and joined Major Reno and Captain Benteen on the hilltop, so McKenna was in that part of the battle and survived.

He was discharged on December 18th, 1879, at Fort Abraham Lincoln at the end of his five-year term.

## George Post

Born in Adrian, Michigan in 1848. He enlisted on June 28th, 1875, and was assigned to I Company of 7th Cavalry alongside Thomas Patrick Downing. Prior to enlisting he had worked as a saddler.

George Post was killed in the battle on the afternoon of 25th June 1876. He is buried on the battlefield with his colleagues.

## William Ryan (O'Ryan)

Born in Limerick, Ireland in 1854. He enlisted on October 2nd, 1875, in New York City and was assigned to H Company of 7th Cavalry under Captain Benteen.

H Company scouted the left flank of the area before joining the battle late. They joined Major Reno and took part in the hilltop fight late in the day.

On February 1st, 1877, William Ryan deserted from the army and was never seen again.

## Darwin Symms

Born in Montreal, Quebec in 1852. He enlisted on August 25th, 1875, and was assigned to I Company of 7th Cavalry alongside Thomas Patrick Downing. Prior to enlisting he had worked as a clerk.

Darwin Symms was killed in the battle on the afternoon of 25th June 1876. He is buried on the battlefield with his colleagues.

## James McNally

Born in Kildare, Ireland in 1847. He enlisted on November 12th, 1872, in Troy, New York, and was assigned to I Company of 7th Cavalry alongside Thomas Patrick Downing. Prior to enlisting he had worked as a labourer.

All of Company I who were at the battle, were killed with Thomas Patrick Downing. However, James McNally had been assigned as an escort for the supply train and so was not with his colleagues. The supply train arrived last in the afternoon and joined Major Reno and Captain Benteen on the hilltop, so McNally was in that part of the battle.

James McNally was discharged from the army on November 12th, 1877, at the end of his five-year term. He died in St Paul, Minnesota in April 1893.

## Patrick Lynch

Born in Carrigaholt, Co Clare, Ireland in 1851. He enlisted on October 16th, 1872, in Toledo, Ohio, and was assigned to I Company of 7th Cavalry alongside Thomas Patrick Downing. Prior to enlisting he had worked as a labourer.

All of Company I who were at the battle, were killed with Thomas Patrick Downing. However, Patrick Lynch had been assigned as an orderly to General Terry at the time of the battle and so was not present.

Patrick Lynch was discharged from the army on July 14th, 1877, at the end of his five-year term. He later worked as a Saloonkeeper in Bismarck, Dakota Territory according to the 1880 Census.

## Patrick Kelly

Born in County Mayo, Ireland in 1831. He enlisted on September 13th, 1866, in New York City. At the end of his first five-year term, he re-enlisted at Bagdad, Kentucky on September 17th, 1871.

Kelly deserted on June 10th, 1873, but was captured, court martialled and sentenced to three years custody. That sentence was suspended, and he was redeployed to I Company of 7th Cavalry alongside Thomas Patrick Downing.

Patrick Kelly was killed in the battle on the afternoon of 25th June 1876. He is buried on the battlefield with his colleagues.

## John Mitchell

Born in County Galway, Ireland in 1842. He enlisted on September 14th, 1871, in Bagdad, Kentucky and was assigned to I Company of 7th Cavalry alongside Thomas Patrick Downing.

Mitchell was on detachment and serving with Major Reno during the battle. He was sent to deliver a message to General Custer and stayed with him during the battle. John Mitchell was killed on Last Stand Hill alongside General Custer on the afternoon of 25th June 1876. He is buried on the battlefield with his colleagues.

# XVI

## The Downing Family

Just over a year after Thomas Patrick Downing joined the army, the Downing family left Savannah, Georgia in May 1872. They moved to Independence Township in Buchanan, Iowa where they got some land and began farming. Downing's aunt Catherine Harrigan Powers also lived there with her family.

Downing's father **Thomas Bartholomew Downing**, died on February 1st, 1905. He was seventy-eight years old. **Ellen Harrigan Downing**, died on February 29th, 1912, also aged seventy-eight. They are buried in the Downing family grave in St John's cemetery in Independence, Iowa.

**Francis Bartholomew Downing** - Born in 1861 in Savannah. He moved with his family to Iowa. There is some suggestion that he was mentally handicapped in some way. His mother refers to having to support an "insane" son in correspondence re Thomas' pension. We can presume that John was sane as he joined the navy. That only leaves Francis as having some sort of issue. Francis did work as a labourer according to census returns. He never got married and died of heart disease at his sister Mary Ellen's house in November 1912.

The Downing family grave at St John's cemetery in
Independence, Iowa
© Des Ryan

**Mary Ellen Downing** - Born in 1865 in Savannah. She moved with the family to Iowa. In 1885 she married a machinist named William Wallace and had two children. Nellie Wallace (1887-1869) and Agnes Wallace (1889-1967). Neither Nellie nor Agnes married. William Wallace died in 1916. Mary Ellen died in Iowa in February 1923.

**John Downing** - Born in May 1868 in Savannah. He moved with the family to Iowa. John enlisted in the Navy in San Francisco in 1891 and served for three years. In 1898 he moved to Anchorage, Alaska where he became a goldminer. He never married and died at the Pioneers' Home in Anchorage on October 19th 1952.

**Kate Downing** - Born in 1872 in Savannah just after Thomas

Patrick Downing left the family. She moved to Iowa with the family. In 1892 she married Daniel Donovan. Kate and Daniel had five children (Anna Donovan Jacobs, Grace Donovan Wallace, Alice Donovan, Don Donovan, and Leo Donovan). Kate died suddenly, probably of a brain aneurysm, in May 1902. She is buried in the adjacent grave to her parents at St John's cemetery in Independence, Iowa.

**Agnes Downing** was born in Iowa in 1876. She never got married and died in Independence, Iowa in 1956.

**Anastasia Downing** (in some records Anna Lastasia others refer to her as Alice) was born in Iowa in 1877. She never got married but cared for Kate's children after she died. Anastasia died in Iowa in February 1932.

# Original Records

Mr Meagher say something about the flag of liberty, but will not swear to his expressions, was sure Mr Meagher heard what Mr Dillon said

Constable Downing deposed that he had heard Mr Meagher addressing the people at Graguenemanagh    Mr O'Brien and Mr Dillon were at Graguenemanagh also, Mr Meagher said he was one of the young generation and that he was addressing one of the old—at the same time turning round to an old gentleman they called General Cloney (laughter)   The prisoner also spoke of the formation of clubs, and of the suspension of the habeas corpus act, he then told the people to I un the "claws of the law, and commit no breach of it, heard Mr Dillon speaking and he asked the people would they allow Mr Smith O'Brien to be arrested, the people said they would not, and Mr Dillon desired all who were for preventing the police from arresting Mr O'Brien to hold up their hands, Mr Meagher and the gentleman with him drove off in the direction of Kilkenny

Cross examined by Mr Butt—Is sure that Mr Meagher said th t the government might keep the rights of Ireland this generation and the next, but that their posterity would inherit it, did not state that on Mr O'Brien's trial

Constable Robert Mahony deposed to Mr O'Brien, Mr Meagher, and Mr Dillon having been in Callan on the 24th July   In continuation, the witness detailed some sentences which he alleged had been spoken by Mr Meagher on the above day, and which were similar to those deposed to by the other policemen

Mr Lynch submitted that the crown might now give in

Constable Thomas B Downing – Testimony in trial
against Thomas Francis Meagher in Clonmel as reported
in the Freeman's Journal 18th Oct 1848

**Marriage Record of Thomas Downing and Ellen Harrigan St Michael's Church, Limerick - 15th February 1855**

*Courtesy of National Library of Ireland*

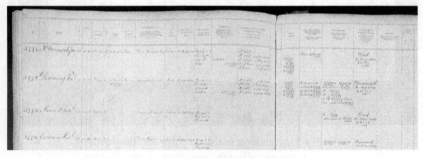

**Baptism Record for Thomas Patrick
Downing – Adare 9th March 1856**
*Courtesy of National Library of Ireland*

**RIC Record of Thomas B Downing showing his
dismissal in 1859**
*Courtesy of An Garda Siochana Archives*

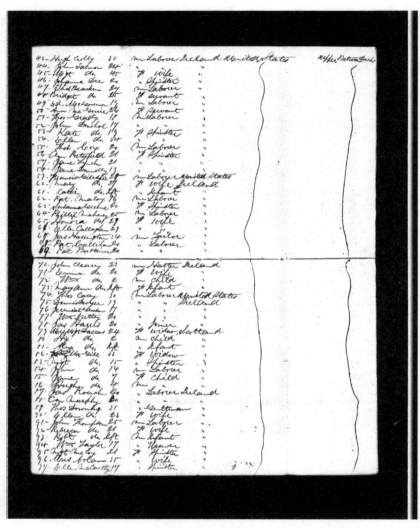

Henry Stetson ship manifest showing Thomas and
Ellen traveling to New York in 1859

**Death and Burial Record for brother Denis Downing –
Savannah 1864**
*Courtesy of City of Savannah*

**Thomas B Downing in Savannah court for beating his
wife in 1866**
*Courtesy of City of Savannah*

Downing Family listed in the 1870 US Federal Census.
Living on St Julian with the Donovan family and Celia
Burke living next door on either side

*Courtesy of US National Archives*

**Final Statement** of _Private Thomas P. Downing_
Captain _Henry J. Nowlan_ Company [ _F_ ] of the _Seventh_ Regiment
of _Cavalry_ , born in _Limerick_ , in the State of _Ireland_ ,
aged _21_ years, _5_ feet _8¼_ inches high, _florid_ complexion,
_blue_ eyes, _sandy_ hair, and by occupation a _Laborer_ , was enlisted
by _Lieut. Nave_ at _Lebanon Ky._ on the _12th_ day
of _February_ , eighteen hundred and _73._ , to serve for _five_ years,
who is now discharged by reason of
_was killed in the Battle of the Little Big Horn M.T. June 25th 1876_

The said _Thomas P. Downing_ was last paid by
Paymaster _Maj. W. Smith_ to include the _30th_ day
of _April_ , eighteen hundred and _76_ , and has pay due from that
time to _June 25th 1876._

### DUE SOLDIER.

For _____ years' continuous service under sec. 2, act August 4, 1854, $ _____ per month.
For retained pay up to June 30, 1872, _____ dollars.
For retained pay under act of May 15, 1872, _Twenty Dollars and eighty six cts_ 20 86/100 dollars.
For clothing not drawn in kind, _One hundred and twenty seven Dollars seventy cts_ 127 70/100 dollars.
For deposits (the date and amount of each deposit to be stated) 6 50/100
_Aug. 5th 1875 Maj. W. Smith Six Dollars and fifty cts._

### DUE UNITED STATES.

For clothing overdrawn, _____ dollars.
For tobacco _One Dollar and seventy one cts_ 1 71/100 dollars.
For _____

He is indebted to _____ , laundress of Company _____
_____ Regiment of _____ dollars.
Remarks:
_O.G. Body recovered & buried on field of battle 1876 under G.O. 77_

I CERTIFY that the above Final Statement, given in duplicate at _Ft. A. Lincoln D.T._
this _5th_ day of _December_ , 18 _76_ , is correct.

[ A. G. O. No. 34. ]

_Captain 7th Cavalry_
Commanding Company.

**Final statement of Thomas Patrick Downing's army affairs**
_Courtesy of Downing Family_

I Ellen Downing being duly sworn according to law do depose very that I am applicant for pension No 228.360. that we removed from Savannah Georgia & came to this County in May 1852. That for some 2 or 3 years before our removal my son Thomas B Downing was earning from 20 to 30 dollars per month, and all of said earnings he paid to me. He worked a part of said time I should think 6 or 8 months for "Beard & Kimball" proprietors of the "Savannah Advertiser" a newspaper —also he worked about 2 years for Messrs C.K. Anderson & Co grain merchants at Savannah and he worked for other persons. It was for these 2 firms & other persons he worked when he earned from 20 to 30 dollars per month & which money he always paid to me in money & it was used by me in my support & towards our family expenses. I have written a number of letters of inquiry for these employers to Savannah in order to if possible obtain their affidavits thinking they or some of them might know that my son paid to me his wages, but I am as yet unable to hear of or from any of them & do not know the present whereabouts of any of them. My said son came with us to Iowa in May 1852 remained & worked on our farm a few months & all of the proceeds of his labor during that time was for the benefit of myself & family —he earned no money but worked with us on the farm & lived with us till I think it was in August of 1852 when he went

**Correspondence One/Page One - Ellen Harrigan**
**Downing trying to get her son's pension**
*Courtesy of Downing Family*

away from home & we soon after learned of
his enlistment in the army. I have caused to
be attached to this affidavit 3 of my said
sons letters they are dated Mar 23/85 - Dec
18 - 1875 & January 25/76 - are the originals -
are genuine & are all of his letters we can
find all others having been lost or destroyed — I have never taken pains to preserve
his letters. I attach & incorporate & make oath
to as a part of this affidavits my communication
to as a part of this affidavit My communication written to of H.G. Dorman
daties July Buchanan Co J H Dorman
dated July Buchanan Co July May of
26 & 1877 for the information of the pension office
1877 for the information of the pension office
I further attach a cert of the birth of my said son
I further attach My residence & P.O. address
is Jesup Iowa

*Ellen Downing*

State of Iowa
County of Buchanan } On the 25th day of May
AD 1877 before me a Notary Public in & for said
county in person came Ellen Downing to me
personally known & she subscribed her name to the
foregoing statement & made oath thereto in my
presence & before me. I further certify that the
9 - 10 - 11 - 12 13 & 14 lines of last page were
struck out & rewritten by interlineation before
signing. I have no interest in said
claim & am not concerned in its
prosecution Witness my hand & seal
W.G. Dorman
Notary Public

**Correspondence One/Page Two - Ellen Harrigan
Downing trying to get her son's pension**
*Courtesy of Downing Family*

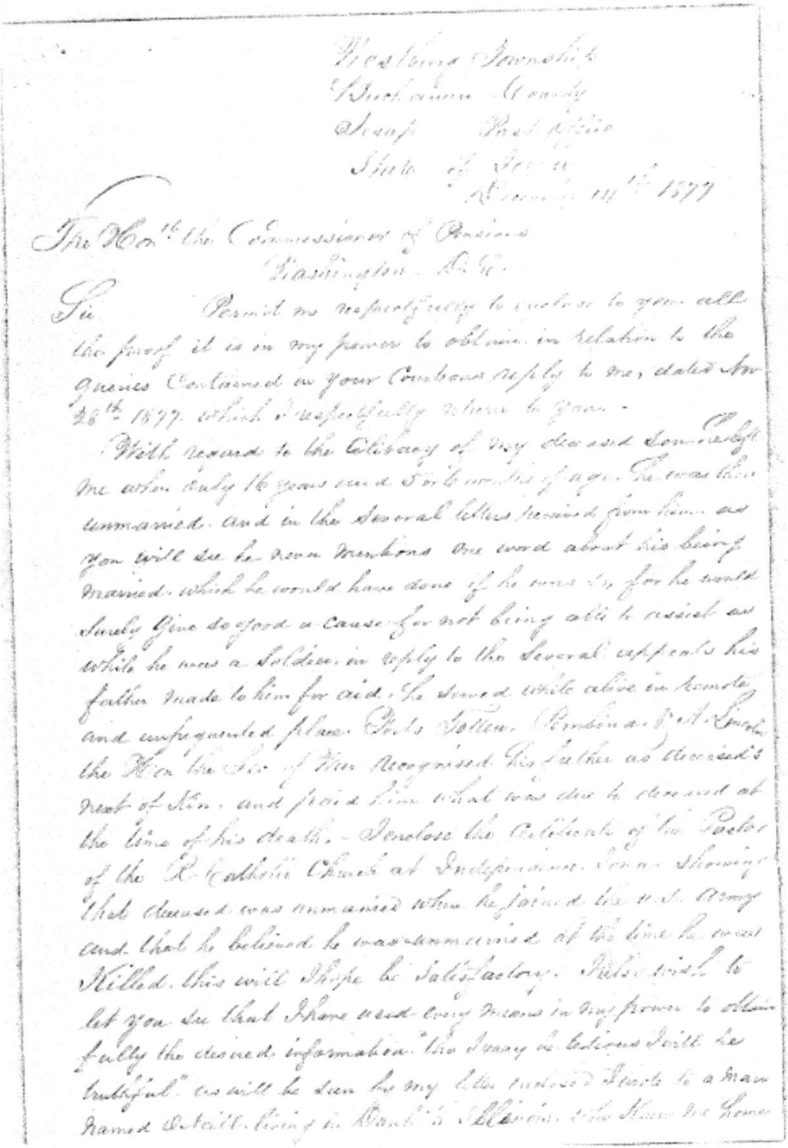
Westling Township
Buchanan County
Jesup Post Office
State of Iowa
December 14th 1877

The Honble the Commissioner of Pensions
Washington D.C.

Sir Permit me respectfully to enclose to you all the proof it is in my power to obtain in relation to the queries Contained in your Courteous reply to me, dated Aug 28th 1877 which I respectfully return to you -

With regard to the Celibacy of my deceased Son he left me when only 16 years and 5 or 6 months of age. He was then unmarried. and in the Several letters received from him as you will see he never mentions one word about his being married. which he would have done if he were so for he would surely Give so good a Cause for not being able to assist us while he was a Soldier. in reply to the Several appeals his father made to him for aid. He served while alive in remote and unfrequented places. Forts Totten. Pembina & Ft. Lincoln the Hon the Sec of War Recognised his father as deceased's next of Kin. and paid him what was due to deceased at the time of his death. - I enclose the Certificate of the Pastor of the R. Catholic Church at Independence Iowa Showing that deceased was unmarried when he joined the U.S. Army and that he believed he was unmarried at the time he was Killed. this will I hope be Satisfactory. I also wish to let you see that I have used every means in my power to obtain fully the desired information "tho I may be believed I will be truthful" as will be seen by my letter enclosed I wrote to a man named O'Neill living in Dwight Illinois who knew the same

Correspondence Two/Page One - Ellen Harrigan Downing trying to get her son's pension
*Courtesy of Downing Family*

at Adare Co Limerick Ireland. I took him to go before
a Notary Public. and make declaration on oath that he knew
me here. as the wife of Thomas Downing. and after an
absence of over Twenty Years. he saw me again at my
home here. but whether I did not properly instruct him what
to do. or from the neglect of the Notary Public. he failed to do
what I required of him, there is only one sentence in his letter
that is of any avail to me. and that is where he told the N. Public
that he knew me. — As regards my relationship to deceased
You will see by the Baptismal Certificate of the Parish
Priest at Adare Co Limerick Ireland. which Honble Sir you
have in your possession. that the deceased was born on
the 6th March 1856. and baptized by the Rev Thos. Standish
O'Grady P.P. Since dead. the parents were Thos. Downing
father. and Ellen Harrigan his mother. as it appears the
mothers maiden name is always given on such occasions
in Sep 1873. 17 Years and 6 months after the baptism of
deceased. another child Anastasia. was baptized by the
Clergyman at Independence Iowa. and the parents names are
given the same as at the baptism of deceased. Viz Thomas
Downing. and Ellen Harrigan. and this during the life of
deceased nearly three Years before he was killed. So Honble
Sir I hope You will be fully Convinced that I am the
lawful mother of my brave boy. and yet the legitimate
wife of his father. They to attach Baptismal Certificate of the
Pastor of the Catholic Church at Independence Iowa.

As regards my husbands disability during the
Year 1876. And Particularly during the month of — of this
Year, permit me Honble Sir to make a few remarks to You
in relation to above. — Of all the sickness or disease. that
a man could suffer or be afflicted with. Ulcers are the

**Correspondence Two/Page Two - Ellen Harrigan
Downing trying to get her son's pension**
*Courtesy of Downing Family*

"Most ... and painful ... to ... in such a place as my husband has ... now ... left hip to his knee the bandages can never be put on to stay in their place and the friction of the clothing add to the soreness. the bandages and cloths on which the salve is applied are always stained with offensive matter besides delicacy prevents a man from showing or even letting persons know that they are suffering from such disgusting sores. My husband did suffer as much in 1876 and perhaps more in the month of June of that year owing to May & June and a part of July being so continued wet. our wet clothing always make them worse than they would be if dry and quiet as the friction of the clothing chafes the skin which is ... and easily irritated. He was as bad during 1876 and as I stated particularly during June 1876 as he was ... and as he was at the several times he was examined by Drs House, Peak & Mellon. I allow a certificate from the latter gentleman certified to by the clerk of the court and seal of his office. Showing that my husband is unable to perform continued manual labor even for one day, which is solemnly & sincerely true. he is not able to perform manual labor but the support of a large family compels him to do the most he can towards their maintenance. It does not Hon'ble Sir require any professional skill or judgment to see the cause of his disability. Sometimes he can scrape the bone with his finger. And the Doctors tell him that while he lives the ulcers will break out as the bone is partly rotten. — I also attach statements from my neighbours showing that my husband has never earned one dollar from any source during the time he is living in this Township. And that his only income is what he can make on the farm

**Correspondence Two/Page Three - Ellen Harrigan Downing trying to get her son's pension**
*Courtesy of Downing Family*

which in their opinion is inadequate to support our family. I also attach the statement of the Auditor of Buchanan Co. showing the assessed value of our husbands property. Real & Personal. for 18¾ 1876 & 1877. The true value the Auditor could not give, but I have given it. in the accompanying certificate of the Township Assessor. the Township Clerk and other Respectable and disinterested persons. even I got it from the Recorder of the Co. Court as will be seen by his statement.

I also attach the statement of the Recorder showing that there is a Mortgage of $1150 &c.) uncancelled. recorded in the books. on the Farm.

In conclusion I will respectfully state. that I have not in one instance given the statement of a person in any degree related to me. nor do I believe is there the signature of one person of the same nationality. I have given you. perhaps at too great a length. all the information I possess about my affairs. and God alone Knows they are true. that we are destitute is true. but the destitution of six poor children is painful to look on. I never thought that so sad a termination would so soon befal my poor boy. and that we would be reduced to the state of misery we are now in.

Only for the relief we got from the Custer Fund we would not I believe have even the name of a home as we paid the Interest up to April 1877. but unless your honor looks with Compassion on myself & family what would happen in 1877. will I fear but Sadness come in 1878. I leave my case and in Your hands and in the protection of my good Lord in heaven and I beseech of you to grant me the allowance in your power to give me. I am &c &c

Respectfully

*Correspondence Two/Page Four - Ellen Harrigan*
**Downing trying to get her son's pension**
*Courtesy of Downing Family*

# The Men of I Company

## Members of I Company on 25th June 1876

| Name | Rank | Age | Place of Birth | Little Bighorn Outcome |
|---|---|---|---|---|
| Myles Keogh | Sergeant | 36 | Ireland | Dead |
| Frank Varden | 1st Sergeant | 31 | US | Dead |
| Robert Murphy | Sergeant | 26 | US | On Detachment Elsewhere |
| Michael Caddle | Sergeant | 32 | Ireland | On Detachment Elsewhere |
| Milton DeLacy | Sergeant | 29 | US | With Pack Train |
| James Bustard | Sergeant | 30 | Ireland | Dead |
| James Porter | 1st Lieutenant | 29 | US | Dead |
| Andrew Nave | 2nd Lieutenant | 30 | US | On Sick Leave |
| Samuel Staples | Corporal | 27 | US | Dead |
| George Morris | Corporal | 25 | US | Dead |
| John Wild | Corporal | 27 | US | Dead |
| Joseph McCall | Corporal | 24 | US | On Detachment Elsewhere |
| John McGucker | Trumpeter | 40 | US | Dead |
| John Patton | Trumpeter | 25 | US | Dead |
| John Porter | Private | 27 | England | In Confinement |
| Frederick Lehman | Private | 28 | Switzerland | Dead |
| William Miller | Private | 31 | US | On Sick Leave |
| George Gaffney | Private | 32 | Ireland | On Detachment Elsewhere |
| James Troy | Private | 27 | US | Dead |

| | | | | |
|---|---|---|---|---|
| Conrad Farber | Private | 39 | Hungary | On Detachment Elsewhere |
| John Rivers | Private | 42 | US | On Detachment Elsewhere |
| Patrick Kelly | Private | 35 | Ireland | Dead |
| John Edward Mitchell | Private | 34 | Ireland | Dead |
| William Reed | Private | 33 | US | Dead |
| William Saas | Private | 28 | Germany | On Detachment Elsewhere |
| Jacob Noshang | Private | 29 | US | Dead |
| Charles Ramsey | Private | 26 | US | With Pack Train |
| John Parker | Private | 27 | England | Dead |
| Charles Van Bramer | Private | 26 | US | Dead |
| James Quinn | Private | 26 | US | On Detachment Elsewhere |
| Patrick Lynch | Private | 25 | Ireland | On Detachment Elsewhere |
| George Gross | Private | 31 | Germany | Dead |
| Frederick Fox | Private | 26 | Germany | On Detachment Elsewhere |
| Henry Allen Bailey | Private | 51 | US | Dead |
| Edward Holcomb | Private | 31 | US | Dead |
| Henry Lehmann | Private | 37 | Germany | Dead |
| James McNally | Private | 29 | Ireland | With Pack Train |
| Marion Horn | Private | 33 | US | Dead |
| Archibald McIlharrgey | Private | 31 | Ireland | Dead |
| David Cooney | Private | 28 | Ireland | With Pack Train |
| John Rossbury | Private | 27 | US | Dead |
| Thomas Patrick Downing | Private | 20 | Ireland | Dead |

| | | | | |
|---|---|---|---|---|
| Herbert Thomas | Private | 26 | Wales | On Detachment Elsewhere |
| Franz Braun | Private | 31 | Germany | With Pack Train |
| George Haywood | Private | 26 | Canada | On Sick Leave |
| Gustave Korn | Private | 24 | Poland | With Pack Train |
| Frederick Myers | Private | 29 | Germany | On Detachment Elsewhere |
| Edward Driscoll | Private | 26 | Ireland | Dead |
| John McGinnis | Private | 43 | Ireland | On Sick Leave |
| David Gillette | Private | 25 | US | Dead |
| Gabriel Guessbacher | Private | 30 | Germany | On Detachment Elsewhere |
| Henry Jones | Private | 23 | US | With Pack Train |
| John O'Brien | Private | 25 | US | Dead |
| Feliz Pitter | Private | 31 | England | Dead |
| Joseph Broadhurst | Private | 24 | US | Dead |
| William Whaley | Private | 27 | US | Dead |
| Edward Kkiyd | Private | 24 | England | Dead |
| Charles Haack | Private | 54 | Germany | On Sick Leave |
| Eugene Owens | Private | 28 | Ireland | With Pack Train |
| Darwin Symms | Private | 24 | Canada | Dead |
| Thomas Connors | Private | 30 | US | Dead |
| Adam Hetesimer | Private | 29 | US | Dead |
| George Post | Private | 28 | US | Dead |
| John McShane | Private | 27 | Canada | With Pack Train |
| John D Barry | Private | 27 | Ireland | Dead |
| Andrew Grimes | Private | 29 | US | On Detachment Elsewhere |
| Francis Kennedy | Private | 22 | US | With Pack Train |

| Mark Lee | Private | 27 | US | On Sick Leave |
|----------|---------|----|----|---------------|

| Country of Birth | |
|------------------|----|
| Ireland | 15 |
| Wales | 1 |
| Canada | 3 |
| Germany | 8 |
| Hungary | 1 |
| Poland | 1 |
| Switzerland | 1 |
| England | 4 |
| US | 34 |
| **Total** | **68** |

| | |
|---|---|
| Dead | 37 |
| In Confinement | 1 |
| On Detachment Elsewhere (Not Present) | 13 |
| On Sick Leave (Not Present) | 6 |
| With Pack Train (Survived) | 10 |
| | **68** |

Printed in the USA
CPSIA information can be obtained
at www.ICGtesting.com
LVHW021928081024
793284LV00008B/287

9 781068 672804